GROUNDED
FOR
ALL
ETERNITY

Darcy Marks

GROUNDED FOR ALL ETERNITY

ALADDIN

New York   London   Toronto   Sydney   New Delhi

To all the kids who refuse to let the world change their perception of themselves. You got this.

❦

ALADDIN
An imprint of Simon & Schuster Children's Publishing Division
1230 Avenue of the Americas, New York, New York 10020
First Aladdin hardcover edition July 2022
Text copyright © 2022 by Darcy Richardson Miller
Jacket illustration copyright © 2022 by Nicholas Kole
All rights reserved, including the right of reproduction in whole or in part in any form.
ALADDIN and related logo are registered trademarks of Simon & Schuster, Inc.
For information about special discounts for bulk purchases, please contact Simon & Schuster Special Sales at 1-866-506-1949 or business@simonandschuster.com.
The Simon & Schuster Speakers Bureau can bring authors to your live event.
For more information or to book an event contact the Simon & Schuster Speakers Bureau at 1-866-248-3049 or visit our website at www.simonspeakers.com.
Jacket designed by Karin Paprocki
Interior designed by Mike Rosamilia
The text of this book was set in Fournier Pro.
Manufactured in the United States of America 0622 FFG
2 4 6 8 10 9 7 5 3 1
Library of Congress Cataloging-in-Publication Data
Names: Marks, Darcy, author.
Title: Grounded for all eternity / Darcy Marks.
Description: New York : Aladdin, 2022. | Audience: Ages 8 to 12. | Summary: Mal and his friends break out of Hell and find themselves in Salem, Masschusetts, on Halloween night, and in order to return to their dimension, they must capture the escaped soul of one of the architects of the witch trials before he permanently upsets the balance of power on Earth.
Identifiers: LCCN 2021046644 (print) | LCCN 2021046645 (ebook) |
ISBN 9781534483361 (hardcover) | ISBN 9781534483385 (ebook)
Subjects: CYAC: Guardian angels—Fiction. | Good and evil—Fiction. | Soul—Fiction. |
Fate and fatalism—Fiction. | Halloween—Fiction. | Salem (Mass.)—Fiction. | LCGFT: Novels.
Classification: LCC PZ7.1.D318 Gr 2022 (print) | LCC PZ7.1.D318 (ebook) | DDC [Fic]—dc23
LC record available at https://lccn.loc.gov/2021046644
LC ebook record available at https://lccn.loc.gov/2021046645

COMMAND

MALACHI

Track: Command
Interests: Anything I'm not supposed to do
Fear: Fate, failing

INTELLIGENCE

LILITH

Track: Intelligence
Favorite Activity: Knowing things, teasing Mal
Fear: Imperfection

MAGICIAN

CROWLEY

Track: Magician
Interests: All things comics
Fear: Like I would tell you

ENFORCER

ALEISTER

Track: Enforcer
Favorite Activity: Competing, sports of all kinds
Fear: Nothing to fear with good friends!

PROLOGUE

At the back of Alighieri's Emporium, behind a mannequin showcasing a plush velvet cloak, is an arched black door with no obvious handle. Most people think it's there for decoration, a forgotten piece of architecture from before the place became a shop.

I'm not most people.

I know the door has a purpose, and more important, I know how to open it.

The letters spelling out ALIGHIERI'S EMPORIUM flicker with artificial flame above a different door, this one narrow, green, and shaped nothing like a rectangle. The flames flicker day and night, and the narrow green door is never locked. Alighieri's doesn't close.

On that afternoon there was a stack of packages by the mailbox waiting to be retrieved. I glanced down as I passed but didn't recognize the name scrawled across the top: Morgan Accolon. The small mystery served as a necessary distraction to my nerves as I climbed the front steps and pushed open the distinctive green door.

The shop's narrow entryway was barely wide enough for my wings. A sharp pinch told me I hadn't quite managed it, and I pocketed the feather that had been pulled free. Leaving that here was asking for trouble.

I wove through gravity-defying stacks of merchandise: occult books, glowing red orbs, bubbling slime-filled flasks, toaster ovens. Anything anyone could need to get up to a little mischief. The ceilings were high enough for flight, but merchandise hung from there, too. That was okay. The shop wasn't really my destination.

Sweeping aside the edge of a very specific velvet cloak, I came face-to-face with a wooden door that made my heart race.

I raised my fist, my stomach a swirl of anticipation.

The door jerked open, revealing a goblin wearing a ridiculous red tie, a piece of pizza hanging from his oversized mouth.

"I didn't do the special knock," I said, my hand still raised uselessly.

He looked at the now-open door, then chewed and swallowed the entire slice in a gigantic gulp. "Do you still want to?"

"The door's already open," I said.

"You could still do it."

"Well, there's no point in it now." I threw my hands up and swept into the room. "Did you get it?"

Tony closed the door, and the light dimmed as we were separated from the flames and glowing objects of the shop proper. He licked his fingers free of pizza grease with his overly long tongue, one purple finger at a time. Then he wiped his hand on his tie, causing it to start playing a song that made it even more ridiculous.

If the room had an organization system, it wasn't obvious. The office was just as crowded as the shop, with the addition of several caged animals, eggs, and tanks filled with hidden movement—stacked here and there among office furniture and packages.

I tapped my foot.

"Relax," Tony said.

"I'm on a time crunch," I said. "Do you have it or not?"

"Of course I have it," said Tony. He grabbed the last piece of pizza from the box perched precariously on a cluttered worktable, took a bite, and slurped the entire slice into his mouth. "Imma profeshal."

I grimaced, but Tony *was* a professional. He always managed to get us early editions of hologames and bootleg copies of movies that were still playing in Dagon, and I knew he did more. At least for other clients. After all, it was what Alighieri's was known for.

He shoved aside the pizza box and a book that screamed when it was touched. He rummaged around until he retrieved a small black bag from beneath a large lavender envelope and held it up dramatically. My heart raced. Some part of me hadn't believed he'd be able to get it.

He tilted the bag, and the crystal dropped into his other hand, glowing with perfect golden light. A spark of creation, distilled from the feather of an archangel. A means to grant your deepest desire. A means to defeat Fate. And it was mine.

"Straight from the Archangel Gabriel, kiddo."

ONE

The scent of torment wafted on the breeze like delicious barbecue, briefly overpowering the ever-present odor of pumpkin and decay. My stomach rumbled, and I idly wondered what my parents were making for dinner.

Leaves skittered along the sidewalk, filling the air with a dry rustling sound, which alternated with tapping as some of the leaves sprouted legs and scurried across the ground. I kicked one out of the way before it could untie my shoelaces, and watched as it ran to hide in the moving shadows cast by the flames flickering beyond the wrought iron fence.

In other words it was a perfect afternoon, and with our

much needed week of vacation before we started a new school year, I had an extra bounce in my already jaunty step.

"There he is," Aleister exclaimed with obvious exasperation. "You walked?"

"It's a nice day," I said, and grinned wickedly at my friends. When you had wings like we did, walking was something you saved for inconveniently tight spaces or short distances, but some days, when I wanted to be in the moment, there was something nice about putting one foot in front of the other.

"Dork." Lilith rolled her eyes, but I didn't take it personally. I knew she loved me. (Tolerated me, whatever, same thing.) "Are we playing or what?"

"We're playing," I confirmed, without picking up my pace at all.

I had no desire to rush that sense of perfect freedom before break. You only get that feeling for an afternoon, and I was determined to enjoy it. Sure, vacation would be for relaxing and adventures, maybe a little mischief and a lot of fun, perhaps even an existential crisis or three, but that *first* sensation of *nothing* to do? Oh yeah. That's what I was talking about.

I dropped my unusually light backpack onto the nearest park bench, stretched my black-feathered wings, and launched myself into the air to join my friends, who were already airborne. The game was King of the Cage, but Aleister sometimes called it Super Smashy-Smash.

We had not agreed on that.

The game had taken years to perfect, and I was quite proud of the result. A combination of the very worst parts of dodgeball and keep-away, with just a touch of trash talk and one-upmanship, it was a game born in Hell.

Literally.

And that was something worth celebrating. When living in one of the great hereafters, birth of any kind wasn't a common occurrence. We were more in the death-and-forever-stagnant variety of business.

The ball whistled through the air, randomly punctuated by the sound of rubber hitting flesh as one particularly hard throw or another was caught or missed. Aleister plummeted a few feet before rising above us all with flaps of his huge wings. Laughs and taunts filled the air, almost drowning out the sounds of agony beyond the fence.

Not that I paid much attention to the wailing of the passed-on anyway. It was like the hum of a refrigerator, always there and just as meaningless.

"I think you're losing it, Mal," Aleister shouted. "That was—"

But whatever insult Aleister had been going to throw my way was drowned out by the clanging of bells, which was probably for the best. Maybe it was just that Aleister was relentlessly positive, and insults, clever or not, didn't come easy to him. As much as I tried, my wit never seemed to rub off on him.

The neighborhood flames grew higher in a sudden burst of light and warmth, and my feathers ruffled as the wave of heat slammed over us. The already enormous fence that surrounded our neighborhood expanded and rose, building upon itself with a mechanical clanking, until the black sky was separated from us by bars, and my gated community became a cage.

Escape drill. Sigh.

We dove to the ground but pulled up at the last second so that we touched down lightly on our feet. Then we grabbed our backpacks and jogged to the nearest shelter. Jogging less because of the drill and more because the closest shelter happened to be in the basement of the local café: Faust's.

With the approach of Samhain, the street outside Faust's smelled of rosemary and apples as new holiday treats were baked up. The changing recipes were always a sign that time was passing, since the weather here was always the same. The leaves were always a display of oranges, yellows, and reds, and the air always smelled like pumpkins and cinnamon, but outside Faust's, rosemary and apples were for Samhain just like chocolate and honey were for Beltane.

We squeezed our way through the traffic jam of loitering bodies at the doorway. They were no doubt moving slowly on purpose. Most were probably hoping they wouldn't have to reach the shelter at all before the drill stopped. Cecily, barista extraordinaire and resident bast, held the door to the basement open with a bored expression. No one was in any rush, including Cecily, who snapped her gum as Aleister shoulder-bumped me into the wall.

"Jerk," I said, punching Aleister in the stomach. He laughed and threw an arm over my shoulder. Lilith pushed us both through the door and onto the stairs down to the shelter. The stairwell was too narrow for flight, so I tucked my wings tight as I clomped my way down.

"Let's go, let's go." Faust, as translucent as ever, waved us on from the bottom of the stairs. He flickered in irritation as Aleister made his way past, tripping over Faust's shoe in the process.

"You don't even need to touch the ground. Why are you touching my feet?" grumbled Faust. "Corporeal existence doesn't just happen, you know!"

"If the stairwell was wider, I could have flown right over you," Aleister said. "I'm just saying."

"Sorry, Faust," I said. "You're the best!"

"No one does it better," Lilith said, planting a kiss on

Faust's cheek. His cheeks blushed red while the rest of his body tried to disappear completely.

We turned before our smirks were too obvious.

As a former human in the hereafter, Faust didn't so much *have* a body as project one. It was short and round and perfectly solid and usable under most conditions, but staying solid required actual concentration. When he was stressed, he flickered and blurred. Some of the less honorable among us thought it was funny to startle him as he was mixing drinks, not that I would ever do that. Except that one time. With the whipped cream.

The basement wasn't empty. Faust's was an officially designated shelter, after all, and this was a busy street. Some of those taking refuge had obviously been customers when the alarm had sounded and still sipped on coffee or munched on apple cider donuts.

I eyed them enviously. Faust's apple cider donuts were *worth* selling your soul for, and Faust had, sort of.

Even though the owner of the café was a former human, Faust hadn't been evil like the other souls contained in the Pit. He had made a deal. All worldly knowledge in exchange for eternal servitude, and all that knowledge just so happened to include recipes for the best donuts ever.

I wasn't sure his deal was worth it, but if it kept me in

killer baked goods for all eternity, I was not going to complain.

"Should we snag a couch?" Aleister asked.

"Nah," I said. "It'll stop in a minute."

It did not stop in a minute.

After five minutes Lilith led us to a ripped blue velvet couch that had been removed from the café upstairs. Five minutes after that, adults carrying bags from two of my favorite nearby shops, Burn This Book and Choirs of Hell Music, booted us off the couch.

I made a mental note to check out the COH concert schedule, since I had missed the last show. The shop hosted concerts in the alley out back, and I had spent hours talking to the siren who owned the store about the bands she pulled in. During boring classes I daydreamed about doing that, discovering musicians and launching them to success. Schmoozing and mingling, with people falling all over themselves to say, "You have the coolest club ever, Malachi!"

Aleister shifted next to me, and the feel of one of my long flight feathers being tugged reminded me why those fantasies would never be anything more than fantasies. I didn't need to look around the room to see that me and my squad were the only ones there with black-feathered wings. Our kind were *special*, with celestial destinies or whatever.

If I'd had horns or a tail or even leathery wings, I could

have been an ordinary resident of Hell, like most of the people who just lived here without worrying about how it all fit into the Big Picture. I'd have something the mortals called "free will" and an entire future of possibilities in front of me, almost all of which were closed to me and my friends. Our sleek black feathers separated us from everyone else and were a clear signal that our futures were locked down by destiny.

"Yo," Crowley said as he flopped himself down next to us. His too-dark sunglasses slid to the end of his nose, and he let the comic that he had been holding fall into his lap. Crowley was the missing member of our squad, and it wasn't overly surprising that he had skipped out on our game, even though he had helped create it. Getting unnecessarily sweaty was Crowley's least-favorite activity.

"Where did you come from?" I asked.

"Over there," he said, gesturing to the other side of the shelter. "I was waiting to see if there were going to be better options."

"Nice," scoffed Lilith.

"There weren't," Crowley said, as if this should make us feel better. And it kinda did, because standing by himself was a totally Crowley option to choose.

"Is that the new *Storm Born*?" Aleister asked.

"Yeah, number six hundred and sixty-six." Crowley puffed

out his chest. "Just finished production. Can't even get it yet, *but I know people.*"

He meant Tony, of course, and my heart jolted, but Crowley wasn't even looking at me. I let out a slow breath as subtly as I could. It had been months since I had visited Alighieri's. There was no reason to think he knew my secret. Crowley was just gloating, as usual.

We examined the comic over Crowley's shoulder, marveling at a new character while he swatted our hands away whenever we tried to point something out, until the act of touching the comic became the goal itself.

"You guys are such jerks!" Crowley snapped as we laughed.

I was lucky. We would be together until the end of time, whether we liked it or not. The Fates didn't care if you had fun with your squad; that was just a nice perk we had managed.

Many minutes later we were still there in the basement, away from all the amazing donuts upstairs, and our comic-book-territory slap fight had become . . . a bit aggressive.

"Hey, Cecily. When's the drill going to be over?" Aleister whined loudly, rubbing his hand gingerly. Cecily ignored him, but her eyes flicked to the clock on a nearby table.

Most of the time during a drill we barely made it down the stairs before the bells stopped, the flames receded, and the fence retracted back to its normal suburban size. What could possibly cause a drill to go on for so long?

An oni in the corner held a newspaper awkwardly in one red-clawed hand. His head was cocked sideways to read the crooked print, and he held a steaming cup of something in the other hand. Behind him his spiked tail swished between the flaps of his velvet tailcoat while his hooved feet shifted uncomfortably

Near him a daemon I recognized named Furfur *snicker* sat on the edge of a chair, idly scratching his elk horns against the wall. I couldn't help noticing that his eyes were flicking between the clock and Faust.

In fact, as I looked around, I realized that almost everyone was starting to get fidgety. They probably had places to be, after all. We were the lucky ones heading into a school vacation, not them.

Lilith settled more comfortably against the wall, reading Crowley's abandoned comic, now that the slap fight had stopped. Aleister had flopped onto his back and was throwing a crumpled piece of paper into the air over and over, and catching it each time before it could land on his face. I slid down the wall on the other side of Lilith, getting as close as I dared and using the comic book as an excuse.

It was a balance. If I was too clumsy and obvious, Lilith would annihilate me, but I wanted to be on her radar, so I was close enough that I could feel the heat of her leg. I didn't look at her; I looked at the comic book she was holding. Close but not annoying. It was a dance.

"Did you guys hear about Belial?" I asked, hoping to impress Lilith with my insider information. "The guy in Abaddon's class?"

"Fifty years submerged in the Styx," Lilith said, with a knowing look.

"What did he do?" Crowley asked, finally lowering another comic he had pulled out of his bag.

"He went after Azael," I said.

"So?" said Aleister. "He's been gunning for Azael since Azael started hanging out with that girl Belial's got a thing for."

"He waited until Azael's wing was broken," I said significantly. Everyone groaned.

"And I suppose Belial's parents aren't going to ask for leniency," said Crowley.

"For waiting to attack the weak?" I scoffed. "No way."

Belial should have known better. If he didn't want to spend fifty years gurgling swamp water, he should have confronted Azael when it was an even match. Or better yet, trusted the girl to know her own mind, and not gotten into a stupid fight like it was going to impress anyone.

"Thank you for your patience," Faust announced to the

room at large, tugging at his pointy little beard and shimmering way more than usual. "I'm sure the alarm bells will stop soon."

"Maybe they're broken?" Aleister wondered out loud, sounding completely unconcerned with that possibility.

"Get real," Lilith scoffed. "Hell's Bells? I don't even think that's possible."

"Hmm," the oni muttered in his gravelly voice, clearly overhearing us. Rude. He set his newspaper and mug down on a nearby crate filled with coffee stirrers or some other café supply. (But definitely not donuts, because I had already checked.) His slitted red eyes peered suspiciously into the distance. "Odd."

"You don't think it's for real, do you?" Cecily asked, her fuzzy feline tail lashing out with nervous energy, while her pointed ears twisted on her head. Her golden eyes, which were normally half-lidded in boredom, were wide with anxiety.

"It's happened before," said Furfur.

"Yeah, but . . . ," said Cecily, her voice wavering.

"No," said Faust. "Definitely not. For that to happen it would take an extraordinary breach of security."

The noise level increased exponentially as everyone began to speak excitedly.

"No way," I breathed. I had assumed a glitch or some

stupid procedural thing that was taking too long, but there was always the remotest possibility of the alarm being real. Could there have been an actual escape?

"Whoa," Lilith murmured. Aleister and Crowley exchanged looks with bright, excited eyes. Smirks and gleeful grins tugged at our mouths.

"There hasn't been a breakout in a century. Jeez, Malachi," Crowley tutted. "Your high-and-mighty parents not up to snuff? Did I hear . . . 'demotion'?"

"They were probably too busy covering for your dad's screwups," I replied. "I heard his spell work went haywire the other day and the L-man let him have it."

"'L-man'?" Lilith said. "Please. Dare you to say that to his face."

I blushed, momentarily embarrassed at being called out by Lilith. Of course, I would *never* call Lucifer that to his face. He was an archangel, after all, and the first of us, but if you couldn't talk smack to your friends, who could you talk smack to?

"And you haven't heard anything, neither one of you," continued Lilith. "So maybe we could try not making up stuff just to irritate each other, because if this is legit, this is bad, guys."

Crowley and I mumbled apologies, while Aleister grinned.

"Why is it bad?" he asked. "Some dinky soul escapes?

They'll get it back in no time. Besides, Lilith, souls are weak. I only brushed Faust's foot, and he went insubstantial, and he's *special*. The regular ones can't even do that. They're all wispy nothings."

"Then why do *they* look so worried?" Lilith countered, gesturing with a nod.

Cecily, Faust, and the oni had huddled together and were deep in conversation with other staff members and several customers. Leathery red wings mingled with horns and tails—but noticeably not black-feathered wings—as the regular residents of Hell discussed the still clanging bells and the possibility of a real jailbreak.

"Eh, relax." Aleister shrugged. "What's the worst thing that could happen?"

I shot him a glare.

Though the devilish part of me was thrilled at the possibilities.

TWO

Mom eventually came and sprang me from the lockdown at Faust's after we'd been in the basement for
hours with nothing to snack on except sugar packets from
the café (I never did find any donuts), and nothing to do but
read *Storm Born* No. 666 over and over again. I didn't care
how awesome it was; there were only so many things you
could analyze about a single comic book.

Granted, the fact that the conversation lasted all afternoon
was a testament to how awesome *Storm Born* truly was.

By the time we got home, it was way past dinner. Dad
was still at work when I went to bed, and even though the
bells had been silenced, the flames still maintained their

protective height, making it brighter than normal and harder to sleep.

If I was being honest, my inability to sleep was due only in part to the flame light itself. I kept wondering what might be lurking in the shadows. Stuff like this never happened, and the excitement had my mind racing.

"I still don't understand how he escaped." Mom's voice was tired, drifting up the stairs. I looked at my clock: 03:30.

"As far as we can tell, he overpowered Balan and slipped out of his cell." Dad yawned, and I heard a creak of a chair.

How could a soul get by one of the powers? The whole reason for our existence was to perform this very job, to keep souls like that locked away. Wasn't that what *they* constantly told me? The whole reason I got to have no choice about what I was going to do with my life was because I was a power, and my duty was *sacred*? And where did Balan work? Eighth circle, I thought.

Whether you called it the infernal regions, Hades, or just plain the Bad Place, Hell was one of the major hereafters. I called it home, but for many human souls it was where they passed on to from the mortal coil. Whether they came here or went to any of the other hereafters was based on a bunch of different factors, not the least of which were their own choices made during life.

If they were good people who cared about their fellow humans, they did not come here.

The ones who did come here *so* deserved it and were imprisoned in the Pit, where they were sorted into one of the nine circles, based on what kind of terrible person they had been. Each soul was relegated to the circle that best fit their most predominant evil.

The eighth circle, which our escapee had managed to flee, was for manipulators, which didn't seem so bad, considering some of the alternatives.

It wasn't as if the soul could manipulate us hellions; we were all used to a nice base level of mischief and were largely immune to whatever energy a mere soul had held on to. And besides, like Aleister had said, Faust, who was special, could barely hold his solid form if the donuts were late, much less hold it together to cause any harm. The souls in the Pit were nowhere near as strong as the portly middle-aged man who owned the best café in my neighborhood.

"But how?" Mom asked. "Our Intelligence hasn't been able to figure it out. And where is he now? It's been twelve hours. How has he not been found?"

She said something else, but it was hard to make out, and that was just not going to work for me.

I slid out of bed and tiptoed to the top of the stairs.

21

"I don't know," Dad sighed. "Everyone is looking, and Lucifer is furious. He'd better be found soon, or heads are going to roll . . . and that just gets messy."

I knelt, pressing my face against the wall to peer down the staircase, and could just make out my parents sitting at the table. They looked tired, their wings drooping.

"This isn't the first time either, and you remember what happened to Camael?" asked Mom.

"Who doesn't remember Camael? I wouldn't want to be Balan. This isn't a normal soul, though. Samuel Parris is . . . well, you know what he is. We've got to redouble security, at least."

Dad rose from his chair and stretched, the feathers at the ends of his black wings nearly touching the walls on either side of him. He was an impressive sight when he wanted to be. Not that I would ever tell him that.

My parents worked in the Pit, cosmic prison guards with existence-ending levels of responsibility. They weren't assigned to specific circles like some others but had to deal with more universal issues. Not my idea of fun. While I wasn't really sure what they did all day exactly, I knew Mom was further up the food chain, and just as I and my friends had been assigned a squad, so had my parents, a long, long time ago. Both of my parents had been Command track, trained as leaders of their squads, and I was supposed to follow in their footsteps. Whether I wanted to or not.

"Samhain is in a matter of days. If we don't find Parris before then, if he gets through . . ." Mom's voice was worried, but I wasn't sure why that would worry her, unless it was because our holiday might be affected. "I already snapped at Ruby, my squad's Intelligence. So, that's going to go well."

"Yikes . . . We'll find him." Dad put his arm around Mom's shoulders and squeezed. "Come on, let's go to bed. It's all hands on deck tomorrow."

"Yeah, I was lucky to get off to pick up Malachi at Faust's." Mom groaned, and simultaneously both of my parents said, "Malachi."

My heart raced. How could they know I was listening? I hadn't even landed on the squeaky board. I rose out of my crouch, trying desperately to come up with an excuse. Sleepwalking, maybe? That was a hard one to disprove.

"We need a babysitter," said Dad, and I threw myself back into my hiding spot. They hadn't seen me.

Wait . . . babysitter?

"You're right. I wonder if Scarlett is available," said Mom. The last part was muffled as she rubbed her face with her hands.

"It's too late to call now. We'll figure it out in the morning," said Dad, and they started for the stairs.

I flew for my bed, and dove under the covers before they reached the top. I closed my eyes and tried to breathe slowly. The extra brightness from the flames would give me away in a second if I wasn't careful. Mom paused by my door and sighed, a note of worry in the exhale.

A babysitter? I did not need a babysitter. I hadn't had one in forever. Ugh.

But there was nothing I could do about it yet, unless I admitted I had been listening in, which was not going to happen. I'd just have to wake up early so I could convince them this babysitter idea was terrible.

No problem.

THREE

A dropped pot startled me awake.

I tumbled out of bed and crashed to the floor. My cheek was wet with drool, and my feet were tangled in the sheets. My parents were already awake! I kicked my legs, frantically trying to free them from the straitjacket that was my bedding. I had to stop them before they started making calls.

After freeing my legs, I soared down the stairs and burst through the kitchen door. Dad was still eating breakfast, but Mom was already at the mirror, making a call. I was too late.

"Yes," said Mom. "I understand."

"Mom. Mom," I hissed, tugging at her sleeve and trying

to keep myself out of view of the mirror. She swatted my hand away. "I don't need a babysitter. Don't get one!"

"I know. Thanks anyway." Mom swiped her hand over the mirror. "Well, that makes six, all busy with other kids."

"Mom. That's great. I don't need a babysitter."

"I know I said I'd be home for school break, but with this escape, I have to work. The emergency protocols have all been activated," Mom said. She flipped through listings in her contact book.

"So? I can totally stay by myself. You've let me before!"

"Mal, there's a prisoner on the loose. You can't be alone," Dad said. "Maybe for another vacation we can talk about it, but not this time."

"You never think I can do anything," I argued.

"Malachi, don't start," Dad said sternly. "This is an emergency. It's as simple as that. You're a child, and this is a potentially dangerous situation." It was the I-mean-business, addressing-his-team voice, something that I definitely did not have yet. I hated that tone of voice, but I tried to squash my temper down and focus on logic instead.

Look at me being all responsible.

"Dad, the fence is still up. We're basically living in a birdcage surrounded by flames. I'll be fine. Come on, please? None of my friends have babysitters."

"Well, I know for a fact that Scarlett is babysitting for Aleister, and Crowley has an older brother," said Mom. "Mal, what did you do to your head?"

"What?" I felt my forehead and noticed a small bump. So *not* a big deal. "Oh, probably playing ball the other day."

"Maybe if you cut your hair, you'd be able to see the ball," said Dad.

"Dad." I shook my head in disgust. My hair was perfect.

"You need to be careful," said Mom, brushing my hair from the spot and kissing my forehead. "Your head is important, you know."

"I know," I grumbled, brushing mom slobber from my forehead. "Anyway, don't try to change the subject. Please, don't get a babysitter. I'll lock the doors. I'll play hologames all day and stay on the couch, totally safe from rogue souls."

"Oh, that sounds good," said Dad, like he did not think playing games all day was a great idea. He stood up to put his coffee mug in the sink. There were dark shadows under his eyes.

"Scarlett mentioned Methuselah . . ." Mom trailed off with a grimace. Dad winced.

"MOM."

This was it. This was the answer to Aleister's worst-thing question. It had to be, because no matter how I strained my imagination, I could not think of a *thing* worse than being stuck with Methuselah on my epic school vacation.

"He's a million years old and smells funny. You can't be serious."

"He's a nice man, and he means well. It's good for him to spend time with young people. Think of it less as babysitting and more as keeping an old man company. Besides, I'm sure we'll finish this whole mess up today, and I'll be off for the rest of your vacation. We'll do something fun, okay?" Mom had the same dark shadows under her eyes that Dad did, but her hair was pulled back in a no-nonsense ponytail, and her wings blended with the black of her field uniform. Silver wings embroidered across the tops of both sleeves indicated her role as Commander. Insignia over her heart showed her impressive rank, and her squad identification.

It had been a while since I had seen her in the field uniform, and even then, only ever for training exercises. Not for real. Mom's squad was elite, and she was high enough up that all the powers and even most of the ordinary residents knew who she was. She didn't need a fancy uniform for recognition. No, this was for the times when they went beyond the offices, beyond the fence, and into the circles of the Pit. When they went there among the souls and demons, they wore their field uniforms, gleaming silver halos strapped to their hips. The uniform allowed movement and protection from physical attacks or other, bigger threats.

The kitchen light reflected off the razor-sharp halo at Mom's hip. This was real. How exciting!

She would be a terrifying sight to any soul in Hell unlucky enough to have her hunting them. But not so terrifying now as she smiled and gave me a gooey mom look.

I sighed and changed tactics. "*Dad.* Don't let her call him."

"Sorry, Mal," said Dad. He patted my shoulder as if that could make up for it. "This isn't a game. Just cooperate. Just this once, without a fight. Okay?"

FOUR

W hen I was young, we didn't have hologames," wheezed Methuselah as I did my best to ignore him.

"Fascinating," I deadpanned.

"I played with a stick. I pretended it was a sword . . . or a stick," Methuselah wheezed again. "Of course, I didn't have a lot of time to play in those days. I worked just to survive. The babies cleaned the floors, and the toddlers had to herd the goats, and when I was five, I guarded the house from marauders. When I was seven, I had to get married, and by then, of course, almost everyone had been eaten by giants."

"Giants? That's not true," I said.

"Not true? Were you there? I think not. Have you even

been to Earth, boy? Terrible place. Mostly uninhabited and smelling of goat . . . no plumbing . . . wrath of God everywhere . . . chickens . . ." Methuselah fell silent, and then, after several seconds of me wondering whether my supposedly immortal "babysitter" had died on my couch, he let out a snore.

It may have been the most amazing sound in the world, at least right now, because that horrible snorting, suffocating sound meant freedom.

Methuselah was an "immortal," a race of very-long-lived beings that existed early on in creation, shortly after Earth came into existence: not human, but not anything else, either. He was not celestial or imp, not soul or demon, not oni or bast or siren or anything like the other residents of Hell. He just . . . was, and he wasn't truly immortal, so dying on my couch seemed like a reasonable concern, but not something I wanted to explain to my parents.

Relieved, I paused my game, the three-dimensional figures freezing mid-action, and helped myself to a heaping bowl of ice cream. Methuselah slept most of the afternoon, which was, quite frankly, awesome. Occasionally the snores were punctuated by words, and once, for about three full minutes, he listed names begetting more names, whatever that meant.

"They left me with the old guy," I spoke into my headset. *"Goblin to the left."*

"Got him," Crowley answered. "I'd take the old guy. My brother has been an ignoramus. The only reason—*to your right*—I can even play now is because his girlfriend called."

"This escape is so lame. Oh, looks like Lilith is on. Hey, Lil."

". . . apples . . . snake . . ." Methuselah snorted and shifted position on the couch.

"Hello, boys," Lilith said. "How's detention?"

"What detention?" Aleister asked. "School's out. *Oh crap, what was that?*"

"Behind you," Lilith interrupted. "Detention as in being detained. No one is anywhere. It's like we're all on house arrest."

"Get that gem," I said. "No kidding. Not how I planned on spending vacation. *Dwarf to your left.* Hopefully this whole thing ends today and we can get back to having a good vacation. *Oh, for the love of brimstone, where did that guy come from?* At this rate we might as well be in school."

And wasn't that a depressing thought? This was supposed to be our last hurrah before the start of a new year. *The* year. I was supposed to have this vacation as a time when I didn't have to worry about fulfilling some kind of cosmic destiny. I was supposed to have this week to just be me, to spend time with my friends *as friends*, not as a squad. It wasn't supposed to be like this.

"*Ha. Got him.* Who are you jailed with, Lilith?" Crowley asked.

"I'm chilling solo," Lilith answered.

"What!" Crowley, Aleister, and I shouted in a rare moment of unity. Methuselah snorted and flailed around before falling still.

"What? Mom's been working. She's barely been home."

Lilith's mother worked directly with Lucifer. I wasn't sure exactly what she did, but Lilith always seemed to know a bit more than the rest of us, which was probably a good thing, really, considering she was our squad's Intelligence.

Or would be, anyway.

"No fair, I'm stuck with Methuselah. My house is starting to smell like old man," I said.

"I've got orders to stay inside until the fence goes down," Crowley said. "And my brother is in charge, whatever that's supposed to mean. Ridiculous. How'd you luck out, Lilith?"

"You all know I'm the mature one," Lilith gloated. "My mom trusts that I'm not going to blow up the house."

"I wouldn't blow up the house. I just want to stretch my wings," I grumbled. "*Hey, that was me, jerk. Don't hit me.*"

"Oh sorry, was that you?" Crowley snickered. *"My bad. You should really get out of the way. Oh, there goes your head."*

"Not cool, Crowley," Aleister said, but he sounded way too amused for it to mean much.

"Dude? Knock it off," I shouted, earning an evil laugh from Crowley and an exclamation of "Pudding!" from Methuselah, who promptly went back to sleep.

"This is not the vacation I wanted," I muttered as I regenerated my character. There was silence over the headsets in what I took as unspoken agreement.

FIVE

D ay two was a lot of the same. My parents were barely home, the fence stayed high, the flames illuminated the sky, and Methuselah slept on the couch. Preparations for Samhain had been put on hold, and the news scrolls speculated on whether public celebrations would happen at all, which seemed a bit much.

By evening I *had* to go outside.

I synced my ankle tether to my skateboard—a necessity if you were skating with wings—and with a push of my foot and a flap of wings, I was up the ramp by our shed, across my favorite leaning tree, and as close to freedom as I'd felt since that brief game of King of the Cage, when everything had gone to . . . well, home.

"MALACHI!" shouted my father in absolute fury.

I missed the heel flip I was attempting and had to flap my wings to keep myself airborne and not nose-dive off my second-story roof. My skateboard floated within range of my ankle, wheels still spinning.

"Get down here now," snarled my father. His wings were extended, and the flames in his eyes burned so bright that I could see them from the air. I had never seen my dad this angry.

I dove to the ground.

"Get into the house," he said.

I did, without even a question or witty response. Self-preservation was a strong instinct.

"What do you think you were doing?"

"Skateboarding," I said, pointing out the obvious.

"The prisoner is still on the loose, and you might as well be a neon sign on the roof of the house saying, 'Here I am!'"

"I was just getting some air, and I think it's obvious people live here. You know, with the houses and all!" Okay, apparently my attitude could overcome self-preservation. It was probably something I should work on.

"Don't be so reckless," my father said. "You have to be better than this. How is your squad going—" He stopped and took an enormous breath. It was too late. I knew what he'd been about to say, and it was a low blow. I stormed up the stairs, using my feet so they pounded all the way up.

"Mal," Dad said. He sighed, and then I heard him switch directions to talk to Methuselah instead. Good, I didn't want to talk to him anyway.

Bad enough that destiny had chosen my future, but to then suggest that I wouldn't even be good at it? GAH! Stab me with a pitchfork.

I slammed my door tight, but in the safety of my own room, my anger didn't mellow out like it usually did. It grew and grew until I was shaking. It wasn't just about being yelled at or having my ride ruined. It was my *destiny* being thrown into my face yet again. Because not only had my birth somehow decreed the rest of my eternity but I also had to be tracked and molded and shaped and trained, without anyone asking me what *I* wanted.

I didn't want to think about this. I didn't want everything to change. And that was the problem, wasn't it? Because Samhain was coming, and with it a new year, *the* year when my squad would all be separated into our specialties. I mean sure, we'd be together forever, but first we had to learn our individual roles within the squad. And that meant separate schools and studies to crush us into perfect little soldiers to save all of creation. But yeah, no pressure.

Why couldn't I just have the week of freedom we had

planned? One more week with my friends with possibilities still in front of me, even if they weren't really possibilities except in my own rebellious mind.

I rubbed my knuckles into my eyes and threw myself away from my bed. My eyes burned and my chest hurt, and even being surrounded by my favorite band posters and books and music and squishy pillows was not helping. I flung open my closet door and dug into the back corner, past boots that barely fit and pants I wore only to dances, past an old skateboard Aleister had given me for my ninth birthday, and an old diary I barely remembered writing in. I was frantically grabbing at anything until my hand closed over the smooth velvet bag hidden inside a ballet slipper too scuffed to use. My fist tightened and I fell back on my butt, my prize in hand.

My breath came quicker, and I forced myself to be quiet, afraid Dad would decide we still needed to talk. Like that had ever done us any good in the history of ever. I closed my hand tightly and felt the hard edges dig into my flesh. My stomach churned even thinking about opening it, but in a burst of rage or panic (who could tell the difference?), I emptied the velvet bag into my hand.

The crystal glowed a warm gold in my palm before I pinched the ends between my thumb and forefinger to hold it directly in my eyeline. A spark of creation distilled from the feather of an archangel's wing, trapped in crystal, just waiting to be used. And just like the power of creation, the spark contained infinite possibilities.

Straight from the Archangel Gabriel, kiddo, Tony had said.

I didn't necessarily believe that Tony, with his hologame bootlegs and tacky musical ties, had traveled to Heaven, although I supposed he could have traded with someone who had. I wasn't banking on the spark being from Gabriel. Lucifer was the only archangel here. It would be hard, but not impossible, to get a few of his golden feathers if you were willing to try, and in the end it didn't really matter *who* the spark came from, just that I had it.

Change in Hell was harder than pulling teeth, which is really quite simple with the proper tools. But I could change *anything* with the spark, including my destiny.

One time.

I took a deeper breath, feeling myself calm even as my stomach continued to twist. I had options. I looked past the glowing crystal into the mirror opposite me. The glow hid what I was sure would otherwise be bloodshot eyes. My cheeks were flushed, but if I ignored the twisting in my stomach, I could pretend it was from the skateboarding. My hair still looked awesome, so that was a plus. My wings were still puffed up from stress, but my feelings were so mixed looking at them that I focused back on my reflected face. I smirked. That was better.

Another deep breath, and I returned the crystal to its bag and shoved it under a pile of clothes in the corner of my room. I felt better knowing I had options, even if those options were terrifying. If I wasn't what Fate had decreed, what was I?

Day three was worse.

By day four the ice cream was gone, the house smelled deeply like old man, and Crowley wasn't even bothering to kill my gaming character anymore. On day five I screamed out my window. A gargoyle may or may not have screeched back at me. Methuselah didn't seem to notice.

Day six . . . my will to survive was weak.

My vacation was almost over. I'd be back in school in no time, alone in my brand-new classes with pompous jerks fighting for dominance. If they even opened school on time, that was.

I wasn't sure what I was hoping for. On the one hand, school staying closed? Yes, please! That sounded amazing! And a super-convenient way to avoid what I was dreading. Maybe it would never open again. On the other hand, what good was that if I was trapped at home with a babysitter? Oh, unholy darkness, what if I had to homeschool with Methuselah?

Our large Samhain gathering of what Mom called "found

family" had been canceled. The town celebrations had been indefinitely postponed. I didn't necessarily want to start my new school, but this wasn't an improvement.

Dust motes swirled above my head. I thought about voluntarily cleaning for the first time in my life but quickly dismissed the idea.

When the first hiss of "Mal" came through my window, I assumed I was going crazy. After all, I had considered calling Dad to ask where the dusting supplies were.

"Mal. C'mon, loser."

I didn't think my imagination would call me a loser, but I couldn't be sure.

There had been that whole internal debate about whether fake lemon helped make less dust or just made the motes smell like fake lemon—unmistakably loser-ish conversation.

"Mote." It was a funny word. Why did a castle moat and a dust mote sound the same? That made no sense.

"Mal!"

This time the hiss was quite possibly the loudest whisper that could still technically be called a whisper. My theater teacher would say it had nice projection to the back rows.

A skill to be used for commanding my squad, of course, not for being an actor. Lucifer forbid it to be used for a fun career.

I pulled myself out of bed and shuffled over to my window to peer out. Lilith, Aleister, and Crowley were all hovering outside, grinning evilly. For a moment it was pure happiness to see my squad all together outside my window.

Then I realized I was standing there in my TUESDAY boxer shorts.

Embarrassing enough if it were Tuesday, but even worse seeing as it was Thursday. I would like to think I had just put on the wrong day, but I knew better.

I grabbed a throw blanket and held it in front of my incriminating boxers as Aleister snickered, Crowley rolled his eyes, and Lilith looked away. Maybe she hadn't noticed?

"This is my room, you know," I said, blushing despite the accusation in my voice. I was supposed to be in charge of them? Ha! Reason three thousand and one for using the alternative hidden in a small velvet bag.

My parents both had the exact role I was supposed to have, and they didn't goof off with their squadrons. Ever. In fact, I had seen my mom make hers cry on the regular. Their squads certainly didn't come over and hang out.

"C'mon, dude! Jailbreak," Lilith said, the light of the flames glinting off her black wings making them appear blue and purple in places. She was dressed in a white top, a delicate gold necklace at her throat, and stylishly distressed jeans.

She was perfect.

And I was in my two-day-old boxers.

"Seriously?" I asked, desperate to change the subject as I shoved myself into jeans while scrambling to hold up the blanket covering my delicates. "How did you ditch your babysitters?"

"Well, I never had one, of course," Lilith said, perched on my windowsill like an angel in repose.

Or something. Whatever.

"My ignoramus of a brother snuck out to be with his girlfriend," Crowley said.

"And his brother's girlfriend happens to be Scarlett, who is at my house—doing a terrible job babysitting, I might add, seeing that I am gone," Aleister said. He was wearing a football jersey that hung large over ripped jeans, and a ridiculous yellow bandana in his dark hair, which was apparently his latest attempt at fashion.

"Let's go," Crowley said, flying a lazy circle in the air.

"Where are we going?" I asked.

"You'll see," Aleister called, his voice fading into the distance.

I pulled a T-shirt on, spreading my wings to fit comfortably through the slots, and grabbed a zip-up hoodie, which sent a certain velvet bag tumbling to the ground. Without the fun I had planned for vacation, my existential crises were coming fast and furious, and I had found myself looking at my last-ditch option more than once. I shoved it into my pocket, blushing slightly even though there was no way my friends could know what I was hiding, and launched myself out my second-floor window, following my friends to anywhere better.

We were careful to fly below the tree line, not wanting to be vibrant silhouettes against the flaming sky, before touching down lightly on the cobblestone sidewalk outside Pandemonium Park.

"Aww, man," whined Aleister. "They canceled the games tomorrow." He gestured to a flyer on the stone wall outside the park. It had previously advertised the annual games that took place here every year the day after Samhain, but now it was stamped with one word: CANCELED.

"Obviously," said Lilith. "Everything's canceled."

"That's such garbage," he grumbled. "I've been practicing for the pie-eating contest. I had it this year."

"Wait, tomorrow?" I blurted. "Today's Samhain?"

"Oh, for the—" groaned Crowley. "Seriously? How do you not know that?"

Samhain, also known as All Hallows' Eve or Halloween, marked the start of the new year, normally a time of celebration, but with the escaped prisoner *still* on the loose, all the celebrations had been nixed, and with my parents working every second of every day, the normal baking hadn't been done.

My house felt the very opposite of festive. Instead of smelling like apples and rosemary, it smelled like spearmint and stale cigars. When combined with my absolute dread of the new year, and my lack of awareness of the day, as evidenced by my sad boxers, it was no surprise that I had completely forgotten today was the day.

That was so depressing.

Crowley pushed open the black iron gate, which swung noiselessly, and we entered the park. The fountain burbled, and the lockdown flames were so bright that the bioluminescent moss seemed dull in comparison, just random splashes of faintly glowing color. The park was empty, and we quickly veered off the cobblestone path to make our way into the woods.

The flame light cast long shadows, and the branches stretched like bony fingers, forming a protective canopy above. Dead leaves crunched under our feet while the spindly-legged variety scrambled up and down the trees like spiders, giving the woods a cozy, inhabited feeling—something the empty park had been missing.

The cinnamon and dead-leaf scent of the woods smelled like freedom, and I took a deep breath. Much better than old-man smell.

While I still had a pang of loss at everything that had

been canceled, I was so grateful to be out of my house that I felt happier than I had in days.

It didn't even matter where we were going. It didn't matter that we were walking instead of flying. All that mattered was that I was out of my house with my friends, finally getting the devilish distraction I wanted.

SIX

I don't care if she is your brother's girlfriend. She's hot," Aleister said, tightrope-walking his way along a fallen tree, his arms extended, wings twitching whenever his balance wavered.

"Don't be gross," Crowley said, throwing a small stick in Aleister's general direction.

"She is, dude. Have you looked at her?" Aleister taunted. "He'd better watch out. I think she likes me."

"She does not like you," Crowley said.

"She does. I can tell," Aleister said.

"She's a senior, and you are a cretin," Crowley said. "Though, she does have questionable taste, dating my brother and all."

"Not for long," Aleister replied, and then snickered.

"You're an idiot," Crowley said.

"You're both idiots," I said, before ripping Aleister's yellow bandana off him. "And this is stupid."

"Hey!" protested Aleister. "I like it!"

"I'm helping you." I laughed and shoved his hands away.

"Whoa," Aleister said, freezing in his tracks. I took advantage of his distraction and pocketed the yellow abomination before turning to see what I had missed.

"What is that?" I asked.

We had nearly made our way through the unrestricted section of the woods and were only feet from the fence, which normally stood a lot lower to the ground. Beyond the black metal protection of the town fence was more of the same forest. That section of Hell wasn't residential, even though the land didn't look any different until you got much farther out. At least it didn't *usually* look any different.

Today it had a strange quality to it. Where the fence had always seemed an impenetrable guardian before, the area in front of me now looked shimmery and insubstantial. It was surrounded by foliage, and only the lower portion of the fence looked normal. The world beyond the fence was barely visible through the distortion.

"It's starting," Lilith said excitedly.

"I can't believe it's really here," Aleister said in awe.

"No way," Crowley said.

"What is it?" I asked, feeling a step behind.

"It's the veil," Lilith said, her eyes sparkling, cheeks flushed with color. It distracted my brainpower for a minute, but then the words finally broke through and made sense.

"Wait, the veil? Like, out of Hell?" I asked.

"It's Samhain," Lilith said. "The *way* is opening."

Samhain was the day of the year when the separation between worlds was thinnest. Not just between the mortal coil and the great hereafters but between other dimensions as well. Sometimes the thinning was so great that things could pass through, but anything with any intelligence stayed on their proper side. Wandering around a dimension that was not your own was asking for trouble.

"No way," I said. "How did you know this was here?"

"I found a note in my mom's office predicting an unauthorized rip around here, but then the escape happened, and she's gotten way behind," Lilith said. "She probably didn't even see the note come in. It was one of those automated-alert things she gets all the time."

"Nice," Aleister said, giving Lilith a high five.

"Shouldn't we tell someone about it?" I asked. "I mean, with Samuel Parris loose, shouldn't they be looking at all the possible exits?"

"Shut up," Crowley said.

Translation: *Malachi, stop being a loser and ruining our only entertainment of the week.*

"I'm just saying," I protested, and almost immediately wanted to slap myself. What was my problem? Why was I channeling my dad?

"Wait, what did you say about Samuel Parris?" Lilith asked. "Is that who the escapee is?"

I was secretly pleased that I knew something she didn't. Lilith was impressed by knowledge, and I couldn't help the proud smirk that curved the edges of my mouth.

"Yeah, I heard my parents talking," I said. "Eighth circle, I think."

"Huh, a manipulator. I wonder what he did." Lilith looked lost in thought for a moment and then shook it off. "Anyway, the fence is up, we're fine. Even if his soul wanted to escape through here, it would have to have been in town before the lockdown started, and there's no way that happened."

This sounded fair, and Lilith was generally right about . . . pretty much everything.

After all, the bells were sounded as soon as a soul left its assigned circle, and the lockdown happened automatically when they rang. Samuel Parris would never have been able to make it from the Pit, through the surrounding wasteland, past the security systems of the metropolitan areas of Dagon and Thoth, and all the way over to our quiet little suburb before our flames soared and our fence closed.

Wherever that escaped soul was, it was out there somewhere, struggling its way through the brimstone geysers of the wasteland or the salespeople of Thoth.

Which meant I could enjoy my own escape worry-free. Score!

"I've never seen a way open up before," Aleister said, and everyone shook their heads in agreement.

"Me either," Lilith said.

Crossing the dimensions was only ever allowed through approved openings, with special permission given out for Very. Good. Reasons. Boredom wasn't one of them.

My parents had crossed, of course, but Mom said it was just a bunch of paperwork and bureaucracy to leave home for nothing special. She said I wasn't missing anything. She clearly didn't understand my interests. What could be more exciting than an adventure somewhere new?

The shimmering grew brighter, and it was almost as if the fence and the forest behind it didn't exist at all anymore.

"Dare you to touch it," Crowley said, an evil smile lighting his eyes.

"No way," Aleister said, taking a half step back.

"C'mon, Mal, touch it," Crowley teased.

"You touch it," I said. As if I'd do something just because Crowley wanted me to; crossroads dealmaker he was not. Though he *should* have been allowed to be one if he wanted to. Who was to say he wouldn't have been excellent at making deals with humans if he was allowed to try?

"Coward," Crowley said, and I laughed derisively.

Aleister got a stick, and we all crept closer to the veil. Aleister pushed the stick toward the shimmering spot, and the end disappeared. He pulled it back. The stick seemed unharmed. Crowley picked up a rock and tossed it through. The rock disappeared without a sound. The veil rippled like water.

"Weird," Lilith said. Her eyes sparkled in excitement. I loved when her eyes sparkled.

"Where do you think it goes?" asked Aleister. "Earth?"

"Maybe it just goes to another hereafter," Crowley said.

He had a point.

Openings in the veil could take you to lots of places. Since it was Samhain and the veil was thinnest between the mortal coil and the great hereafters, it seemed more likely that it went to Earth or one of the other mortal dimensions, but it could potentially go to Purgatory, where those who seemed redeemable went, or even Heaven, or any number of other dimensions. There really was no telling . . . well, not from this side of it anyway.

"The alert predicted that it went to Earth. What, you want to test it?" Lilith asked in disbelief. Something in her tone suggested an eagerness to do just that.

"Go on, Mal," Crowley said. "Go check it out. Tell us if that's really the mortal coil through there."

"You first," I scoffed, though I had to admit I had the urge to try it. I had been stuck inside for *way* too long.

"Is that an order?" asked Crowley, smirking as my temper flared enough to send the flames flickering in my eyes and make my wings spread a little.

We jostled each other and kept throwing rocks, leaves, and sticks through the veil, taunting and daring each other to cross the veil, or at least put a hand in, maybe a toe?

We kept moving closer.

Lilith's excited laughs, higher-pitched than our mocking tones, ran a thrill up my spine. Soon we were stretching our hands closer, seeing who would be bravest.

My hand was nearly touching the veil. I swore I could feel something along my palm, something faint like bubbles popping against my skin.

This was so unlike me. Okay, I was daring and adventurous, charming, and generally awesome, but there *was* that little sense of responsibility that always kept me from doing the truly stupid, despite what my father may have thought. Still, I leaned closer . . .

And then suddenly I was through, a feeling like icy water plunging over my body, and I fell, slamming face-first onto a concrete street.

SEVEN

What the everlasting fire!" I shouted, instantly angry. Freaking Crowley!

I turned to curse him out for pushing me, but no one was there.

I looked forward, and rather than foliage and a shimmering fence, there was a busy street with "people," which didn't look anything like what I was used to. The older-looking "people" were walking, children were running, and the sky was blue.

The sky was *blue*.

I had never seen a color like that in the sky. Nothing so bright and infinite. I didn't like it. I sat up, absentmindedly brushing my hands on my pants, rubbing the dirt out of my skin.

At home the flames cast a homey orange glow that reached upward from the horizon, fading to a comforting black at the top of the sky and cradling our neighborhood like a cozy blanket. Warm and dark and safe, just like home should be.

This . . . this was not warm and cozy. This was cold and clear, sterile. Instead of snuggling us in warmth, this sky was like an observation window, and I felt like I was the one in the tank. This was not just another part of home. Was I in another hereafter? No, that didn't feel right. Where could I be?

You know, you never think remembering how many dimensions there are is important when they talk about it in school.

Looking around, I saw that each person glowed with a soft aura, and I knew instinctively that the aura predicted their final destinations; red were ours; blue were Heaven's, and the murky swirls of gray were those whose destinies weren't so clear. Those would sway either one way or another or be judged in the afterlife. Possibly they would simply languish in Limbo as lost souls.

I was momentarily cheered that the blue and gray auras outnumbered the red by huge quantities. Fewer souls for us meant less work, which meant home didn't need me to fulfill any stupid predestined role. They could do without me. Metal vehicles, souls waiting for their hereafters, terrifying blue sky.

Check, check, check. The alert had been right. I was on Earth.

Aw, brimstone.

I was so going to kick Crowley's butt, but when I turned around, there still was no shimmering, no fence, no veil of any kind. I waved my hands vaguely in front of me, but nothing. No tingling. No disappearing. Just empty air.

That was when the panic set in.

Dad had freaked when I'd left the house to skateboard, even though I was literally *on* the house. What would he do if he realized I had left not only the house but the entire dimension?

I tried to think, but my brain decided to turn into an alarm system of noise and static, which made thinking remarkably difficult. My parents went to Earth only for business, with the proper paperwork and through the proper gates. They may have said more, but it was all "blah, blah, blah."

I swallowed a lump in my throat, which was not from being close to crying or anything like that. All I had to do was get from the mortal coil back to the great hereafter. *My* great hereafter. This wasn't a problem. Humans did it all the time. This wasn't a big deal. *Think, Malachi. Think.*

I blinked my eyes rapidly for no reason in particular (certainly not to clear unshed tears away) and began walking. The opening had to be nearby. It *had* to be, and I was sure I'd feel it whenever I found it. It was Samhain. The veil was thin.

I'd be okay. I'd be back in no time, and then I'd *kill* Crowley.

That cheered me slightly.

The human kids, who seemed to be everywhere, ran from door to door, yelling and screaming. The craziest thing was that no one seemed to mind! Adults opened their doors and bribed the kids to leave by dropping handfuls of stuff into the bags the children carried.

There were a few imps and other creatures running around that at first made me feel a little better about Earth, but then I realized that the tails, fangs, and other features were all fake—nothing more than costumes.

Disappointing.

And also, slightly offensive.

In fact, now that I knew what was imitation, I realized that despite the glowing auras, humans looked a lot like powers—wingless powers, of course, but the hair and skin came in the same range of shades. There were so many, though, it seemed to be the only kind of people this world had.

As I was searching my new surroundings, I caught sight of my reflection in a storefront window. For about half a second, I was proud that I only looked slightly worried rather than completely-out-of-my-mind panicked, but then I noticed something so horrific that my brain screeched to a halt.

I was wingless, too. How had I not noticed that?

I stepped closer and turned to look in the glass. My wings were gone. Okay, maybe I had occasionally wished them to be something different, but that was only because I wanted a *choice*. I didn't want my wings to dictate who I was, but I loved them. They were strong and sleek, and the black feathers made me look totally awesome. I couldn't lose them!

I was going to hyperventilate.

I was going to absolutely lose my cool.

I was in another dimension, and I was wingless.

Even worse, I had no idea how to get back.

I was sure I looked ridiculous, frantically searching for any sign of home or help, but for once I couldn't care less about what anyone thought. Let's see how calm they would look, being dumped into a strange dimension and missing necessary, and pretty awesome, body parts. A spiteful voice at the back of my mind said, *Isn't that what the crystal is for? Don't those awesome wings make you feel trapped?* But what did that voice know? Nothing, that's what.

A major freak-out was just on the verge of taking over when I saw it. A small sign, but it caught my eye anyway: SALEM WITCH HOUSE. That was just what I needed. A witch could help me get back home, no problem.

Good thing I had kept my head. That's me, confidence under pressure.

EIGHT

The village was covered in pictures of witches. Seriously, everywhere. On signs, windows, and even some of the weird vehicles, so I was optimistic that the witch was powerful enough to get me home. Having a goal kept me focused, and I found the house easily.

"Brimstone," I cursed. Apparently, I wasn't the only one who had sought out the witch.

There was a line of humans that wrapped around the house. I considered marching to the front, but it was probably best to get an idea of how this witch worked and not do anything to offend them, so I did what most people did when in the presence of a line: I stood at the end of it.

The line was slow-moving and would have been worse if I wasn't so fascinated by seeing real humans in the flesh. Curious, I poked one. They felt the same as us, but it was fascinating to see my finger sink through that glowing aura.

Eventually I discovered that humans didn't like to be poked, and so then I was just standing in line again, imagining how my parents would choose to kill me when they found out I was here. Assuming I ever got out of here. Assuming I ever got my wings back. And wasn't that a loaded thought? Best to ignore it.

I bounced on my feet, urging the line to go faster, but if that had ever worked in the history of lines, it wasn't working now.

"Mo-o-o-o-m-m," whined a kid in front of me. I wasn't sure how humans aged, but he looked young, past cute and chubby, but still whiny. "How much longer?"

"We're almost to the front. Shhh," hissed the kid's mother. Both their auras glowed a murky gray, more blue than not, but still room to brighten with a little more goodness.

"This is boring. I wanna go trick-or-treating."

"We will. After we're done," said the mother.

The kid huffed, plopped himself to the ground, and crossed his arms in anger. Right outside a witch's house! He was so going to be turned into a frog.

The kid looked at me and stuck out his tongue. I frowned.

Humans couldn't read thoughts, could they? No, no way. That was stupid.

The line could give the Pit a run for its money in torture methods. Standing, waiting, never moving, ugh, but it gave me plenty of time to think. A witch would want payment. Normally it would be something unique or rare that the witch could use as a spell ingredient. At home I'd expect to trade a feather from my wings, but, well . . . you know. I wasn't sure what else I had to offer.

Instead of letting it all drive me insane, I decided to wonder about the weird term the kid had used, "trick-or-treating." I knew what tricking was. I mean *Hell-o*, obviously! And treating was usually paying for someone else, wasn't it? Like when I paid for Aleister's ice cream at Frozen Over because he had forgotten his wallet for the sixteen thousandth time.

Whatever trick-or-treating was, the mother didn't seem overly concerned, and so I was back to waiting.

There was a sign on the outside wall indicating that "Halloween" was sold out and only those with pre-purchased tickets would be admitted, but that didn't make any sense. Witches didn't take tickets. They took blood and teeth, feathers and bones, and other spell ingredients. I decided I wouldn't worry about the sign. It was probably just a trick to fool the unworthy.

"Mom," the kid insisted.

"Alex," snapped the mother. "You won't miss anything. Just please be good." The kid made an annoyed sound, and the mother looked at her watch. She held slips of paper in her hand, presumably the tickets for the unworthy.

The line moved forward, and a woman near the door called, "Tickets, please" before taking them from people and waving folks through. I jumped at the voice, startled by the first commanding tone I'd heard here, and worried for a moment that the witch had taken me by surprise, but this woman had a name tag on, and no one looked particularly impressed. Just a minion, then. She did seem to care about people having tickets, though, and that could be a problem.

"I'm sorry," she said, stopping a sharply dressed woman from entering. "We're completely sold out. You have to already have tickets."

"I know," said the woman. "I was just hoping I could buy one. The rest of my group has them, and I wasn't really planning on being in town. It was kind of a last-minute thing."

"I understand, but it's Halloween and we're fully booked," said the minion. "We'll have plenty of space tomorrow."

The woman argued a little longer before finally waving goodbye to her friends and heading off. I frowned. I had to see that witch, and I had no idea how these so-called tickets were even obtained. Blood contract, probably.

My foot lurched as my sneaker was kicked. I looked down. The annoying kid had sagged lower onto the sidewalk, melting into a slump of boredom personified.

I froze, a plan forming in my mind.

I crouched down. "Hey, kid," I whispered, glancing up to make sure the mother wasn't paying attention. The kid, Alex, rolled his eyes to look at me without moving any other part of his body. Impressive. "You know, they're closing trick-or-treating in five minutes. If you don't leave now, you're going to miss it."

Alex's eyes widened, and his chest swelled as he took in an enormous breath before jumping to his feet and grabbing his mother's arm.

"*MOM* . . . We-have-to-go-now-we're-going-to-miss-it." He punctuated the jumble of words with jumps that pulled his mom's arm down. The next part happened the way doom always happens, in slow motion.

Her arm jerked. The arm whose hand was holding, as it turned out, a full cup of coffee. Black liquid spilled down the front of her clothes. Alex went silent as his mom gasped. Everyone in line quieted as we watched and pretended not to watch, so that the sound of the paper cup bouncing off the concrete was audible.

Without a word the mother grabbed Alex's arm and pulled him away from the line, leaving the Witch House altogether. I slid the slips of paper from her hand as she passed.

No tickets? No problem.

NINE

In 1675, Jonathan Corwin was heir to one of the largest Puritan fortunes in New England when he bought this stately home. If you look in here, you can see a typical bedroom of the time. Now, please do stay behind the rope."

After waiting in line *forever*, I wasn't sure what I'd been expecting. Maybe not an immediate audience with the witch, but it certainly hadn't been a boring tour of old furniture.

"Excuse me?" I interrupted. The woman leading the tour smiled at me. I smiled back, because let's face it, my smile is fantastic. "Where's the witch?"

She frowned. "Which witch?" She giggled. I grimaced.

"This is the Witch House, right?" I asked, thinking I was pointing out a rather obvious fact.

"Oh, no. We call this the Witch House because it demonstrates the living conditions during the period of the Salem witch trials. But Jonathan Corwin himself was important to the trials. He was a magistrate and would have heard and stood in judgment over the accused."

"But there's no witch here?" I interrupted again, afraid the woman was going to go on another history lesson.

"No," she said. Her smile dropped for a moment in irritation before she quickly re-formed it.

I should have known! A real witch wouldn't take tickets, and there was nothing in that house a witch would need. There were no spell ingredients. No sigils of protection. I hadn't seen any familiars wandering around. What was the point of all this witch stuff if there was no witch?

I was so furious that it was easy to push the fear of my one plan being an utter failure way down where I shoved everything else I didn't want to think about. I forced my way through the humans, my usual charm almost nonexistent as I backtracked through the house. It was difficult, since the hallways and staircases were so narrow, but I couldn't waste any more time here.

I twisted through bodies, smiling apologetically as my movements against them sent their auras swirling. They were almost all blue or that murky gray, but I managed to step on the foot of one who glowed red. I figured it was the least I could do as a nod to home.

As I stepped off the staircase and back onto the first floor, I caught movement out of the corner of my eye, and at first I assumed it was just the remnant of a swirling aura that caused my head to jerk to the side. It was the opposite direction from where I wanted to go, but resisting my curiosity had never been my strong suit.

I ventured toward where I had seen the movement, but as I took in the foyer and small dark room beyond, it seemed that I was alone. Everyone else had moved on with the boring-as-virtue tour, and the minions hadn't let more humans in yet. I paused, frozen in place, waiting to see what had attracted my attention. It was a long moment of stillness before something moved.

There! Something in the darkest corner of the room, the parlor, if I was remembering the minion correctly.

I crept closer and bent down. The thing jerked back and disappeared, but I knew where it was now.

"C'mon, little guy," I whispered. "I know you're there."

The shadows stayed stubbornly still.

68

"I promise I won't tell," I said, keeping my voice low. "How did you get here? Can you show me?"

The shadow darkened and slithered. The edges grew slightly longer, reaching toward me.

"It must be tough with that sky," I said. "Maybe it will get dark later. I'm pretty sure that's how it works here."

The shadow lengthened even further, stretching impossibly far from the corner until, with an audible sound, it popped free. A chubby little shade sat on the floor, splay-legged with a thumb popped into its mouth in front of me. It was adorable, and way too little to be this far from home.

"Do you want to come with me?" I said, pulling my T-shirt out and away from my stomach. If the baby shade stayed under there, and I zipped up my hoodie, it would be dark enough to keep it safe. "I don't know the way home yet, but I'm sure I'll find it soon."

The shade fell forward, rearranging its limbs as it advanced. Shades weren't necessarily from home; many of them stayed in Limbo or even Purgatory, but we had them at home, too, and it would be better for this little guy to be there rather than stuck on Earth.

The shade's presence so far from home made me feel much less alone. That was probably why I didn't notice the room darken until the darkness was almost all there was.

The shade was yanked upward, and I snapped my gaze up.

"Oh, you're *not* alone," I said, standing back up.

A face scowled at me from the ceiling before all the shadows in the room pulled back and returned to their normal places. The room brightened considerably. Only a slightly darker corner gave away that anything was out of the ordinary.

"I wasn't trying to kidnap it," I protested. "I swear." If a shadow could express disbelief, the one in the corner was doing just that.

I decided to make myself scarce, and in no time I was through the kitchen and the gift shop, then pushing open the door to the outside world and the still waiting line. The blue sky was just as jarring, and now that my one plan had failed, it was even more nerve-racking. But I wasn't the only one who was in the wrong dimension. The presence of the two shades was proof of that, and that was honestly a relief.

I squinted and tried to let my eyes adjust to the too-bright light from the fireball in the sky. *Okay, town, where are you hiding the witch?* How did anyone see in this world? In fact, the longer I was out, the worse it was getting. I rubbed my eyes, but it didn't help. The light was shifting.

It got brighter and brighter until I knew there was a blinding white light behind me. What could cause that? Something awful, probably. Monsters? Weapons of mass destruction? Dad?

With not a small amount of dread, I turned.

TEN

The sound of a choir reaching a massive crescendo rose with the light I now faced. Brighter than any aura. Brighter than the small spark of creation in my pocket. My eyes managed to adjust, and then a form became clear through the whiteness. Its wings extended, creating a large silhouette. For a moment I hoped (and feared) it was one of my parents coming to bring me home.

But it was something much, much worse.

"Behold, I am an angel of Heaven," said the form, in a melodic feminine voice. "Come, child, I have come to bring you to paradise."

The angel extended her hand. Her gown and wings were

so white, they were barely visible against the blinding light, and her hair was so fair that it shone a pale yellow barely discernible from the golden halo that glowed brightly above it. She was one of the seraphim. There was a reason they were called the burning ones, and my angry retinas were proof.

I took a deep breath and then did what any sensible person would do in the same situation.

I screamed and ran.

I ran until the sound of the choir faded, and the light dimmed to what I could only assume was a normal Earth level. My feet pounded against the pavement with jarring force as I ran for my life. I never thought I'd ever *need* to run for my life. Fly, sure, but not *run*.

I almost fell once when my muscles instinctively flexed where my wings should be, ready to launch into flight, but without my wings I just ended up doing a weird shrug and stumbled when my feet hadn't been ready to keep running.

It wasn't pleasant, but the seraph didn't seem to be following me, so I supposed it was worth it. I got more than a few weird looks and one thumbs-up from someone running in the opposite direction.

I slowed my pace and eventually loped to a not-so-graceful walk. My feet hurt. My side had a stitch.

"Ugh, running sucks," I groaned, gripping my side.

"Dude, arch supports and Band-Aids on your nipples."

I looked up in utter confusion to see a man jogging in place. He had a sweatband across his forehead and a water bottle strapped to his arm.

"What?"

"They're the keys to making running *not* 'suck,'" said the man. "Well, that and good tunes." He pointed to his ear and continued running past me. I looked in the direction he had come from, but if there had been anything chasing him, I couldn't see it.

Band-Aids on your nipples. Brimstone! Earth was so weird.

But the weirdness cleared my panic and let me take stock of my situation.

The seraph hadn't followed me, and now it seemed I was in a much busier part of town. Despite the line trying to get into the Witch House, the area immediately around it hadn't been that crowded, but right now I was surrounded by humans. I didn't know if any of the heavenly host had permission to appear before mortals, but she wasn't here now, so I was hoping not.

I hadn't thought the seraphim left Heaven. At least not often. Maybe she would go away. Or maybe I should have asked her how to get home? No, she had said she wanted to take me to Heaven.

I shuddered. Destiny changes or not, I was no heavenly angel.

And then a thought stopped me cold. My heart raced and a sweat broke out across my forehead. Did Heaven know I was here? Was the seraph here for *me*?

"Whoa there," a woman said. Her arm shot out, holding me back. She smiled kindly, one eyebrow raised like she found me amusing. Her aura glowed a pretty blue. "Wait for the signal."

She gestured in front of me to a light box with a red hand on it. My foot was balanced on the edge of the curb, and as a metal vehicle raced by, the breeze sent my hair across my eyes. I stepped back to safety and shook my head. I had almost been smooshed.

"How am I supposed to deal with a full-grown angel?" I blurted out.

"Aw, that's sweet," said the woman, laughing lightly. "I'm definitely not an angel, but saying 'thank you' is always a good bet."

"Thank you?" I said, completely confused, until I realized she had no idea what I was talking about. Probably for the best, really.

The woman winked. The red hand changed to a green person, and an annoying beeping sent people moving. My eyes darted to the town around me even as I was swept along with the crowd. *Something* felt wrong. I tried to ignore it because *everything* was in fact wrong.

I didn't know what it was that drew my attention to the man on the cross street. His aura was a murky swirl of indecision. His clothes weren't particularly impressive, but something made me do a double take. Just in time to see him dash off the curb despite the red hand surely telling him to stop.

There was a screech like a banshee's yell, a thump, and a held breath of silence.

Then the screaming started.

ELEVEN

I ran over without thinking. The driver was out of his vehicle, looking shell-shocked, his hands trembling through his pale blue aura. "The light was green. I—"

"Someone call 911!"

The man held his hands to his head, the driver's door still open. "He came out of nowhere."

"James," a woman yelled, parting the crowd. Reaching the horrific scene, she stopped, apparently stunned, and then she clung to the body slumped over the vehicle's hood. "Someone, get help!"

The glass front of the vehicle was cracked in a spiderweb pattern, caved in, and barely holding on to its form, as if a good breeze would send it raining down onto the front seat.

The glass was tinted pink from blood, and where the liquid slid from the flat plane, it ran and spread into the cracks, painting them scarlet. The body of "James" was still and lifeless.

His aura was gone.

Before the crash his aura had been that swirling gray that meant he'd need to be judged first. From there he'd go to one of the great hereafters. There was a roughly one-in-three chance that he would end up right where I wanted to be. Well, sort of. He wouldn't go to the nice residential section I was from, of course, but the part outside the fence, where it always smelled like barbecue, which was close enough.

I had never seen a mortal pass on. Was it already done? Had I missed it? The humans were obviously upset, but maybe they didn't realize that Earth was only a temporary stop on the way home. Not just for me but for them, too.

Blue and red lights and the wail of a siren came closer. For a moment I assumed the bright blue that approached was just another part of those lights, but in moments I realized it wasn't from the lights on the vehicles at all; it was the aura of a boy. The brightest azure I had seen yet.

He pushed right past me and placed his first two fingers on the neck of the body across the car, something none of the adults had done. More lights reflected off the metal and glass, this time mostly red, and I looked over my shoulder to see large white vehicles approaching.

With all the flashing lights, and the abnormally bright sky, it was probably understandable that I didn't notice the shimmering light rising from the body at first. But once I did, my head snapped up, and in the process I met very familiar eyes across the vehicle.

Crowley.

Oh, thank Lucifer. I wasn't alone! My heart surged with relief.

Of course, I wouldn't even have been in this mess if it hadn't been for Crowley.

My eyes narrowed, but I'd have time to deal with Crowley when we got home; now wasn't the time for death glares. Besides, even if he was to blame, *maybe* in the deepest part of my heart I was still a tiny bit happy to see him. *Maybe.*

Our eyes locked, and Crowley's eyes widened in surprise, but right now we had more important things to worry about, and with a few ridiculous head gestures and a nod, I knew we were on the same page. Maybe the soul, if that was what the shimmering light was, wouldn't be of any help, but it was worth a shot. We had to follow it.

Besides, the newly arrived adults were wearing identical

uniforms, and I had already encountered a seraph; we didn't need to add human authorities to the mix. Being anywhere else seemed like a good idea, even if the soul didn't lead us home.

The boy with the bright soul stepped back from the body. I didn't dare spare him a glance, but then the sparkle drifted, and I was facing the boy as I tried to keep the soul in sight. He didn't seem to see the light himself, but he noticed my eyes move, and he cocked his head curiously to the side. And then the sparkle took off.

"C'mon," I snapped to Crowley. We removed ourselves from the crowd as gracefully as possible, and then bolted as soon as we were clear.

"We're thinking that's that guy's soul, right?" Crowley asked.

"Gotta be," I said, with more confidence than I felt. "They must look different here. Maybe we can follow it to a doorway home."

"Is this a good idea?" Crowley asked, but he didn't stop running. "It could be heading to Heaven."

"No way," I said. "I saw his aura before he died. He's going to be judged first. If we can follow him, we can take the door home."

"You gonna sweet-talk the Jackal?" Crowley asked. His breath came out in pained huffs as we ran.

"If it will get us home?" I asked. "Yes!"

The sparkling light we were following would have to go to a place we called the Gray but others called Limbo, the Between, or the Underworld, and there were probably a million more names that I didn't even know about. It didn't matter what it was called. It was all the same thing, and it was ruled by Anubis, affectionately known as the Jackal.

Once the door to the Gray opened, we'd follow the soul inside, and while the Jackal was doing his thing with the feather and scales, and the recently deceased soul of James, we'd slip on past, open door number two, and voilà—home sweet home.

It was foolproof, except for the fact that I wasn't 100 percent sure this was a soul at all, and as much as I thought Anubis would be cool, I also wasn't 100 percent sure he'd let us pass through without being all responsible and telling our parents. But before we could deal with any of that, we had to keep the soul in sight, and that was proving remarkably hard to do without wings.

It was like the soul was trying to get away from us. It twisted and turned through the air, zigging and zagging as if it was doing its best to avoid being kept in sight. Running wasn't any better this time, and my feet caught on raised stones. The stitch in my side threatened to come back.

We wove in and out of kids, vendor carts, and adults—

some dressed in suits and ties, others in fur and fangs, and still others in glitter and wings. I wasn't sure what was normal human attire or whether it all was, but there was no time to think about that now because the soul was getting away.

It was hard to keep the shimmery spot in sight, and as it moved farther away, I began to panic. This might be our only chance, and if we lost it . . .

"Hey! Watch it," shouted a voice as we crashed into a group of teenagers. We tried to weave through them, but the multitude of bodies slowed us down, and the soul was getting farther and farther away.

"What's your problem, man?" argued the voice just as I broke free.

"You're my only problem," Crowley snarled.

Of course.

I turned, and Crowley was chest to chest with a boy a good deal taller. If we hadn't been in a major hurry, I would have laughed, because they were both staring at each other with the same imperious look. I groaned and whipped my head back around, but the soul was barely visible.

"Crowley!" I shouted. Crowley glanced my way, and I gave him a furious *Hurry up, you moron* look.

"Fine," Crowley said. He strong-armed the taller boy with a stiff shove, sending him to the ground and leaving him stunned. I didn't feel bad because we didn't have time for guilt, and besides, the boy's aura had a pink tinge that looked like it would develop into a nice red any day.

It was only moments later that we started to gain on the sparkle. I ignored the pain in my side and my aching muscles and pushed faster.

And then I noticed that the sparkle was no longer moving.

Crowley and I stumbled to a halt, our breath coming fast and hard. I clutched my side, and Crowley rubbed his thigh.

"Ugh, it's like being tortured in the Pit," groaned Crowley.

The sparkle was right in front of us now, but it had changed.

"This isn't the sparkle. It's a reflection," I said dully. I pressed my hand against the glass of a shop window. "It's just a reflection of that fireball in the sky." I turned and looked. The fire was getting lower, and the blue of the sky was changing.

"Actually, the ball is incandescent gas," Crowley said. "Not a fireball."

"Not relevant," I said. "Why'd you have to start trouble? You made me lose track of the soul!"

"I didn't *start* anything. That *human* started it," Crowley said. "What was I supposed to do? Apologize and ask for my leave?"

"When we're trying to find a way home and have a one-in-a-million chance of following a soul home? Yeah, you play nice and keep moving."

"Whatever, it probably wasn't going to work anyway," Crowley said. "Anubis would never have allowed us in when there are judgments to be made. You know the rules."

"Yeah," I ground out. There were So. Many. Rules. "If you have a better idea, I'd love to hear it. Should we just kill someone?"

"Why not?" asked Crowley. "Haven't you noticed all the glowing humans? Pick out one of ours and push it into traffic. We'll follow it home."

I knew Crowley wasn't serious. When we were five years old, he found a black kitten trapped in a broken piece of fencing. The kitten was wet and dirty, and the rest of us wouldn't touch it because its eyes were all gummy. Crowley freed that kitten and cradled it in a towel for hours until his parents found a healer that was open.

I tried to keep the image of Crowley nursing that kitten to health as we stared at each other on an Earth street, contemplating pushing one of its residents to an early demise.

"We're not killing anyone," I said, rolling my eyes, and then I paused and considered, because you should never rule out too many options too soon. "At least, not unless we have to."

TWELVE

I'm starving," Crowley said, after way too much staring. "If we're not going to kill someone, we should eat."

"I don't think they're giving it away," I said, suddenly very aware of the awesome smells coming from the nearby food kiosks.

I looked over at the closest shop. The humans were giving stuff to the owners before they got food. Sometimes it was paper and other times it looked like pieces of plastic, but it was noticeably *not* like the few coins I had in my pocket.

"Do you have Earth money?" Crowley asked.

"How would I have Earth money?" I asked.

"I don't know. You got here first," Crowley said. "I assume."

"Yeah, didn't I tell you? I got a job, got married, got a bunch of half-human kids now. Dude, I couldn't have gotten here much sooner than you did," I said. "Actually, why are you here? I thought you pushed me."

Crowley's eyebrows climbed so far into his hairline, it looked like he might have shaved them off. "Why would I push you?"

"To be a jerk."

"My style of being a jerk is making fun of your ridiculous boxers—because oh yeah, I noticed—not pushing you into another dimension," Crowley said. "You were standing in front of me at the veil. Obviously you would have gotten here first."

"Fine," I said, agreeing only because I knew that if Crowley had pushed me, he would not have gone through himself. He would have waited for me to find my way back and then gloated forever. "If you didn't push me, how'd we get through? And why don't we have our wings?"

"Do I look like Lilith? It's not my job to know why we don't have wings. I assumed Aleister fell and knocked us in."

"Aleister? Star athlete Aleister accidentally fell on top of us?"

"He has his moments," Crowley said.

Aleister's natural ability with any physical activity was only surpassed by his enthusiasm for any activity. Balancing and playing around on half-rotted logs with leaves running between his feet was nothing. Normally. But add in the elation from escaping a week's lockdown, and suddenly Aleister falling over his own feet and knocking us into another dimension seemed completely plausible.

"So, you think Lilith and Aleister are still home?" I asked. My stomach growled as a breeze carried the scent of something amazing my way.

"Probably," Crowley said, edging closer to a particularly good-smelling kiosk that was sizzling in a way that made my mouth water.

"Does that help us?" I asked, watching as a woman squeezed sauce into a hot pan, sending steam soaring. "Can you magic something between us and them?"

"Maybe," Crowley said. "But I can hardly be expected to work without food."

"Are you kidding right now?" I asked.

"Hungry." Crowley folded his arms over his chest.

"Stranded in another dimension," I helpfully pointed out.

"Hungry," Crowley repeated.

I was 98 percent sure Crowley could use his magic even when he was hungry, but I was also 99 percent sure that he was stubborn enough to let us rot in a strange dimension until he got what he wanted.

I rolled my eyes. I supposed if it was a choice between

being stranded forever and stealing some food, I was going to have to steal some food for my spoiled magician.

"THIEF!"

For the briefest fraction of a second, I thought I was being called out for just *thinking* about stealing. Which seemed a little unfair, and seriously inconsistent, since no one had yelled "Murderer" when I'd been thinking about pushing people into traffic. But then I realized that the human who'd yelled wasn't even looking at us, so apparently my thoughts were safe. *For now . . .*

At a nearby stand selling T-shirts, hats, and some light-up spinny things that no matter how long I looked at them never revealed their purpose, a tug-of-war of epic proportions was happening. I supposed one of the humans was the "thief" and one of them was the yeller, but who was who was beyond me.

"C'mon, food," Crowley said, yanking on my sleeve.

I shook my head at the foolishness and left with Crowley. The kiosks were too small and too closely watched to be an option for charming or stealing.

We entered a café that strongly resembled Faust's. The door gave a funeral-dirge chime as we entered, but with the vast number of people inside, no one noticed. Coffee machines burbled and hissed, a human behind the counter called out names, and other workers assembled sandwiches and other plates of food. Music played over the speakers, while screens on the walls played soundless movies. A counter with a glass front displayed a huge assortment of treats.

The ever-present witch imagery was here, too, but there were also fake gargoyles in the corners, and fake bats hanging from the ceiling. Fake spiderwebs spanned corners of the rooms, and fake creatures moved rigidly next to fake candles.

"Why is everything so fake?" I asked before I could think about it. "And if everything else is fake . . ." Did that mean the witches were fake too?

"Are you going to finish that thought?" Crowley asked when I fell silent.

"No," I said. "I don't think I will."

We moved closer to where the food was being ordered and served, and I ran through all the ways I had ever used to charm my way to free stuff. Bat the eyelashes, smile so the dimple shows, pout the bottom lip just a tiny bit.

None of which were going to work with a café this busy. The staff here had strained smiles as they raced around, sweat beading on their foreheads. I didn't think they were going to be up for conversation. Maybe they'd take some of the coins in my pocket? *Excuse me, miss, what's the current exchange rate for infernal denarius to whatever it is you use here?* I snorted.

"I said light mayonnaise," snapped a man as he barged past me, shoving me into the human next to me. "Does this look like *light*? It's dripping down the sides! I waited here forever, and this is what I get? How is making a sandwich so difficult?"

"I'm sorry, sir," said the woman at the counter. "We can make you a new one if you'd like."

"Can you? Are you capable of that?" The man threw the sandwich onto the counter, sending the top of the bun bouncing out of the basket. "No wonder you make minimum wage. Worthless."

"Do you want a new sandwich?" asked the woman again. She wasn't smiling, but she also wasn't stabbing him with a fork. She had amazing self-control.

"Obviously!" snapped the man.

"Name?" she asked blandly.

"John McConnell," he snarled.

"We'll get right on that," the woman said, clearing the counter. The man stomped off to the side of the café to join an embarrassed-looking woman. The red glow from his aura turned the wall pink.

"What circle, do you think?" Crowley asked.

"Wrath?" I guessed. "C'mon, I have an idea."

We maneuvered our way through the people waiting and a fake jack-o'-lantern or three before we closed in on the pickup counter. I leaned against the wall and waited.

Crowley nudged me. I looked over, and he pointed up. "Gremlin in the rafters," he whispered.

"Huh," I said, watching the tiny green creature pulling on a nail. "I saw a shade earlier—well, two actually, at this place called the Witch's House, which is such a lie because it was just filled with old furniture. Nothing witchy about it."

"That's a good sign," Crowley said. "The shades and gremlins are getting through somehow. We can go that way too."

"Too bad a gremlin isn't going to help," I said.

"We'll just have to find something a little more agreeable," Crowley said. I wasn't sure what the odds of that were, considering the realms we were talking about. Speaking of which . . .

"Hey, earlier I had an encounter with—"

"McConnell?" called a person at the counter.

"C'mon," I said. I shoved through the people waiting. "That's me."

The man holding the basket looked at me and raised an eyebrow. He glanced to the corner where the real McConnell was looking aggravated at something else. "This is for you?"

"Totally," I said. We stared at each other. I smiled, bright and innocent.

"Whatever. The owner will be here any minute, and he hates customers like that. Take it; I promise we didn't spit in it," the man whispered, before handing the basket over. "Watch out for the extra jalapeños in the middle, though."

"Got it," I said, returning his smile.

Crowley and I grinned and pushed our way back through a swinging rear door. It led us out to the side of the building away from the main entrance, and we made our way across the street to a bench.

"Wow," Crowley and I said as we sat down. The sky had changed while we were inside the café. The fireball had sunk low, and the sky was a swirl of purples and reds, pinks, and oranges. It was like an abstract painting of home.

"This is better," I said, gesturing to the sky.

"Seriously," Crowley agreed, opening the sandwich in the basket I held. "Now, that was justice. Well done, fearless leader." He bowed with an elaborate hand gesture.

"Whatever," I grumbled. In the middle of the sandwich was a clump of green with white seeds. "Those must be jalapeños."

Crowley grabbed one, sniffed it, and stuck it into his mouth.

"Well?" I asked.

"About the same as the medium sauce at Baphomet's BBQ," he said.

"Awesome."

We ate in silence for a few minutes. I let my eyes unfocus and watched as the auras of the passing humans blurred together. Food and company had a remarkably calming effect.

"I figured I'd find a witch and ask for help," I said. "Haven't had any luck yet."

Crowley made a noise. "There's not much magic here; not sure how much a *witch* will help. And have you noticed that everything here is—"

"Fake?" I said. "Yeah. But if there isn't any magic, why is there so much witch stuff?"

"Easy," said a familiar voice. "A major historical miscarriage of justice turned into a tourism excuse hundreds of years later."

"Lilith!" I said, much too loud and far too enthusiastic to be cool. Ugh, fail. How could she possibly look so perfect standing there, wingless, and just as stuck as the rest of us? Her pale blue eyes and blond hair, which were such a rarity at home, didn't stand out as much here against the lighter sky, but still made my heart all squiggly.

"Hello, boys," she said. She spread her arms out. "Welcome to Earth."

"Was this your idea?" I asked. "Did you plan this when you got the alert?"

"What? No," Lilith protested, dropping her arms down to her normal stance. "I assumed Crowley pushed me, and I had no idea you guys were even here."

"That's what I said!" Lilith and I high-fived, as Crowley protested with a disgruntled, "Hey!"

"Crowley thinks Aleister fell into us," I said.

"That's possible," Lilith agreed. "What have you been up to?"

Crowley and I exchanged a glance.

"What have we been up to?" I mused. "Looked for a witch, failed, followed a soul, failed, attempted to steal food, succeeded." I held up the last bite of my sandwich before popping it into my mouth.

"You did what?" Lilith asked flatly.

"Our fearless leader thinks we should find a witch. I think there's no magic here worth speaking about, but the food is decent," Crowley said.

"Not the witch and not the sandwich," Lilith said, rolling her eyes. "You followed a soul?"

"Yeah," I said, tossing the basket and wrapper into what I hoped was a trash bin. "We saw someone get hit by a car and figured we'd follow the soul home."

"Are you insane?" snapped Lilith. "You could have ended up in Heaven!"

"Please," I scoffed. "Do I look like an amateur? I saw the guy's aura before he died, and he was going to be judged first. I figured the Jackal would let us go home, wherever the guy ended up being sent."

"Oh, you figured you could just charm a god into doing whatever you wanted?" Lilith said. She could sound as disbelieving as she wanted. That sparkle in her eye told me she had complete faith in my smooth-talking abilities.

"Well, it's not like we know where the gate back is," Crowley said, brushing a crumb off his shirt. "We had to seize the opportunity, and now that I'm fed, I suppose I could see if we can magic some way to message Aleister."

"*You* may not know where the gate is," Lilith said. "But I do."

"Of course she does," muttered Crowley.

"You're lucky I ran into you guys," Lilith said.

"Why? Were you going to leave us here?" I asked. *Of course not, Malachi. I could never abandon you, of all people, to the cold wilderness of the mortal coil. I would search high and low for you—*

"It's not like I knew you were here," Lilith said. Which . . . wasn't quite the declaration I was looking for. She leveled a glare at Crowley. "Are you sure you didn't push us?"

"No, I didn't push you. I wouldn't be here if I did!" Crowley exclaimed. "You know how Aleister gets when he's been inside too long."

"Where to?" I asked as we began to walk.

"Okay, so here's the thing," Lilith said. "We can't go back the way we came in because we went through a wild opening. We have to take an official gate back, and I really don't want my mom finding out. Can you imagine? The press would have a field day. Scandal in Lucifer's own office. Ugh."

"Your plan is to stay here forever, then?" Crowley asked.

"No," Lilith answered, blushing slightly. "My plan is to bribe the guard not to report us."

"The guards can be bribed?" Crowley asked. "I feel very secure."

"Only sometimes," Lilith said. She shrugged. "Well, usually. Okay, maybe like all the time."

"That's disturbing. *But* surprisingly convenient. What's a good bribe?" I asked, wondering if it would be one of those weird bribes like a whisker from a kitten or a dewdrop on a spider's web.

"From Earth? Nougat," Lilith said promptly.

"What's nougat?" Crowley asked, swerving out of the way of two running kids wearing masks they probably couldn't see out of.

"Nobody knows," Lilith said in a spooky voice with a wave of her fingers before getting serious again. "Just kidding. It's sugary crap, made with . . . stuff. Anyway, it's only found in certain chocolate bars on Earth. All we need is a bunch of those, and I think we'll be good."

"All right, where do we get the nougat?" I asked.

"People are handing candy out to kids tonight. It's a custom called trick-or-treating."

That was what that kid was whining about! Mystery solved.

"So, we should steal it from the kids?" Crowley asked, cracking his knuckles. "The one with the cape looks slow."

"Or we could just knock on doors ourselves," Lilith said slowly. "You know, participate in the ritual?"

"I like my idea better," Crowley said.

"We need costumes," Lilith called as Crowley stalked a particularly clumsy girl in red and blue holding a golden sword. He peered into her bag, earning an outraged, "Hey!"

"I definitely like my idea better," Crowley called back.

"Why?" I asked.

"Because costumes are stupid," Crowley said. "Unless you're cosplaying, but we do *not* have the supplies here to do that properly."

"Not why do you like your idea," I said, rolling my eyes. "Why do we need costumes?"

"That's not normal Earth attire," Lilith explained, gesturing to the humans around us. "They're in costume. You have to be in costume to get the candy."

Free candy always has a catch.

Surprisingly enough, we managed to pull together some almost, if not actual, costumes. Crowley complained the entire time.

Lilith managed a halo made of wire and tinsel, which was

funny considering the obvious, and a little unnerving given my seraph encounter from before, and yet she pulled it off. She was already wearing a white frilly shirt, and she had found a gold scarf that she wrapped around herself dramatically. If she'd had her wings, and if those wings hadn't been black, she would have looked like a heavenly angel.

Still hot, though.

Crowley and I hadn't been so lucky. For the sake of my own dignity, I decided not to dwell on what I was wearing, but I didn't try to hide my snicker at Crowley's disgruntled expression. I wasn't sure what he was supposed to be, but Lilith declared it "okay enough" with an expression that said it was definitely not "okay enough."

We had managed to get a few bags like the ones the humans were carrying. A street vendor had given them to us when we were scrounging pieces of costumes. At least, I was pretty sure the vendor had given them to us. Maybe we stole them? "Let's get this over with," Crowley said, shuddering slightly. "We've been here too long already."

Brimstone. I had started to relax. Why had I let my guard down? I didn't even know if Earth ran on the same time cycle as home. Did Mom and Dad know we were gone yet? Had they already been looking for days? Months? Years?!

No, that was ridiculous. Lilith would not be this calm if

that was the case, but Crowley was right. We had been here too long.

"Okay," Lilith said. "We just go up to a door and knock . . . I think."

"They do this all the time?" I asked, warily watching the kids at the house next door.

"Every All Hallows' Eve," murmured Lilith, not moving any closer to a door.

"It doesn't make any sense," Crowley said, also staying stubbornly put.

"I know," said Lilith, taking a deep breath. "When in Rome, though."

She walked a few steps ahead, and Crowley leaned in to whisper, "Are we in Rome?"

I shrugged, before reluctantly following. My sneakers scuffed the ground in protest, which I allowed for only a couple of steps before walking properly. I loved these shoes.

We approached the door and stared at it. It was brown, with little grates across the tiny windows at the top, and had a door knocker. We gave each other significant looks, and finally, with an exasperated sigh, Lilith raised her hand and knocked.

The door opened and the woman, a matronly older human, greeted us with a smile, which fell almost immediately, and a bowl of candy, which luckily did not.

"Okay . . . ," said the woman. "Well, it's good to see home-made costumes again. That store-bought stuff is so impersonal, and I can see you made your costumes all by yourselves."

She used that high-pitched voice you use with puppies or especially slow preschoolers. Her smile was large again, and I struggled not to blush while Crowley shifted his feet awkwardly.

"Well?" asked the woman.

She was clearly expecting something, but what that was, I had no idea. Our costumes were not going to get any better. But then among the other street sounds I heard a gleeful yell of "Trick or treat." The source was a small boy, who held out a bag to the person at the door, as if begging strangers for candy was the easiest thing in the world. The person dropped several pieces of candy into the bag, and the boy was off.

Show-off.

But a show-off who clearly knew the words to the ritual.

"Trick or treat?" I said.

"Is that a question?" asked the woman with a teasing smile.

"I . . . have no idea," I said, frowning. The woman frowned too.

"Here you go," said the woman, tossing a handful of shiny cellophane into each of our bags.

She paused while we stood there awkwardly for several

long seconds, and then, with a grimace, she closed the door in our faces. It was probably for the best.

Knocking on doors and saying strangely threatening phrases did not get less awkward. Thankfully, we figured out early on that "Snickers" and "3 Musketeers" were nougat mother lodes. We may have looked like maniacs pawing through the humans' offerings, but at least we were efficient.

Even still, it felt like forever before Lilith finally declared, "Okay, I think we're good."

"Good," Crowley and I said, while simultaneously ridding ourselves as quickly as possible of our not-costumes.

Lilith tossed her faux halo into a trash receptacle and was about to throw the scarf after it when she seemed to think better and instead used the scarf to pull her hair up into a tight ponytail.

"C'mon," she said. "I know where the official gate is."

The streets of the city had become reminiscent of downtown Dagon during festival week, and walking toward the unknown gate, I could almost pretend we were home enjoying the festivities. A juggler dressed as a decaying clown threw flaming torches into the air. A belly dancer painted like a lizard woman danced in front of a hat. Random people threw coins and paper in. I heard an electric guitar and the thump of drums in the distance.

We had been locked inside our houses all week.

I ate a few non-nougat candies and watched the action.

"C'mon, keep up," called Lilith.

Of course, if we went back now, we'd be locked inside our houses all over again. Our town's Samhain celebration may have been canceled with the lockdown, but this place's celebration was in full swing.

"Mal?" Lilith questioned when I hadn't moved.

"How long have we been here?" I asked.

"A few hours. Why?" she asked.

"So our parents will be working for at least . . . four more hours," I said.

"Probably . . . ," said Lilith, frowning.

"So we have time to look around?" I asked, raising an eyebrow.

And for once, vacation was going exactly as it should.

THIRTEEN

Now that I had some company, and we knew there was an official gate and we could bribe security whenever we wanted, I wasn't feeling a particularly urgent need to get home. I mean, sure I wished Aleister was with us, but other than our missing squad member, there wasn't anything good waiting at home. Just cranky parents, a decrepit babysitter, and panicked dread for the start of the new year. I squeezed the crystal in my pocket in response to the panic that always brimmed at the thought of my new school. Then I took a deep breath and released it slowly into the cool air.

"We deserve some fun," I said. "Aleister would want us to have fun."

"Would he?" asked Lilith.

"Yes!" I said. "He's already missing this. Think how disappointed he'll be if we don't even have any cool stories."

"Yes," Crowley said, a mischievous spark of flame lighting his eyes. "This is a good idea."

"I don't know that it is," Lilith said. Easy for her to say. She was the only one without a jailer.

"C'mon, Lil," I said, fluttering my eyelashes, clasping my hands in front of me. "Please?"

"You know you want to," added Crowley.

Lilith sighed.

"I mean, we're probably the only ones from home to ever have spent real time on Earth during All Hallows' Eve," I said nonchalantly. "Undiscovered, blending in, even. Think of all the insider information you'll have."

Lilith's eyes became calculating, and I knew I was winning.

"But," I continued, "I suppose we can be good and just go home like we're supposed to. I'm sure you can learn about their customs in a book." I paused just long enough that when I threw the next comment, I knew it would have maximum effect. I shrugged. "Dina can probably explain it to you anyway."

"Dina!" growled Lilith, throwing her arms into the air. Crowley and I traded grins of victory. "She thinks she's so smart. Do you know she honestly believes that Earth is a conspiracy? Like this place supposedly doesn't exist at all, and all the souls we get are actually just made-up distractions from the Powers That Be to blind us to some greater conspiracy."

I laughed. "Seriously?"

"Oh, yes," said Lilith. "And Lucifer's in the know. Apparently, he's secretly a deep Heaven agent, you know, because he was born there."

"Wow," Crowley said. "I had heard about her leaf theory."

"What leaf theory?" I asked.

"She thinks the *ambulafolia* aren't really plants, but zombified desiccated hands."

"Wow," I said. "Well, Lilith? What's it going to be? Experience human culture and get a once-in-a-lifetime learning adventure, or let *Dina* explain it you?"

"Fine, I give in!" Lilith laughed, and then shook her head, pointing at me. "But those are not the only two options."

"Eh," I said, and then turned to Crowley. "Tell me more about these hands. Where did they supposedly come from?"

Lilith made grabby gestures at us, and we relinquished our candy. She sorted out the nougat and secured it, like we couldn't be trusted with bribery material, before handing the rest over to us for snacking. In no time, we were weaving between people and exploring.

We discovered that the town was called Salem and that All Hallows' Eve was A. Big. Deal.

There were shops and cafés and restaurants, street vendors and kiosks, performers and theaters, and probably most exciting, there were humans everywhere doing human things.

Almost without thinking, we followed the sound of music and found a stage set up between two haunted-house attractions. There were screams from within the houses, which were quickly followed by laughs. The rumble of thunder, howls of some great beast, and other clanging noises that almost reminded me of the alarms at home came from enormous speakers outside.

Out in front were humans either scaring those waiting in line or trying to lure others in. "Come in, dearie. Take a look around," a woman in front of one of the houses said, reaching for me as if she'd snatch me, but it was just an act. She let her hand drop before it touched me. I laughed, and Lilith pulled me away from the woman, toward the music. I let her because hello! Lilith.

The band onstage wore makeup to look like red creatures, almost like oni, but like a child's drawing of what an oni was, rather than the real thing. The red skin was too flat, like primary-school paint, nothing like the purple and ruby tones of the skin of real ones. The singer wore a black top hat that had holes to allow horns to poke through the brim, but the horns were simple black cones with nothing like the unique curves and streaks of color found in the real things. The costume was a poor imitation, but I didn't think it was meant to be insulting.

Even still, the singer carried himself like he was powerful. His voice felt dark like magic, and it was a sound that would have held its own against my favorite bands at home.

There were shadows of things moving above the stage, lining the light bars and scaffolding. I couldn't exactly tell with the flashing lights, but I knew the shadows weren't natural. There were *things* up there. Things that belonged here just about as much as we did, like the shades I'd seen at the witch's house and the gremlins at the café.

I let myself get lost in the music, surrendering completely to the rhythm as I danced. I had no sense of time or urgency. There were no predetermined roles, no cosmic destinies to worry about here. Just thumping bass that rattled my lungs and a melody that I would probably forever associate with Lilith, and the swirling of auras. Even Crowley got into it. All of us, free to do what we wanted, hanging out as equals. It was something we wouldn't be able to do for much longer, and something I was desperate to enjoy as long as I could.

Fireworks flashed above the stage, filling the air with rumbles and a sound like foil crinkling. The flashes of light reflected off upturned smiles and shining eyes. Lilith pulled out her pocket mirror and captured a few seconds of memory. I stuck out my tongue, and she laughed, saving the image. Aleister was going to be so jealous, and I wished he were here. This was near perfection; exactly what I needed out of this break.

"C'mon," I said as the band took their final bow. "Let's find where those fireworks are coming from."

"And get some water!" Lilith added.

We staggered through the crowd, our legs wobbly from all the dancing—dancing without wings was way more work—and found ourselves back on the main drag.

"We should do this every year," said Crowley. "You keep an eye on your mommy's alerts, and we take a trip through the veil."

"Yeah, right," Lilith said. "There's still a chance we won't even get away with this."

"I'm surprised the humans have fireworks," Crowley said as the sky burst into light again. "Do they have magicians too?"

"I didn't think they did," said Lilith. "But they're creating the fireworks somehow."

Between Lilith and Crowley's back-and-forth over the questionable magical ability of humans, and the thundering of the explosions overhead, I almost missed the sound at first.

"Shut up a second," I said. "Did you hear that?"

We froze as we waited to hear something out of the ordinary. We didn't have to wait long. "Stop, please!"

The voice drifted up from an opening in the ground. We crept closer, scenes from horror movies playing through my mind, and a little voice in the back of my head whispered, *This is how they get you*, even as I moved closer. Because what was the alternative? Ignore someone who needed help just because there could be something scary involved? I thought not.

The opening in the ground was actually the top of a staircase leading down, rather than just the hole in the ground I originally thought it was. We should have ignored it and moved on. Strange dimension, stairs below the ground. It was all very sketchy.

But the voice had sounded scared, and that was enough for me.

Nasty-smelling steam surrounded me as I started down the stairs, which were covered in squished gum and puddles of stuff I didn't even want to identify.

Crowley and Lilith followed behind me.

The snap of accusations and whimpers of fear were all we could clearly hear as we snuck down the stairs to what appeared to be an underground station of some kind. Without my wings I was feeling a little disadvantaged, but it was no different from fighting with an injury, right? That was something I had at least trained for.

"Hurry up!" demanded a large man standing on the platform. "I know you have money. I saw it!" He towered over the small woman in front of him. She was wearing a long dress and a cloth on her head, and shook like a pixie on a sugar high.

"I don't. I swear!" She was petrified.

The man moved closer to her, and she backed away warily, right toward a trench in the ground. As he encroached on her space, his murky gray aura steadily gained a red tinge.

"Hey!" I yelled. "Leave her alone!" The man looked at me, and I took the last step onto a cement floor.

"Mind your own business, you little brat," he snarled.

"Leave her alone," I repeated. "She's not doing anything to you."

The man shook his head like he was bothered by something, like a centaur shaking a firefly away. I thought I saw a shimmer by his head, but before I knew what was happening, he pushed her. She screamed and fell into the trench.

I ran to the edge. Something sounded like it was coming fast, and the whole tunnel started to light up. A train? Was this trench for a train? Oh, brimstone! We had those at home, and if the earthly ones were as large and fast as the hellish ones . . .

"Train," I yelled. Crowley swore.

I pushed past the man, who was now standing frozen, staring at the woman in horror, as if he couldn't believe what he had just done. The shimmer I thought I had seen was now a full-fledged sparkle swarming the man's head, but there was no time to think about that now.

"Grab my hand!" I yelled to the woman on the tracks below.

"I can't! My dress, it's caught."

I jumped into the trench. The ground was shaking. The light was growing brighter. The sound was unbearable.

I ran to the woman; her dress was caught on a spike coming off a rail. How she had caught it in the two seconds she'd been down here, I didn't know. I pulled, but it was seriously stuck. Crowley jumped down beside me, and we both yanked as hard as we could. The fabric ripped, and with a stumble, the woman was free.

Crowley boosted himself out of the trench with Lilith's help and turned immediately to reach a hand out to help. I looked down the tunnel and saw headlights. I had to move fast.

"We'll help," Lilith told the woman. "Grab on!"

I pushed the woman, ramming my shoulder beneath her butt to help lift her up to Crowley and Lilith. They pulled both her hands, and she lurched back up onto the safety of the concrete platform.

"Malachi, hurry!" yelled Lilith.

I could see the train. I know I shouldn't have looked, but there's something about death advancing on you that just makes you look.

I tried launching myself up like Crowley had, all the while thinking it would have been way easier with my wings. But Lilith had helped Crowley up, and she was currently juggling a very panicked human who was clinging to her and sobbing into her shoulder. The wind was rushing, heat and noise blasting me, and then I was falling back. I wasn't going to make it, and I didn't have time for another jump.

But then, miraculously, I was grabbed by hands; one delicate and strong, one large and vaguely sweaty.

Crowley and Lilith stopped me from falling, and I would have been relieved, except there was no time for that. The train was rushing past, and the backdraft tried to pull me down to the tracks. I held on to my two friends for dear, sweet, amazing life. They yanked hard, and we all stumbled farther away from the edge.

The man who had been so threatening before was running up the stairs like a coward. There was no hint of a sparkle, but his once gray aura now glowed red.

"Thank you," said the woman. "Thank you." She hugged each of us. I don't think my arms even lifted to return the hug, because I was in a very clear state of What. Just. Happened?

When we'd come down the stairs, that guy had been acting Pit-worthy evil, but then he had run away like he couldn't believe what he had done. And what had that shimmer around his head been? It was almost like the soul sparkle we had followed, but there was no reason for a soul to be here; no one had died. But then again, the train had had a headlight, so it had probably been just another trick of the light. Right?

Unless the sparkles we had been seeing weren't what we thought they were. But if they weren't a recently departed soul, what were they? Was it just a coincidence that the sparkle had been there when James's soul had departed his body? Did attacking this woman just happen to be the final choice that tilted the scale, or was there something else going on here?

"I think it's time for us to go home," said Crowley.

For once Crowley and I were in complete agreement.

FOURTEEN

Our walk to the official gate was just another depressing turn in a vacation of depressing turns. We followed Lilith with a wary eye and sharp ear as she led us to a stone witch statue in the middle of a small clearing. The witch smiled broadly, warm and welcoming, and sat astride a broom on a cloud, with a crescent moon behind her. She had one hand raised in greeting. I didn't know if it was a statue of a real person or just another fake witch, but with any luck I wouldn't be here long enough to know the answer.

"How do we turn it on?" I asked, randomly pressing spots on the statue. "Do we have to move it?"

I shoved the statue. It moved about as much as one would

expect a stone statue to move. Crowley stood at a distance and studied it like he might see something we wouldn't. Lilith ran her hand lightly over the statue's arm.

"Oh," Lilith cried as the stone hand closed over hers. Lilith yanked her hand back, and the statue's arm bent at an unnatural angle.

"You broke it," Crowley said.

"I didn't mean to," Lilith said, rubbing her own wrist and looking at the witch's bent arm with some concern. "I just thought it might activate . . ."

"I don't think it's broken," I said. "Look."

The statue slid slightly to the side with a grinding stone-on-stone sound that sent an irritated shiver up my spine. A narrow opening in the ground was revealed, emitting a familiar flickering glow, and I was struck with an unexpected pang of homesickness.

The opening grew until it was a shimmering gap in the cement, large enough for a narrow purple-and-green tollbooth to rise from the ground. The top of the booth was covered in black fabric, which was held aloft by thin purple posts.

I looked around nervously, but the nearby humans didn't seem to notice anything unusual. Moments later the booth was completely aboveground, looking out of place in the human world, but also as if it had stood there the entire time. Inside, a small imp sat on top of a tall stool behind the counter, his long nose hanging so low that it nearly touched the surface of the counter, which held a stack of papers on one end and a clipboard currently situated beneath a tattered book in front of him. Next to the booth was the way home, just barely visible as a distortion in the Salem air.

"Names?" the imp asked in a bored voice, reluctantly sliding his book to the side, and not even glancing up from the checklist now revealed on the clipboard in front of him.

"Well, that's what we were hoping to talk to you about," said Lilith. "Here." She placed the bag of nougat candy on the counter, directly over the checklist. The imp delicately pawed through the candy, apparently counting the pieces.

"Does this have nougat?" asked the imp, holding a 3 Musketeers up to his nose. He inhaled with such force that the candy stayed stuck to his nose even as his hand dropped away. He lowered his head with an exhale, and the candy fell to the counter.

"Yes," said Lilith. "And you can have it, in exchange for a favor."

The imp's eyes sparkled. "What kind of favor?"

"The kind where you just let us through the checkpoint without logging us."

"There are rules, you know. Security and whatnot. Can't

have people sneaking in," said the imp, rolling a candy between his fingers.

"You know we're not trying to sneak in," said Crowley.

"Perhaps not, little ones, but you are trying to sneak *back* in," said the imp. His name tag read TERRENCE. "How many pieces of nougat are here?"

"Thirteen," answered Lilith. "Which you know. You already counted it."

"I don't know. . . . For three of you . . ."

"You can't leave that booth and get any candy yourself, and I don't see a lot of humans eager to get in," I pointed out. "Speaking of which, why aren't they even looking over here?"

"The gate is camouflaged unless you have a connection to Hell. And you have to be right here," added Terrence, considering. "If you stood over there, you wouldn't see it either." The imp studied us, a greedy glint in his yellow-green eyes. "Fine," he said, tearing into a piece of candy and tossing the chocolate into his mouth. "I won't log you. Go on through."

My stomach jumped in excitement. We were going home, and if we hurried, Methuselah might never even have noticed I'd left. Crisis averted, plus a little adventure on the way.

The opening behind Terrence wavered like the veil we had crossed through to get here; the human street behind it was blurred but still visible.

"Go together," said Terrence, his mouth full of candy. "You crossed together; you've got to cross back together."

"Okay," I said. The three of us stood shoulder to shoulder and grinned. We were going to get away with it. No one would ever know.

Maybe this vacation wasn't so bad after all. Sure, for most of it I had been stuck inside doing nothing, but a visit to Earth? None of my classmates had ever done that. This had definite bragging rights written all over it.

Well, quiet bragging rights. It wouldn't do to have my parents find out.

Together we stepped toward the gate. One more step, and it would be over. I held my breath, readying for that icy crossing. Another breath and we'd be home.

Which was why it was so confusing when we suddenly found ourselves bouncing off the veil like it was made of rubber and landing none so gently on our backsides, right back onto the Salem street we were trying to escape.

FIFTEEN

"What the blazes?" I shouted.

"Oh. So the truth comes out," said Terrence in triumph. "Trying to leave someone behind, are you? Nu-uh, children. That ain't happening. Can't bribe your way out of that one."

"What are you talking about?" I asked, picking myself up off the ground.

"The magic has its own rules for security. The same number that goes out, comes back through. No exceptions."

"But we're all here," I argued, furious. Home was so close and yet so far. I mean, I could still see it!

"Clearly you're not," said the imp, shoving another piece of nougat into his mouth. A small dribble of chocolate-colored drool ran down his chin.

"Aleister," said Lilith softly.

Crowley groaned.

"If we're missing someone, it's Aleister. It was the four of us at the veil. He must have come through too," said Lilith. She brushed her blond hair off her forehead and searched the streets, as if Aleister would materialize in front of us. "I should have realized when I found you two that he might have gone through as well. I mean, I'd thought *I* was the only one."

"Me too," I said. Crowley nodded. Why hadn't we thought of that? We had been surprised to see that each of us had crossed but still hadn't suspected that the same could be true for Aleister?

"So he's probably here too," Lilith said.

"Great. How are we supposed to find him?" I asked.

"That's your problem, not mine, but you'd better hurry," said Terrence, swallowing hard. The imp slammed his hand against a button within the booth, and the witch's arm twisted back into the correct position. The booth started to descend. "Tick-tock, children. And bring more nougat. Extra kid, extra nougat."

We watched in silence as our way home dropped into the pavement.

Crowley swore.

Lilith sniffed, and with her back facing us, she wiped her face with one hand, while the other started tapping a nervous rhythm on her leg.

"You have your pocket mirror," I said. "Does it work for more than just pictures and hologifs? Maybe Aleister has his?"

I knew where mine was—on my bedside table at home. I hadn't thought to take it. Why would I when my closest friends had been with me?

"No," Lilith said, her voice strangely wet. "There's no signal."

"Lil?" I asked. "You okay?"

She straightened her head and shook it, but then she sniffed again. She didn't bury her face in her hands or anything; she just looked up into a nearby streetlight.

"Lil, it'll be okay," I said.

After several awkward attempts, I finally placed my hand on her shoulder, and froze as Lilith suddenly turned into me. I felt wet spots through my T-shirt and hoped it was tears rather than snot, though that probably wasn't what was important. Even if this was one of my favorite shirts.

I hadn't developed a charming way of comforting yet, so I was still standing there, doing nothing, until my brain rebooted, and I finally wrapped my arms around her. My fantasies of this had involved a lot fewer tears.

Crowley walked toward us, and he and I exchanged a concerned look. I couldn't even remember the last time I had seen Lilith cry. Not when she'd gotten hit in the face by one of Aleister's ridiculously hard throws during King of the Cage.

Of course, now that I thought about it, Aleister's throws were always ridiculously hard. Probably why he called the game Super Smashy-Smash.

Lilith spoke into my chest. "I thought the worst we had to worry about was our parents finding out. I didn't consider that we might not be able to get back."

"We'll get back. We know where the gate is. We just need to find Aleister, and we *will* find him. We'll be home in no time."

"And then we can torture him," said Crowley in a gentle voice. Lilith laughed, and I grinned.

Lilith looked up, a watery smile on her face, and it suddenly sank in that my arms were around her. Like really, truly around her. And then she realized the same thing, because the watery smile became a mischievous smirk, and I blushed before letting my arms drop.

Lilith wiped her eyes. "All right. Ready, boxer boy?"

Oh, unholy darkness. Lilith had seen me in my boxers. This vacation could not get worse. They hadn't even been my good boxers. Crowley laughed and pushed my jaw back up from where it had dropped open in disbelief.

Lilith smiled. "Let's find that overgrown puppy and get home."

"Excellent," I said, trying and failing to regain my bravado. "Kind of ridiculous, though. I mean, if we have to cross together, why doesn't the gate *keep* us together?"

"If we'd gone through an official checkpoint, it would have. We went through a wild gate, and it just sort of spit us through," explained Lilith, seeming more confident now that she was on solid knowledge again.

"If I can find a few supplies, I should be able to do a locating spell to find him," Crowley said. "Unless our plan is just to wander aimlessly."

I looked around. The sky had darkened to a comforting black. The glow at the horizon, which had been similar enough to the flames at home to give me a small sense of comfort, was now completely gone.

I took a breath, let it slowly drift out into a waft of fog in the chilly air like dragon smoke, and said the famous last words of horror movie characters everywhere: "Let's split up."

SIXTEEN

It's eightish now," I said, glancing at a clock on the side of a nearby building. "Let's give it two hours, and we'll meet back at the statue. Crowley, if you can get your spell working, great. If not, just . . . look around, I guess."

I didn't know if Crowley could get his locator spell to work, and I wouldn't be any help anyway. Walking behind him asking, "Is this it?" while Crowley tried to find what he needed was probably not the best use of our time. Splitting up meant Lilith and I could divide the town to look for Aleister while Crowley tried to spark his magic.

It was definitely a bad idea. A logical, terrible idea.

"Good executive decision," Lilith said. She tossed me an

approving nod, while I pretended *not* to understand what she was *not* saying.

Unlike me, my squad was fine with their destiny-dictated roles. They loved them, embraced them, never even questioned doing something else, which was frustrating and . . . lonely. Lilith's way of persuading me to accept my role was to be super encouraging anytime I did anything that remotely resembled making a decision.

"All right, Lil," I said. "You head that way and I'll go this way?" Lilith nodded. "Everyone, stay safe."

The streets were full of older teenagers and adults in costumes that had gotten more elaborate and more terrifying as the night went on. Most of the little humans were gone. People regularly tried to hand me flyers for various shows, some of which I was pretty sure I wasn't old enough to see. If only this were home, I'd have been spending my night sneaking into shows I had no right seeing, but I couldn't even muster up the disappointment.

I was secretly terrified that after all our searching we might not find Aleister. What if the wild gate had flung us farther apart than just this town? What if he'd been flung to another part of Earth altogether? We'd never find each other, and we'd never get back home. My parents would look for me eventually, of course. In Hell. Where I belonged. They'd never find us here.

I swallowed down the lump that threatened to choke me. We would get home, and everyone would be fine.

I searched the faces of anyone who looked remotely like Aleister, and some who looked nothing like Aleister at all. I kept seeing *something* out of the corner of my eye, something that wasn't there when I turned to look. I knew there were creatures hiding in the shadows, intruders like me, but I wasn't worried about them. I *was* a little concerned about the humans.

Sometimes . . . well, I didn't really know what was normal, but things felt *wrong*. Like they had when that guy James had run out into the street without worrying about the vehicles, or when the people had fought over a T-shirt before Crowley and I had grabbed dinner, or when the man had pushed the woman onto the tracks of the train. Then there were the snippets of conversations I caught as I searched.

". . . never seen him like that before."

". . . dancing on the table! I am not kidding you."

"So I said, you can take that job and shove it right up your—"

Earth was unpredictable, I decided. And even though there were lots of places and people that felt exhilarating, I didn't like those moments when things felt off-kilter. I wanted to go home, even if it meant babysitters, just to get away from the wrongness of it all.

Stores, cafés, alleyways, and graveyards all came up empty. None of the visiting critters were helpful. Either they couldn't speak to me or they weren't willing to. I thought I might get some help from a hobgoblin, but his smirk and his giggling friend told me I'd be better off ignoring his "advice." I hoped Lilith and Crowley were having better luck.

And then I saw someone who was not Aleister but shouldn't have been here anyway. I knew what a real tail looked like. None of the costumes I had seen here could replicate the twitch and movement of the real thing. And this tail was familiar. I reached out and snagged the short tail peeking out between the flaps of a long, hooded coat, and tugged.

"Hey!" The figure spun and turned. Furfur frowned. The hood was large, which let his horns stay hidden in its shadow and made him look taller than he was. "What are you doing here?"

"What are *you* doing here?" I asked.

"I come every year," he said, smoothing the lapels on his trench coat. "Teenagers. They think summoning 'demons' is fun. They don't know what they're talking about, and they never do a binding. So, bing bang boom, I come here. Their summoning wears off at the end of Samhain, and I go home."

"Yeah, but you're not a demon. Daemons and demons are different," I said. Daemons were natural creatures that had no specific alignment to good or bad, while demons originated from souls corrupted by their own evil into something entirely new.

"Obviously," he said. "Didn't you hear the air quotes?"

"So they summon the 'demon' Furfur." I snickered. What a ridiculous name for a demon. Not that a lot of true demons had proper names.

"Laugh it up, kid." He huffed, and then pointed at me. "Free vacation."

"Have you seen any other of *us* here?" I asked. "I'm looking for someone."

"Not one of you, no," he said. "Others, though. The usual kinds. But . . ."

"But what?" I asked.

"I don't know, kid." Furfur frowned. He scratched at the base of one of his elk horns. "Just be careful. Something is different. . . . Just be careful."

"I will," I said. I really needed to find Aleister.

While it made me feel better to see someone from home, Furfur's method of returning was not going to work for us. We hadn't been summoned, so there was no waiting out a spell for us, but Furfur telling me to be careful? That was a bad sign.

Finally, when sweat had started forming under my arms and my hoodie was relegated to being tied around my waist like a belt, I saw it. I wasn't enough of a fan to identify the team, but I would know a sports jersey anywhere.

"Al!" I shouted. There was no response. I jogged to catch up, but Aleister turned the corner between two buildings.

"Hey, watch it, kid. I'm working with fire here! You're going to get hurt." The street performer, dressed in a black bodysuit with flame designs running up the sides, held his torch high in one hand. The other hand held up a bottle of something undoubtedly flammable. He kept them far apart. Over-worried much? It was only fire.

"Sorry," I shouted, not sorry, as I ran, skirting around the performer and weaving my way through a few people standing ready for the performance.

"Aleister!" I shouted as I turned the corner into the alley, getting angrier and more desperate by the second.

Nothing.

If Aleister had been there, he was gone now.

I yelled and hit the wall with the edge of my fist. The boy had never turned, and he hadn't responded to my call, not even a flinch, so maybe it wasn't Aleister.

Or maybe it was, and Aleister had a reason why he didn't want to be found. If that was the case, we were all screwed.

No, that couldn't be. Above all else, Aleister was completely loyal to his friends. There had been more than one time when one of us had asked for help and Aleister had said yes, before we'd even explained what we needed or wanted. It was never a question.

He would have been overjoyed to see me. Right?

The alleyway grew brighter behind me, and for a wonderful moment of ignorance, I wondered how much fire the street performer was using. It seemed excessive. The light continued to grow, and my stomach sank.

Not again.

I didn't want to turn around. But then again, I didn't hear a choir, so it was possible it was all my imagination. Yeah, definitely my imagination. The light faded, but I just knew I wasn't lucky enough for that to mean I was alone.

With enormous trepidation, I turned my head.

It was not my imagination. The seraph, because of course it was her, smiled gently. In her hand she offered a plate of cookies. Without the overwhelming light, I could see her better this time. She was an adult, slightly taller than me, with golden-hued skin that almost blended with her hair, but the expression on her face wasn't what I was used to seeing on adult faces. It was . . . naive, maybe? I wasn't sure if that was a Heaven thing or if it was a ploy so I'd let my guard down, but I wasn't falling for it.

"Please don't run," she said gently. "I have cookies."

The smell of freshly baked cookies made my stomach rumble audibly. The seraph's smile widened.

"Come, these are for you. I know you're hungry," she said. "You can have them."

I hesitated. She seemed sincere, and maybe she could help me find Aleister. Plus, the cookies *did* smell delicious.

Steam rose from the plate, and there was a delectable shine on the chocolate chips, melting and gooey. Melting and gooey were my favorite kinds of chocolate. It was tempting.

But temptation was something I knew a lot about.

"I'm not going to hurt you," she said, and I almost, *almost* believed her. "I'm going to take you to paradise."

Fear jolted me into action, and I tried to run, but since I hadn't turned completely, my feet tangled, and I fell hard to the ground. My reflexes still weren't used to me not having wings. My right hand pressed into a shard of broken bottle on the ground of the alley, and I scrambled to my feet and ran.

If I got dragged to Heaven, I'd never get home, never see my parents or friends again. Worse, it would be my fault that Lilith and Crowley would be stuck. Without me to complete the group, even if they found Aleister, they'd be stranded on the mortal plane forever.

"No!" cried the seraph. "Wait!"

The weight of all-powerful eyes nearly made me fall again.

I ran out of the alley and turned randomly to the left, hoping to lose the angel, but once again I slammed into someone on the street, and we fell to the ground in a crumple of bodies.

"What the heck, man?" groaned the body I'd crashed into. "Watch where you're going!"

I scrambled to my feet, or at least tried to, but it took me an extra moment or two to untangle our limbs.

"Let me up!" I demanded, finally getting my feet solidly on the pavement. My panic must have become obvious, because suddenly my crash victim changed his demeanor entirely.

"Is something after you?" he demanded. His hands gripped my shoulders painfully tight. I had seen this boy before. It was the one who'd seen me watch the soul leave the man hit by the car. The one whose own soul glowed brighter than anyone else's.

He looked behind me as if he could see what was coming. I looked back as well, but there was no sign of the cookie-wielding angel.

"I'm sure it's . . ."

"What?" demanded the boy. "Drugged-out wacko? Kidnapper? Sales rep? Are we going to need weapons?"

"For a sales rep?" I asked. I was momentarily distracted, but still flicking my gaze behind me.

"Some of those reps are aggressive," he said. "Or was it something else? Maybe something . . . *different?*"

"I don't know," I said. "Maybe it was my imagination."

Did celestials appear in front of humans? If I explained what I was running from, would he believe me? And if he did believe me, would he side with me, or the seraph?

"I've got a great imagination," said the boy. "Try me."

"It's nothing," I said. Better not to gamble. "Just running. For exercise, you know? So much fun."

He stared at me.

"Really," I said. "Got Band-Aids . . . on my nipples and stuff."

He raised an eyebrow. I blushed. He looked back the way I had run from. I brushed my hands together and hissed in pain. I turned my right hand over. It was cut. Badly.

"Does your idea of fun always involve bleeding?" asked the boy.

"Don't judge me," I said, with whatever bravado wasn't leaking all over the ground. All red, and wet and uncomfortably splashy.

The sensation of being watched made my stomach twist in fear, or maybe that was the splashing, but when my eyes jerked to the alleyway, the seraph was nowhere to be found. I frantically looked around in case I was missing something obvious, but my search was stopped in its tracks when my gaze locked on to the boy's eyes. Amazing green eyes.

SEVENTEEN

That's going to need stitches," Green Eyes said. "Are your parents nearby? Do you live around here?"

"No," I said, trying to cup my good hand under the injured one to catch the blood.

"Do you know where the hospital is?" the boy asked, sighing like he knew I absolutely did not know where the hospital was, nor could he trust me to get myself there.

"No, but it's fine," I said, knowing that it was not fine.

I didn't know if a healer could figure out I wasn't human. Even with my wings gone I strongly suspected there were other ways I was different from human kids. In fact, splashing my blood all over the road was probably a bad idea as well. Blood magic was powerful stuff.

"It's not fine. I can show you where the hospital is," he insisted.

"No, it's okay," I said. The cut was starting to make me woozy, and I wrapped it in the bottom of my shirt, before closing my eyes and taking a deep breath.

"My name is Sean," the boy said. "C'mon, if you're not going to do the smart thing, you might as well come with me. I can help you with that."

I hesitated. I should not have been wandering off with strange humans, but my blood was already soaking through my shirt, and I didn't know what else to do. I didn't know where Crowley and Lilith were and wasn't sure they could do any more than I could.

"My name's Malachi," I said. "Maybe if you just have a bandage."

Sean snorted and pulled a black cloth out of his pocket. I caught the slightest shimmer of gold script but didn't have time to study it further before he was yanking my hand toward him. He studied the cut and frowned before pulling a shard of glass out.

"This may pinch," he said, before wrapping the cloth

tightly around my cut. I had only a second to think, *Wow, that tingles,* before, "Ow!"

"Sorry, there's probably still some crap in there. C'mon," Sean said.

I stared at him openmouthed until I realized he wasn't going to wait for me, and I hurried to catch up. We walked a few blocks, heading farther into a residential section, while I silently berated myself and wondered if I should turn back.

My hand throbbed, and my shirt was wet with blood. I couldn't believe I had been so clumsy. I vaguely wondered how much blood loss caused fainting. I should have been looking for Aleister right then, not walking with a random human who, for all I knew, wanted to trap me and sell me into servitude. I was pretty sure that was a thing that happened. At least it was a plotline in movies.

Sean led me through the yard of a small house that I would have ignored otherwise. It was completely invisible in its averageness, and the weirdest thing about it was that it was physically hard to look at. Every time I tried to take in the details, my eyes decided that the tree next door or the mailbox across the street was much more interesting. They weren't, and my aversion could not have been normal. Was I finally finding real magic in Salem?

This was a bad idea.

Sean twisted the doorknob. It didn't move, and seeming satisfied, he took out his key and unlocked the door. I stood on the step, hesitating. Going into a stranger's house when your senses were tingling was a guaranteed recipe for disaster.

But Sean's soul was bright and clear, and I was potentially leaking out all over the street. Cautiously I stepped over the threshold, and nothing dramatic happened. Win.

The kitchen was clean, except for a few cereal bowls by the sink, but it appeared old, as if no one had bothered to update the kitchen as time had passed it by. The house was sparsely furnished, with no visible photos or knickknacks. It didn't look lived in, though this was the first human house I had ever been to, so what did I know?

The air in the house felt charged in a way that it hadn't been outside or in the stores I had wandered into. Maybe all human homes felt like this, but if I hadn't known they were missing, I could have sworn that all my feathers were puffed up. Thinking about my missing wings depressed me, so I took one quick reassuring glance at Sean's glowing soul and decided I wouldn't worry about the charged energy of the house.

The crackle of some sort of radio filled the silence as Sean pulled out a first aid kit that was conveniently located right next to the door. It sounded like there were emergencies everywhere.

"Sit," said Sean.

I sat on a vinyl-covered kitchen chair as instructed. There was a large bowl of candy in the center, and Sean shoved it to the side to make room for the supplies he was pulling out.

"Okay, let's see it."

I held my hand out, noticing when I did that it didn't hurt as much as I'd expected. Sean pulled the cloth loose and whipped it away before I could really study it, and oh yeah, there was the pain. The inside of the cloth glittered gold with unfamiliar symbols that I probably couldn't have interpreted even with more than just the brief glance I'd gotten.

I frowned. The black cloth hadn't looked wet at all, which seemed impossible, considering the blood that was still leaking out of me. My stomach rolled at the splash of crimson on the table.

"It needs stitches," Sean said, and threaded a needle. My heart raced.

"What are you doing with that?" I said.

"You need stitches," Sean repeated slowly, holding up the needle in one hand and tugging on the thread with the other.

"Stitches," I said, my mind working sluggishly on the idea. "Right, and stitches are . . . when you . . ."

I looked at the needle. I looked at the thread. I looked at my hand. No. No, no, no, no.

"Sew skin together, yeah," Sean said.

"No, I'm good," I said, standing up. The burst of adrenaline was not a great thing, since it sent the room spinning, and I dropped back into the chair with an angry thump.

"Hey," Sean said. "I told you to go to the hospital, but you didn't, so plan B it is."

Okay, clearly humans didn't have healers, or maybe they did, and they were at the hospital, but this was some barbaric stuff right here. But my hand was bleeding, and I couldn't heal it myself, at least not quickly, so I guess it was arts-and-crafts time.

"Have you done this before?" I asked, my voice coming out higher-pitched than I would have liked in front of eyes that green.

"Yeah," said Sean. "A few times, and I've seen it done a lot more than that."

"That's weird," I said, then remembered I was in another dimension with different norms from what I was used to. "Isn't it?"

Sean shrugged. "This is going to hurt. Hospitals have things to dull the pain."

"No hospitals." I swallowed hard and looked at the ceiling.

"Right," he said, and got to work. The needle pierced my split skin, and I gasped. The world exploded into black and white, but I stayed determined. I was glad I hadn't eaten any of the seraph's cookies. I swallowed again and tried to think of literally anything else.

Two times four is eight. The capitol of Hades is Congress. The forty-second level of Universe Adventure *has a secret petunia of power inside the whale. Lilith's wings shine purple under the light of the flames. That glint she gets in her eye when she knows she's got the upper hand. Ow. This really hurts.*

"Hang in there," muttered Sean.

Four times four is sixteen. Oh jeez, I hope I don't throw up. The Pit is ever-expanding, and the energy released keeps the flames burning. Mom makes the best pumpkin pie; the crust is all crumbly. Lilith got whipped cream on her nose the last time she had some. I wonder if Sean likes pie.

I don't know what it was that made me look down. Sean's house was probably infested with an ardad—an annoying little creature that leads you to make poor decisions—because there was absolutely no reason for me to look at the travesty I knew was happening on my hand. And there it was, the black thread trailing from my skin to the needle like I was a stuffed animal overly loved and in need of repair.

"What, black is the only color?" I gasped. The room spun for a moment in a horrible parody of flight before I could resolutely focus on the ceiling again.

"Black goes with everything," Sean said.

There are nine circles in the Pit. First is for Apathy, second is Jealousy, third is for Theft. Ow. This really hurts. Fourth is Greed, fifth is Wrath, sixth for the Liars, the seventh holds the Violent, and the ninth circle holds the Cage. Ow, ow, ow. Parris escaped the eighth circle, which holds the Manipulators.

"I think gold's more my color," I said, swallowing hard against the nausea.

"Almost done," said Sean.

Thirteen deep breaths and a recitation of the choirs of angels later, Sean snipped the final thread, and I sighed in unholy relief. My hand was a row of neat black stitches, but it was sealed, and my blood had stopped running quite so freely. Sean wiped the cut with a wet paper towel and placed a bandage over the now-sealed wound. That was way better. Out of sight, almost out of mind.

Sean went to clean his supplies and throw the bloody paper towels away, so I stood up. The room only spun a few times. Progress. I swiped my hand across a mirror mounted on one wall. Maybe I could find something that would lead me to Aleister.

"What are you doing?" Sean asked.

"Trying to look for something," I said.

"That's a mirror," he said.

"Yes," I said. "Is it broken?" It didn't look broken.

Sean frowned at me. His mouth opened and closed a few times before he finally said, "Maybe you should rest."

"I'm okay," I said.

"Humor me," said Sean. "Sit down. I'll get you some water."

I should have been heading back already, but Sean had helped me, and I didn't have any way of paying or returning the favor at all, really, so I owed him. I sat out of obligation. That was all. It had nothing to do with wanting to be near the brightest soul and greenest eyes I had ever seen.

Sean finished washing his hands and sat down across from me, handing me a glass of water. Our eyes met for a moment before we quickly looked away. Sean rifled through the bowl of candy and grabbed a piece before dumping the entire thing out onto the table. He gestured to the mass of sugar, but I wasn't sure my stomach could handle it yet.

"You sure you're okay?" asked Sean.

"Yes," I said, taking a sip of water and looking around the house from where I sat. If this was the only human house I was ever going to be in, I was going to take advantage. Wait, was that a protection sigil in the other room?

"Good, because if you keel over from loss of blood or some head injury you're not telling me about, things are going to get weird. Well, weirder."

"Are things weird?" I asked. That was salt on the windowsills and sage hanging in the corner . . . all things I had expected to see in the Witch House.

"It is, *out there*," he said. "Speaking of all that, what was chasing you before? I promise you can tell me."

"Uh . . . ," I started. I blamed the still-throbbing pain for my lack of eloquence and the fact that I hadn't thought up a good lie. "I'm sure I just overreacted."

He rolled his eyes. "You were there when that guy got hit by that car. You saw something."

I mean, clearly pain was a factor here, or maybe shock from my lack of wings, or the effects of the mortal coil, but I was usually way quicker with a story than this. Or maybe I was just distracted by what looked like a warding symbol peeking out from under the slightly crooked area rug in the other room.

"After the crash, your eyes tracked something," insisted Sean. "Look, I'm pretty familiar with stuff people think is crazy. I'll believe you. Are you psychic?"

"I . . . I was watching the soul," I said. *Maybe.* I wasn't convinced anymore that that was actually what it was. I studied Sean's face, but if he was thinking I was crazy, I couldn't tell. I continued cautiously, "I was watching the soul when you saw me that time."

"You can see them?" Sean asked, excitement clear in his voice. "So you *are* psychic."

"I can see them," I agreed hesitantly, because even if what we had seen here hadn't actually been a soul, I could definitely see them at home.

"Is something after you?" Sean asked. "I can help."

I had no idea where to start. I couldn't explain my situation, because there were things Sean was not allowed to know, and I couldn't explain the sense of wrongness I had encountered, because I didn't know this world. How could I define what was wrong when I didn't know what was right?

I didn't even know what the shimmers and sparkles I kept seeing were. If I had seen anything at all.

I thought I had . . . but maybe what I thought was strange behavior wasn't strange here anyway. Maybe humans were just unpredictable.

"I'm not sure," I said. "What's different today?"

"Notice all the sirens? The fights? The random dancing?" asked Sean. "Of course, it is Halloween and a full moon at that. People go crazy, act a little weird. Especially when both happen at the same time. It could just be the normal chaos. Nothing more than that . . ."

I didn't think Sean believed it was nothing, but I wasn't sure what to say. I flexed my hand. It still hurt, but it felt worlds better without the whole coming-apart-and-leaking thing. I looked at the human while I thought of what to say.

If we'd been home, I'd have turned on my most charming self and seen if I could make Sean blush, but this was a temporary stop, and that super-bright soul of his was a bit intimidating anyway. Not that I would ever admit it.

"I thought something was after me," I said. "I think I freaked out. I'm just spooked because of all the *weirdness*, but anyway, I don't think it's anything to worry about. Just someone in costume."

Sean studied my face, and I could tell he knew I was lying. I felt bad, but I didn't know what the human attitude was regarding celestial angels. Would Sean side with me, or the seraph? It wasn't worth chancing.

"Well, if you decide it *is* something to worry about, you can ask me for help. I'll say yes."

"Thanks," I said. Our eyes met, and for a moment it felt like the floor dropped out. Not just in that swoopy way of hormones and pretty faces, but in the way it feels when a particularly strong spell steals your attention and the world disappears. I looked away. My hands shook. What was that?

Sean took a few breaths, like he was going to say something, but he stopped each time, while he kept fiddling with the candy.

"What?" I asked, not at all prepared for an answer and trying to work my way politely back out onto the streets to look for Aleister, and away from whatever that feeling was.

"Does the phrase *l'appel du vide* mean anything to you?" asked Sean.

And that—that was not what I'd expected. Sean ripped open a bag and fiddled with the small bright-colored candies that landed on the table. He wouldn't meet my eyes.

"Should it?"

Sean shrugged, a light pink tinge to his cheeks. "Don't know."

The clock chimed once, and I jerked my head to look at the large grandfather clock. Nine forty-five. Brimstone! I jumped from the chair.

"I've gotta go. I'm meeting my friends at ten. Thanks for everything," I said, flexing my injured hand again before freezing completely. The candy I thought Sean had been absently fiddling with was instead lined up into the exact shape of the symbol displayed proudly on the gate to the eighth circle. What the Heaven! He had no business knowing that.

My head snapped up. Our eyes met. The kitchen disappeared and instead there was the same symbol in bold flames over black iron gates. For a heart-stopping moment I thought I had arrived home, except there was no heat from the flames, and I knew that Sean's eyes were still on me. I could see them, just the tiniest bit like they were superimposed over everything else. I jerked my head away, and instead of flames there was terrible wallpaper. My breath came in pants, and my heart wanted to burst from my chest. *What was that?*

Sean's face looked as shocked as I felt, and I was not going to wait until he recovered. He shouldn't have known about any of this.

"I really have to go," I said. My voice shook. "Thank you for everything."

"Wait!" said Sean, and for a moment I thought he was going to stop me, demand an explanation for what had just happened, and then of course I would have had to demand one right back. I didn't want to do that. I didn't want to have to deal with a human who knew too much about us, not even one who had helped me.

I turned to look at him anyway. His soul was still as bright as ever.

"Um, here." Sean thrust a bag at me. "I hate nougat, and um—I meant what I said before—about helping if you decide it wasn't nothing. Helping is kinda what I do."

"Okay." I took the bag gingerly. Did he know we needed this, or was it coincidence?

It felt like there was more to say. The silence was expectant, waiting to be filled, but what it was waiting for, I had no clue. I had no idea where to start or if we even should. If Sean hadn't seen what I had, then there was nothing to deal with. If Sean didn't understand the symbol he'd formed out of brightly colored sugar, there was no threat. It was best not to know.

Sean swallowed hard and studied me. What he was looking for was just one more thing we didn't need to address.

In the end we didn't fill the silence. I nodded my head, gave a weak smile, and left.

EIGHTEEN

I'm not a wimp, but unholy night, my hand throbbed while I walked. I embraced the pain, because it was better than the shaky panic of unease that followed me out of Sean's neighborhood.

At first I was worried that the blood all over my shirt would bring unwanted attention, even with my hoodie back on, but as the night had worn on, the revelers had gotten older and the costumes had become more gruesome, and now, even if someone noticed, I totally fit in.

I wondered if my shirt was the only one covered in real blood. I decided to add that to the list of things I was better off not knowing.

I kept a wary eye out for suspicious humans—taking note of soul colors like it was my job—heavenly angels, and even for Sean. It wouldn't have surprised me to see him following me. As much as I liked him, that wasn't going to be helpful, and it was better for everyone involved if we didn't see each other again.

When I returned to the statue, my stomach dropped. Crowley and Lilith were waiting, but there was no Aleister in sight. They were probably just as disappointed to see me coming back solo. We were going to have to go out searching again.

I tried to fight the rising panic at that idea. What if Aleister was avoiding us for some reason? What if he had been flung farther away, and we never found him? What if the seraph came back before we did?

And then what about Sean? Something told me he was more dangerous than I thought. Just because he was still slated to go upstairs didn't mean that his goals would be the same as ours. In fact, wouldn't he be *more* likely to help the seraph if it came to that? No, we had to go home, and without Aleister, we weren't going anywhere.

"Please tell me you found him and he's just taking a potty break or something," I said.

"That *would* be like him, but no such luck," Crowley drawled. "However, since you've obviously failed as well"—he looked at my bloodied shirt and raised an eyebrow—"we'll have to move on to plan B."

I was beginning to hate plan Bs.

"Mal, what happened?" Lilith grabbed my bandaged hand, and I let out what was *not* a gasp of pain. I'm sure it sounded manly, and not like I was going to cry.

"I just cut my hand. It bled for a bit." I shrugged, because that's what you do when you want to look blasé and cool.

"Your shirt is covered in blood," Lilith said.

"It's okay," I said, shrugging again. Extra shrug, extra cool.

"Getaroom," Crowley coughed, and my cheeks got hot, which was definitely because of gangrene setting in and not because I was embarrassed. I turned and scowled.

"So, what's plan B?" I growled.

"Most of the magical stuff in this town is fake," Crowley said. "Or at least, if it works, it only works for humans, but I was able to find a small but functional scrying mirror in one of the shops, so I swiped it. My magic is . . . not spectacular here, but I should be able to at least locate him."

Crowley set the scrying mirror on the pavement, adjusting its position until it lay perfectly flat on the ground. "Do you still have that stupid bandana you yanked off Al?"

"Oh, um." I patted my jeans and found the crumpled thing in my back pocket. Probably would have been good to remember that when my hand was leaking. "Here."

Crowley set it down gently next to the mirror and unfolded it like the wrong move would blow us to smithereens. If Crowley's magic was unstable, that might not have been far from the truth.

"Anything?" Lilith asked.

"What are you looking for?" I asked.

"Got it," said Crowley triumphantly, holding up something nearly invisible between his thumb and forefinger. "Let's hope this is actually from Aleister and not his hound."

I kept my fingers crossed and whispered a tiny prayer to Eiael for luck, but nothing too specific. Just enough to make this token spell have a minute chance of working. The last thing we needed was for the angel to figure out we were somewhere we shouldn't be and rat us out to our parents.

Crowley pricked his index finger with the pin of a button badge that read HAUNTED HAPPENINGS and began to mutter over the mirror, his pricked finger tracing symbols next to the hair, and just as I resigned myself to the idea that this was never going to work, the mirror started to glow. Lilith and I fell to our knees to crouch over it with Crowley. The three of us were crushed together, elbows jabbing into one another's sides as the surface of the mirror glowed and swirled slowly into focus . . .

. . . to a giant panting tongue and glowing red eyes.

We groaned.

"Ugh, freaking Damien!" I said, throwing myself back onto my butt. Of course the hair would be from the hound! Damien barked.

"Malachi?"

"Aleister?" I asked, shoving myself toward the mirror again.

"Move, Damien," said Aleister's voice, even though all we could see were white fangs and drool. "C'mon, I'm serious. SIT!"

Damien sat. And behind his massive black head, happy drooling jaw, and glowing red eyes was Aleister.

"Dude," he said, throwing his arms into the air. "Where did you guys go?"

"Where are you?" Lilith asked. "Because you were with us, but Damien wasn't."

"I'm in my room," Aleister said, shoving Damien away so that he could look at us more clearly through whatever surface we were appearing on. Damien immediately threw himself back onto Aleister's lap. "I haven't been with you since you guys disappeared in the woods. I called around and waited. I even threw a message through the veil, but you never replied. I thought about following, but I don't know, seemed kinda reckless. Besides, I knew you'd need someone to cover for you. Where are you, anyway?"

Seemed kinda reckless. I mouthed the words. Crowley shook his head.

"We're on Earth," Lilith said. "And we thought you were here too. We tried to cross back, but the guard said we weren't all together."

"Well, obviously the stupid bureaucrat was wrong," said Crowley.

"You have to tell me all about the human world when you get back," Aleister said. "Ugh, move whatever you're scrying with slower. You're making me sick."

"Hey, Lil, pull the hand on the statue," I called, psyched that we were not going to have to wander around this city again . . . until I saw Lilith. "What's wrong?"

Lilith gave a quick, insincere smile. "Nothing." She shook her head. "It's nothing." She pulled the hand on the statue, and it slid across the cement, drowning out the sound of Aleister demanding to be turned in certain directions so he could look around.

"You again," grumbled Terrence the imp once the booth had risen to its full height. Then, after careful consideration, his face took on a calculating look. "Got any more nougat?"

"Aw, brimstone," Crowley swore.

"What's nougat?" asked Aleister from the mirror.

"Yes, we do," I said, pulling out the bag Sean had given to

me, and thus saving my friends from certain parental doom.

"Excellent. Let's see." The imp held his hand out eagerly, wiggling his fingers in a greedy gesture. "But, uh, not for nothing, children, I ain't seeing another person here. You can't cross without your full and complete party."

"The only other person with us by the veil was Aleister," Crowley said. "And he's still home."

Aleister waved from the scrying mirror. "He's right, you know. We were the only ones there, and I didn't go through. Your sensor thingy must be busted."

"Yeah, maybe having him on the mirror will make it better," I said. "And I have his bandana, which has his energy and probably more hair on there somewhere, so we should be good!"

"Yeah, but . . . ," Lilith said, a frown forming on her face. "You know what? Never mind. You promise this won't get back to anyone? Strictly off the list?"

"I never saw you," Terrence said, a string of drool starting to spill out the corner of his mouth. Disgusting.

"All right," Lilith said, and stepped back. I handed the bag of nougat over to the imp, who tore into it immediately. He gestured vaguely to the shimmering gate before sticking his head entirely into the bag.

"Okay. Hands?" I asked.

"I don't have any hands," Crowley argued, shrugging his shoulders to display one hand holding Aleister's image and the other holding a bag with an unfamiliar lightning-bolt logo on it.

"You went shopping?" I asked. "How?"

"Never underestimate the lengths I will go to for comic books." Crowley grinned. "Especially ones we haven't seen before. I'll be the only one with copies."

"Wow," I said. "Whatever, I'll just hold on to your arm."

I grabbed Lilith's hand with my good hand, squeezing it reassuringly, and placed my injured hand on Crowley's arm. This was it. It was time to go home. We were getting out of here.

I'd have to throw away this shirt, which was honestly a bit of a killer—it was one of my favorites—and lie about my hand, but maybe I could make it sound like it was Methuselah's fault. Bonus.

Lilith squeezed my hand, just a quick, involuntary thing that drew my attention. I turned. She was biting her lip and looking away from the veil. My stomach dropped, but I ignored it. Whatever was wrong would be better once we were home.

I nudged her to get her attention and smiled before gesturing to the veil with my head.

Ready.

Set.

Go.

NINETEEN

I t really shouldn't have been surprising.

"What the blazes?" I shouted. "You said if we were all together, the barrier would open for us. Well, we're all here. There was no one else!"

My eyes started to glow. I didn't need a reflection to know. I could feel the flames starting to flicker, and even with all my anger I was relieved that at least this part of me was still there. The fact that it was a part I usually avoided didn't matter at all right now. Not when everything was so uncertain.

The imp didn't even look up from the bag of candy. Chocolate was smeared everywhere, and drool was pooling on the counter of his booth in a disgusting swamp of brown saliva. I snatched the bag away. It was wet. Gross.

"Hey!" Terrence protested.

"What gives?" I repeated, forcing my eyes to settle down into a less blazing color.

The imp considered us while he finished chewing what was already in his mouth. He wiped his mouth with his arm, smearing the chocolate across his face and up to his eye, leaving his shirtsleeve a filthy mess. Finally, after a million years, he swallowed.

"Full parties only. That's the deal. It's the conservation of energy. Added security. Same number in and out unless you're a new soul entering. Then you can fly solo. If the gate isn't opening, it's because you're not all here."

"Well, we are. Maybe it's broken."

Terrance laughed.

"It was just us in the woods. The only other person with us was Aleister, and he's still there! We were by a wild gate, and we fell through. It was just us. We would have noticed if there was someone else," I said, but the back of my mind was nudging me like it didn't agree.

"There was someone else. Hell is very particular about its laws, as you well know, and this one is nonnegotiable. The gate doesn't break," said the imp, reaching for the candy, his fingers opening and closing as he snatched at it. "It's not my fault. I've done my part."

"So, what? There was some invisible person that we just didn't notice? We were all there and . . . and . . ." I stopped talking as my brain demanded I take notice.

I, and pretty much everyone else, had assumed that if Crowley hadn't pushed us, then Aleister had nudged us all through. Sure, maybe not on purpose, but Aleister had more exuberance than a hellhound and half as much grace, at least when he was overly excited and had been cooped up for too long.

I knew I had been pushed from behind. I remembered the feel of it. Didn't I? I had to have been pushed. I would never have jumped.

But somehow my brain wasn't confident in this recollection.

Lilith's blue eyes grew wide, her mouth dropping open as thoughts raced across her face. Crowley sighed heavily and muttered something suspiciously curse-like.

In an epic determination of denial, I frantically searched for other explanations, but I knew my first thought was correct.

Lilith had already figured it out. Crowley smiled in disbelief and started to shake his head. I grimaced, Crowley's eyes rolled heavenward, and he dropped his bag of comic books onto the ground.

Not everyone who had crossed through the veil was here. There *was* someone missing, and we were in so much more trouble than we had ever been in before.

It wasn't until the smiling witch statue took its proper place as guardian of the gate that we dared voice the horrible conclusion that had occurred to us all.

"What?" Aleister called. "Why didn't you come through? What's going on?"

"We'll call you later, Aleister," Crowley said before whispering the ending spell and placing the mirror in his pocket. "You guys can't really think . . ."

"That we let the escaped soul out of Hell?" I asked. "That Samuel Parris is loose on Earth because of us? Yeah. That's exactly what I think. And it's what you think too."

The night was colder and darker without Terrence and the gate.

"We could be sent to the Cage for this," Lilith said.

"We have to get him back," Crowley said. "Fast."

"How are we supposed to do that?" I asked. "Our parents have been looking all week, and they're professionals. It's a one-way trip into Hell for souls. They can't cross back out. Are we even sure about this?"

"There are exceptions," Lilith explained. "Souls can leave if they're with a power."

Powers. Us, that would be us. I thought I was going to be sick. My knees went weak.

"So if we hadn't been messing around by the veil, Parris would still be in Hell," I said. "Which brings this back to being our fault and, again, a Cage-worthy offense."

"Not if we get him back," Crowley said, a calculating expression on his face.

"How's your magic?" I asked.

Crowley held up a hand, and a wisp of barely visible smoke drifted lazily up. I cringed. That was not a good look for our only magician.

There were no homey flames on the horizon, no comforting skitter of leaves—at least not ones that were running around themselves, just dead things being pushed by the wind. I was thankful for the streetlights, since the dark was suddenly scary in a way it had never been before.

Everything would be okay.

I just had to keep saying that.

"You knew," I said, turning my attention to Lilith. "Before we tried to cross, you knew it wasn't going to work."

Lilith said, "If the gate just needed whatever Aleister energy was still attached to his bandana, then it would have let us through the first time. It didn't let us through then. There's no reason to think that bringing Aleister up on the scrying mirror would make a difference. We were only supposed to use that to find him, here, on this side of the veil."

"Why didn't you say anything?"

Lilith shrugged. "I could have been wrong."

"You're never wrong," I said. And if it sounded bitter, well, even I had moments when I was less than perfect. "What are the odds of being forgiven for this?"

"If we don't fix this," Crowley said, "we will pay the consequences."

"Agreed," Lilith said.

And I suppose I knew that was the answer. The Powers That Be wouldn't *want* to send kids to the Cage, but they would. Maybe Lucifer would let us out after a while, but a while could be a *really* long time for an infinite being.

"Um, so here's the other thing," Lilith said, because apparently there needed to be a *But wait, there's more!*

"We only have until dawn. When the sun rises, the veil closes . . . until next year," Lilith said, cringing as she added that last part. "That's why Terrence told us time was running out."

"But my parents travel all year," I protested.

"Yeah, to Purgatory and Heaven. Earth is pretty well

locked down—you know that whole free-will, nonintervention clause—except for this one night." She thought for a moment, cocking her head to the side in an adorable tilt. "Well, exceptions can be made at specific points during the year: solstices, equinoxes, eclipses, but those take major power and permission. Neither of which we actually have."

"So how do we capture a soul, assuming we can even find it?" I asked. "What do they use at home?"

"A morningstar," Lilith said, first with confidence and then with a look of utter despair.

Yeah, I knew that answer. We all knew *that* answer. The medallion was practically the first picture we colored when we were in preschool. I was just hoping that Lilith knew something I didn't. She was supposed to be our squad's Intelligence, after all.

Morningstars were medallions imbued with infernal magic, used to trap and hold souls belonging to Hell. They were made of a rare metal found only in the farthest regions of Hell and were always heavy and warm to the touch. I had never used one. But I knew how they worked, and how they felt. I had held one in my hand in school. The spiky pentacle over a rayed sun design had caught the light and pressed into my fingers.

"Which we also don't have. Obviously," Crowley said,

rolling his eyes and taking out one of the comics he'd procured. The cover showed a white figure with little spikes on their head.

I noticed he wasn't reading the words, which made me smirk for a second. You've got to focus on the positive when facing absolute doom. Seeing a crack in Crowley's bravado, as small as it was, was my momentary silver lining.

"You could use a personal belonging. If the object was significant, there would be a memory, you see." The woman's voice, coming from beside us, became muffled with chewing. "Memories want to be reunited."

We all froze.

"You'll need some Latin, too, but it would work." She sighed.

There was no choir. No heavenly light. Her wings drooped, and the white robe was smudged with chocolate and cookie crumbs, but there was no doubt that the woman sitting on a conjured chair next to us now was a heavenly angel.

The same seraph who had been stalking me all day.

TWENTY

P lease don't scream," she said, holding one hand up and rubbing her forehead with the other, a plate of cookies in her lap. Her halo shifted with the gesture before returning to its place to glow steadily over her head. "I have a terrible headache."

"Is she a—?" Crowley started, eyes wide, his comic book dropping to his side.

"Yes," I confirmed. Lilith glared at me, and in her non-verbal dialogue practically screamed that I had been hiding things from her. She sort of had a point.

"You know, I am trying to take you to *Heaven*. Paradise? You know?" The angel sniffled. "You've escaped Hell. You should be jumping at the chance. I'm a terrible social worker." She began to wail and then shoved a cookie into her mouth.

"We didn't escape," Lilith said, her voice shaking only slightly. "It was an accident. We're trying to go back."

"Why would you want to go there? Hell is a terrible place," said the seraph.

"I mean, it's a little slow on the weekdays, but it's the suburbs. It's not terrible," I said. "It's not like we live in the Pit."

"Suburbs?" she asked, looking puzzled and sniffling a few final times.

"Yes, the *residential* section," Crowley said with a look that clearly implied she should already know this. "Where do you think all the employees live?"

"Well." The angel stopped. "I mean, isn't it all just one big torturous pit of . . . torture?"

"We don't live in the Pit," Crowley said. "We haven't even been there."

"There was that field trip one time," I interrupted.

"Yes, but we didn't go past the offices," argued Crowley.

"The point is," Lilith interjected, "that we live with our parents in a nice residential area, not with the souls and demons in the Pit. Why would we want to go to Heaven?"

"Because it's Heaven," said the seraph, happy to be back on familiar territory, but clearly she still wasn't quite getting it.

"Look, as much as my parents irritate me sometimes, I still want to live there," I explained. "We all do."

"But that's just the thing," said the seraph. "I can't leave you with demons. You need to be brought to Heaven before they corrupt you, too. You're all so innocent."

I snorted. Crowley raised an eyebrow.

"Wait . . . demons?" Lilith asked.

"Yes, your parents."

"Our parents are not demons," Lilith said. "And we're certainly not going to turn into them either. Demons, that is, not our parents."

"Speak for yourself," Crowley said. "I'm not turning into my parents, either."

"I'm sure they're very nice," the seraph said. "But you see, I can take you to Heaven right now. There's no need to worry."

"We don't want to go," I said very, very slowly.

"Yes, you do," said the seraph, just as slowly. "You just have Stockholm syndrome."

What was that supposed to mean? I glanced at Crowley, who was staring at the seraph like she was insane.

"Okay . . . I think we should start over," said Lilith. "I'm Lilith. That's Malachi, who you apparently have already met, even though he didn't say anything like he should have, and this is Crowley."

"I'm Cassandra," the seraph said.

"So, Cas," Lilith started.

"Cassandra," corrected Cassandra. All right, we were not going to be buddies.

"Right, sorry," Lilith said. "What were you saying about a personal possession being used to contain a soul?"

Cassandra straightened and brushed a few crumbs off her gown. "If you have an object that was important to the soul in question, then when you touch the soul with the object and say, '*anima coniuncta*,' the two will combine into one. It's a sort of metaphysical object memory. You can hold the soul inside the object until the counter-spell is spoken, '*anima separate.*'"

"So we just need to find an object that belonged to him," Lilith said. "What do you know about Samuel Parris?"

Cassandra frowned. She waved her hands, and an ancient book with tattered yellowed pages appeared, floating before her. She muttered, "One sixty-five, one sixty-five . . . ," and the pages flipped of their own accord until she stopped them with a sharp poke of her finger.

"'Reverend Samuel Parris was the puritan minister in Salem, Massachusetts, during the Salem witch trials, one of the most horrific cases of mass hysteria in American history,'" Cassandra read. "'He was also the father of one of the afflicted girls and the uncle of another.'"

"He was a reverend?" I asked. "From . . . here? Exactly where we are?"

Parris was from this town? Had the opening taken us here because it used to be his home?

"Yes," Cassandra said. "A terrible one, who orchestrated the Salem witch trials of 1692. More than two hundred people were accused and twenty were executed. Samuel Parris collected quite a bit of the accused's belongings and property. It was just awful."

"Afflicted girls?" Crowley asked.

"Girls who said they were victims of witchcraft. Their accusations were taken as truth," Cassandra said. "You see, Parris excelled at causing chaos. All to his benefit, of course. It's not that difficult; humans are always looking for an enemy. He preached at the meetinghouse at the corner of Forest and Hobart."

Cassandra waved her hands vaguely, and glowing lines raced across each other as a map drew itself in the air. I memorized the route just before Cassandra realized what she was doing, and with an angry swipe, the book and map were gone.

"Why are we talking about this?" Cassandra demanded, and for a moment her glow brightened ominously. "What did you do?"

"Nothing," I said. "We didn't do anything."

Cassandra studied our faces for a few moments, but we must have looked honest, because her glow lost the harsh edge and then faded away altogether.

"But," I said, "we think he may have slipped through the veil and returned to Salem."

"But if this is true, it's terrible," Cassandra said, suddenly standing, dropping her plate of cookies in the process. Instead of shattering, the plate, and the cookies with it, disappeared just before it hit the ground. "Oh dear." She looked down, frazzled, at her rumpled appearance, cookie crumbs and chocolate smears staining her gown. With a wave of her hand, she was clean and glowing brighter than ever. "I have to alert the office."

She started to leave, then turned and looked at us hesitantly. We all took a step back. She scowled momentarily and disappeared.

"Let's check out that meetinghouse," I said. "Fast."

TWENTY-ONE

We were able to find the intersection of Forest and Hobart Streets in no time. And it wasn't like I'd been exactly *expecting* a little glowing ball of Parris soul hovering over the object we needed to bind him (how convenient would that have been?!), but I had been expecting something *more*. Like maybe a building, but instead of a meetinghouse there was a small, paved area surrounded by grass, and a blue signpost holding a plaque.

Lilith approached the metal plaque and began to read: "'Directly across from this site was the original Salem Village meetinghouse where civil and military meetings were held, and ministers including George Burroughs, Deodat Lawson, and Samuel Parris preached. The infamous 1692 witchcraft hysteria began in this neighborhood.'"

A chill went up my spine. I really missed the warm glow of flames and the friendly cover of blackness at home, which was so different from the empty dark of the Salem night.

"'On March 1 accused witches Sarah Good, Sarah Osburn, and Tituba were interrogated in the meetinghouse amidst the horrific fits of the "afflicted ones,"'" Lilith continued. "'Thereafter numerous others were examined including Martha Corey, Rebecca Nurse, Bridget Bishop, Giles Corey, and Mary Esty. Many dire, as well as heroic deeds transpired in the meetinghouse. In 1702 the meetinghouse was abandoned, dismantled and removed to this site until the lumber "decayed and became mixed with the soil."'" Crowley muttered something about people being thorough, but Lilith ignored him. "'In 1992 a memorial was erected to honor the witchcraft victims, and to remind us that we must forever confront intolerance and "witch-hunts" with integrity, clear vision, and courage.'"

"It's gone," I said.

"You know," said Lilith, "I never really give much thought to what's in the Pit. They tell us in school, of course, but you never *really* think about what it holds. Or why. Our parents' jobs—our jobs—are really important."

The familiar argument of *My wings don't define me* tried

to claw its way out of my throat . . . but it was a weak protest. The job *was* important. For *someone* to do.

I had seen images of souls in the Pit before. They were so insubstantial, foggy white specters, oblivious to anything but their own suffering. It was hard to see them as a threat. But they hadn't always been like that, and there was a reason why they were there. There was a reason why they *had* to be locked away.

"We shouldn't have been messing around by the veil," I said.

The Pit wasn't just punishment. It was necessary to keep the universe in balance. It was necessary to keep evil and its influence locked away where it couldn't drive out the good. Where it couldn't infect creation like a virus. Something like that could turn a perfectly peaceful world into chaotic madness.

You know, like Salem at this very moment.

I froze. Hadn't I thought things felt wrong? Hadn't Sean said things were crazy? Didn't that imply that the chaos was not just because of Halloween or the full moon?

I wasn't naive enough to think that a manipulator couldn't be dangerous. I knew they could. Hitler had made a pretty big splash when he'd arrived, and he was held in the eighth circle, but it was rare that a manipulator caused mass damage. The harm was usually on a much smaller scale.

Most souls weren't even aware of their surroundings, and they certainly didn't change. Dead souls were static, but not Parris. And now he was not only free from his prison but loose in the mortal coil.

I found myself angry at my friends again. If we hadn't been messing around by the veil, Parris would have still been in Hell. Maybe not in the Pit where he belonged, but still contained. Still surrounded by his guards. I knew I was being unreasonable. They hadn't meant for it to happen, and even though I had given token protests, I hadn't really thought there was any danger either.

"It's not like we knew it was going to happen," Crowley said, echoing my thoughts. "And what did they expect, locking us away all week? During vacation! It was supposed to be awesome, and it sucked—the whole thing. I would say this is not even the worst part." And then his rant faded away, and his face fell. "Though I could be wrong . . ."

I followed Crowley's gaze and turned, and any questions about what exactly had happened at the veil and whether we truly had brought Samuel Parris through with us were answered with surprising clarity.

He should have been nothing more than a shimmer of light, the faintest glimpse caught out of the corner of your eye. In fact, exactly like the thing I had been seeing all night. So there was no way I should have been looking at a fully realized man. A fully realized man that could only be Samuel Parris.

Okay, he was see-through and flickered occasionally, but I could *see* him.

Pointy nose, curly dark hair that fell to his shoulders, a black suit and weird white ruffly thing at his neck; it was all visible. And it shouldn't have been, not at all. He looked more like Faust than the imprisoned soul he was supposed to be.

We backed into each other, forming a tighter group as we looked in horror at the thing that should not have been. Parris smiled and took a deep breath, though a soul shouldn't need to breathe. Shouldn't be able to, really, what with the no-lungs thing. He flickered and was gone.

"That's not right. How is that possible?" Crowley asked.

"I—I don't know," Lilith stuttered. Whether she was shocked more because of Parris or because she didn't know the answer was probably a toss-up. I could count the number of times Lilith hadn't known an answer.

Seven. The number was seven.

"We are in so much trouble," I said, wondering if perhaps taking Cassandra up on her offer was really such a bad thing. How bad could Heaven be? I was sure I'd be adopted by a perfectly nice family who wouldn't blame any of this on me. I could learn how to play a harp, and hopefully I would get my wings back. They might end up all white and fluffy instead of black and razor sharp, but that was a sacrifice I was willing to make.

"It's not possible," Lilith said.

"Clearly it is," Crowley said. "We need something to capture him."

"The sign says the humans let the building crumble to the ground and disintegrate, because of what they did here," I said. "Anything associated with Parris was probably destroyed, and there's no way we're going to find a morningstar here."

If something was so hated that the ruins of a building associated with it had been left to fall and disintegrate, a concept I couldn't really process, then why would they have kept anything from inside the building? I couldn't understand, and that was the problem.

I wasn't human, and this wasn't my world. And yet Crowley and Lilith were looking at me as if I would immediately have a plan, like I would have all the answers. How was I supposed to do that?

My heart raced, and irrational anger swelled at my friends, and okay, I know that was just a response to the panic, and maybe just a tiny bit of guilt from my hidden spark, but how dare they put this on me! Just because we had been cosmically assigned stupid roles didn't mean we had stepped into them yet, and "leader" or not, I didn't know this world any better than they did. I closed my fist over the crystal in my pocket.

It hadn't even been my idea to go into the woods. I had been perfectly fine going slowly insane in my house. They were the ones who had gotten me into this mess, and yet now it was all up to me to come up with a plan!

A very quiet voice in the back of my mind reminded me that I loved my friends and that they weren't any guiltier than I was, and that we would all need to work together here to get home. I told that voice to shut up and let me be petty for five freaking minutes!

My friends were expecting me to come up with something, to have a plan and take charge, but that wasn't me. And wasn't that the whole problem?! The take-charge leaders were my parents, and no matter what the Fates thought about family lines, there was always the white sheep of the family, and that was me. What was I going to do?

We needed help. Someone who was willing and able and knew a whole heaven of a lot about the mortal coil.

Someone local. Someone like—

"What. Was. That?"

Sean.

TWENTY-TWO

In what was a definite improvement over our last two impromptu guests, Sean stood at the corner underneath the lone streetlight, not looking nearly as shocked as I would have expected. Maybe walking, breathing dead people were a thing here, but I hadn't found that to be true yet.

"I mean, you guys saw that, right?" Sean asked. "Because it looked like you saw that."

"What are you doing here?" I asked.

"Had a feeling I should be looking for you."

"Do you know each other?" Lilith asked, with another accusatory glare in my direction. I cringed.

"Sean helped me with my hand," I said. Wow, my secrets were piling up. "How did you find me?"

Sean bit his lip and drummed his fingers against his leg. He took a deep breath, studied Lilith and Crowley for just a second, and then shrugged. He pulled a black scarf with glittery gold runes written across it out of his pocket and waved it in the air. It was the same scarf that had been wrapped around my cut hand. The same scarf that had tingled oddly, and unnaturally stopped my bleeding.

"I had a connection," he said sheepishly.

"Wait," Crowley interrupted. "What kind of connection?"

"Hey!" Sean yelled as Crowley ripped the scarf from his hand.

"You let him have your blood?!" Crowley snarled at me. "Are you insane? You let a hu—a *stranger* have your blood?"

"I didn't give it to him," I said primly. "I fell, and he helped me get cleaned up."

Sean wrestled the scarf away from Crowley and tucked it back into his pocket. Lilith looked at me in stunned silence.

"Hey, I don't mean any harm," Sean said. "I was just trying to help, and that's it. But then . . . well, I felt like I should find you. To see how your hand was doing, of course, not for any weird mystical reason or anything."

We stared.

"I'm a normal human," said Sean. He blushed.

"That's a weird thing to say," I said. "But my hand's fine."

"And that's the *only* reason you came looking?" Lilith asked. "To check on his hand?"

"Well," Sean said, "also to determine why there's a ghost, or whatever that thing was, haunting my town."

And wasn't that the question. What was Parris now that he had escaped his great hereafter? Was he a ghost now?

"Thank you," Lilith said. "For helping Malachi. And checking on his hand, apparently. But we don't—"

"Actually," I said, "this is perfect. What do you know about capturing a rogue soul?"

"Not a lot," Sean said with a raised eyebrow. "But I know someone who might. . . ."

Whether it was the plan my friends wanted or not didn't matter, because despite their glares in my direction, they followed me just the same. I winked, and Lilith and Crowley gave simultaneous eye rolls that somehow made me feel better.

Which was good, because the atmosphere of the dark, crowded streets had changed to feel dangerous with expectation. Maybe it was in my head, but I didn't think that was it. It felt like we were just waiting for the ignition that would set the whole thing ablaze. And maybe even worse was the foreign sense of glee that accompanied that thought. I was not having fun, and that glee didn't feel like mine. But if it wasn't mine, then whose was it and why was I feeling it? What was wrong with me?

I shook my head, trying to shake off that alien feeling, and focused on the neighborhood Sean led us to. It was nothing like the one he lived in. Rather than bland and forgettable, this street was one adorable house after another until we reached an apex-level-cute house.

The windows all held flower boxes overflowing with orange, yellow, and red flowers. A colorful welcome flag with a witch silhouette swayed gently in the soft breeze. The lights on either side of the front door held bulbs that flickered with artificial flames. Gingerbread detailing along the eaves made it look like you could almost eat the house. The railing on the front steps was decorated with artificial orange and red leaves.

"It's this one," Sean said, already climbing the steps.

"Give us a second," Lilith said, grabbing my arm before I could follow, and halting me dead in my tracks. Sean frowned. Crowley's face was carefully blank, and that more than anything else made me wonder if I was in trouble.

"Go on," I told Crowley and Sean. "It's fine."

"Wait—" Lilith started, and I knew she wanted Crowley to stay with us instead of following Sean, but I interrupted.

"It's fine," I repeated. "We'll be right there."

Crowley raised an eyebrow but followed Sean to the top of the stairs, and after a knock and what sounded like an excited squeal, the two went in.

"What's the matter?" I asked when we were alone, watching Lilith pace away from the house.

"What's the matter?!" Lilith repeated. "Why are we following a human? You just sent Crowley into a strange human house! We should be going home."

"We can't go home unless we find Parris, and we have no way of doing that," I pointed out. "Crowley is perfectly safe. Can't you see Sean's soul?"

"Yeah," Lilith said. "It's bright. I'll give you that. But that just means he's not coming to us, not necessarily that he's on our side. We know nothing about him!"

"He helped me before," I said. "He doesn't need to know who we are or where we're from, but we need the help."

"I don't like it," Lilith said dismissively.

Maybe anyone else would've taken her at face value, believed she just didn't like putting our faith in a stranger, but I had known Lilith since her pigtails had stuck out straight and she'd insisted on being called Princess Sparklepants. I knew it was more than that.

"What is it really?" I asked.

"You didn't say anything about him or the seraph," Lilith said, not even pretending that there was nothing else wrong.

"I didn't think it was important," I said.

"I know you're in charge," Lilith started, and I groaned.

"Lilith, don't!"

"It's true," Lilith snapped. "Just because you don't *want* to be doesn't change the fact that it's determined. But even though *you're in charge*, it doesn't mean you can hide things from us. Even if Al's not here, we're still a team, and we can't work as a team with secrets between us."

"I know that," I said, turning away before Lilith could see the guilt in my eyes. Not because of Sean or Cassandra but because of the spark of creation weighing heavy in my pocket.

"Is this the last surprise?" Lilith asked.

"Yeah, Lil," I lied, my stomach twisting. "You know everything."

TWENTY-THREE

In my defense, I really did think about telling Lilith about the spark right then and there, but everyone had secrets. *Clearly* Lilith only meant no secrets about Salem. There was no reason to feel guilty, no matter what the stupid voice in the back of my head thought. The spark was a last resort, and we weren't there yet, voice!

I had a million reasons why not to tell Lilith about the crystal in my pocket, despite my promise (not the least of which was that I wasn't even sure I was *ever* going to use it), and I went through them all meticulously.

That was probably why it took Lilith's muffled scream to make me realize that we weren't alone anymore.

I spun to the sound and nearly staggered. A man dressed as a skeleton had grabbed Lilith's wrist and yanked her close. She looked unimpressed, but her skin around his grip was turning red. "Isn't it past time for bed, girlie?"

And to make matters worse, the man had friends. The four of them began to spread out from behind their leader, trying to surround us.

"Isn't it past time for your chauvinist crap?" she snarled.

"Let go of her," I said, in a voice that rivaled my dad's in warning tone.

I knew my eyes were glowing red again, flickering like the flames of home, but if the idiots in makeup cared, they didn't show it. They circled us as I desperately tried to make eye contact with Lilith.

"Awfully late for you two to be out alone," drawled Guy Number Two, who, like the others, was dressed as a skeleton. His version wore a suit and top hat, and his face was painted to form a skull in shades of black and white. In his hand he held a broken bottle, the edges of the glass twinkling as the streetlights hit them.

"Ah!" Guy Number One cursed as Lilith kicked his knee and pulled her wrist free in one smooth movement. She landed in a defensive stance. I quickly joined her, and we stood back-to-back just the way we had trained, wary of the humans moving closer.

Why couldn't they have been real skeletons? These guys didn't look like they had the same anti-violence values as the bone men at home. In fact, they looked dangerous, and it had little to do with their costumes, and a whole lot with the deranged looks in their eyes.

I balanced my weight evenly, feeling the subtle shift behind me of Lilith doing the same.

"That wasn't very nice," noted the guy in the top hat.

The other skeletons moved forward, and one of them cracked their knuckles ominously.

"Think you're a tough guy, kid?" asked Top Hat, shifting his weight and bringing his arm back. "If you cooperate—"

I punched him in the throat.

The man retched, and I lunged for the next before they realized what was happening. From the sounds of rustles and thumps behind me, Lilith was doing the same. I was sure it was a simple matter of moving on—when an arm was suddenly around my neck.

The arm was clothed in black—top hat man had recovered—and it had the grip strength of a hydra. He lifted me off my feet, and I grabbed the arm around my neck, trying to get more air, while I scrambled with his other arm, trying to keep the jagged glass of the bottle in his hand from touching my throat. My eyes bulged, and the world took on a sparkling sheen, while my throat burned but didn't bleed.

And then I was loose and fell to the ground, where I landed in a crouch, more from muscle memory than any actual intention. I gasped there for a few breaths while the world lost its glitter.

"Leave you alone for two minutes . . . ," said Crowley, far too amused at my near-death experience. It would serve him right if I died and went home without him. Let's see how smug he'd be, stuck here forever.

"We had them," I said, before coughing to clear the roughness in my voice.

"Yup," agreed Lilith. "Totally under control. Thanks, though." She gestured at the crowbar Sean was holding.

"Not that you really needed help. Where'd you learn to do that?" asked Sean, pointing to the skeleton men at our feet, rather than to the one he had smashed.

I shrugged. "School."

"Okay . . . ," said Sean slowly.

"Oh. My. God!" squealed a new, very enthusiastic voice. "That was amazing! You were all like 'Take that, psycho,' and they were all like 'Grr, we're bad guys,' and then Sean was like, 'Off with your head, Bonehead!'"

"And this is Charity," said Sean, pointing to a girl

standing on the last step in front of the house, with her hand still on the railing. She had rainbow streaks in her dark brown hair, and wore a shirt that read WITCH, PLEASE! Her eyes crinkled with her bright smile, which brought out dimples in her cheeks, and she somehow matched the house in cuteness, something that didn't seem possible. Charity bounced off the last step to join us.

"Hi! Nice to meet you! What do you think of Salem? I mean, it's not like this, like, *ever*. It's way more exciting than usual. I mean, don't get me wrong, super dangerous, but still so exciting! But anyway, it's really not safe out here, and I made popcorn, so we should go inside."

Sean placed his hand over Charity's mouth. "Chill."

"Everything all right?" Crowley asked me under his breath as Sean and Charity continued chattering quietly.

I looked at Lilith, because quite honestly, I wasn't sure. She smiled and nodded. Relief and guilt settled oddly in my stomach, like that time Aleister made us try chocolate ice cream with pickled pumpkin, but I didn't really want to deal with more messiness, so I responded with a confident wink.

Fake it till you make it. It was practically my slogan.

I shook out my hand as we followed the humans up the stairs, because ow, fighting had not made that feel better, and if Charity's house was adorable on the outside, it was even more so on the inside. There were black cat statues and pointy hats, white pentacles on the wall, and sage bundles tied with purple ribbons. There were witch silhouettes and pumpkins, and on the wall above the door, elaborate script read BLESSED BE. There were knickknacks and old books, crystals and cauldrons, and the entire room smelled like exotic spices, which seemed to come from incense sticks on an end table that emitted faint clouds of smoke. The walls were lined with pictures, coats of arms, and crests. Latin words were splashed across the walls in glitter. There were vials labeled UNICORN TEARS that couldn't possibly be real, and more to look at than I could take in even if I ended up stuck here forever.

"Wow," I said.

"Isn't it ridiculous?" asked Sean, gesturing to the room at large.

"Oh, excuse me, Mr. Squat in Any Abandoned House You Find," said Charity with a huff. "Some of us like comfort. I mean, *really*, we come here every year." Charity turned to us and elaborated. "We Airbnb it when we're not here, so we kitsch up the place to go with the feel of the town, but I think it's awesome just like it is. When I have my own place, I'm totally taking everything here. Right, Sabrina?" She kissed her fingers and tapped them against a picture of a smirking girl with bloodred lips and hair so blond, it was white. "You too, Kiki," she said, tapping the next picture over, but this one was clearly a drawing of a girl in a blue dress with a giant red bow on her head. She was sitting on a broomstick, and I was reminded of the statue that wouldn't let us go home.

I didn't know who the pictures were of, and I didn't understand a word Charity said, other than to assume that perhaps Sean's house was not a normal human house, but then again, maybe this wasn't either.

"Like Dad would ever come back to the same house every time, where enemies would know our movements," Sean scoffed. "Never mind renting something like that out to literal strangers when we weren't there."

"We're not surrounded by the forces of evil, Sean," said Charity.

"Tell my dad that," said Sean.

"He's just paranoid because of all that Order of— Ow, don't kick me!" Charity said.

Sean made frantic gestures to stop Charity from speaking, and Lilith gave me a look that seemed to say, *See, this is what I was saying.* But everyone was allowed to have secrets, Lilith! This didn't make Sean any less trustworthy. Maybe he just meant his dad was really into organization and didn't want strangers touching his stuff. That was totally normal and not at all a reason to think that someone would betray their friends for their own selfish desires.

"Malachi?" Crowley asked.

I startled, only to realize that everyone was staring at me expectantly. "What?"

Crowley rolled his eyes. "Would you like to join us?"

Charity thrust a bowl of something puffy and buttery in my face. "Are you traumatized from your recent attack? Sometimes food helps, because after an adrenaline dump like that—"

"We're good," Lilith interrupted. "Besides, we came here for a reason. Unless this was all a nefarious trap to get us to a second location, ha, ha, ha."

"Yeah, of course," Sean said, looking thoroughly taken aback by Lilith's near accusation. "I was just starting to explain the situation when all—all *that* happened."

"By the way, I am so sorry about that," Charity said. "I know it's not my fault, but this is my neighborhood, so I kinda feel responsible. I mean, I've been burning sage and silver candles all day, but that doesn't really purify whatever that is going on out there."

"Is it not always like this?" Crowley asked, studying a piece of the stuff in Charity's bowl.

"Like a war zone?" Charity asked. She laughed brightly. "Nope, definitely not normal. Unless the town goes crazy every time we leave. Oh my goddess! Sean, do you think it goes crazy every time we leave?"

"No! What?" Sean said, before looking back to us. "Our moms . . . work together, and we've basically grown up together. We don't live here full-time, but we come here enough to know the town, and this is not the Salem we know."

"Right! Which brings us to this rogue soul you were telling me about." Charity's eyes gleamed in excitement. "Are we talking standard ghost or someone who's crossed on over from the other side? I mean, the veil is *thin* tonight."

Was that something humans were supposed to know?

"Do things often cross over here?" Crowley asked with a troubled expression. "From the great hereafters?"

"Great here what now?" Charity asked. "Like from an afterlife? No. Every Samhain we have some issues with spirits awakening and others drifting through Limbo. The ones who wake up usually aren't an issue, but sometimes you have to help the ones from Limbo cross over, or at least trap them if they're angry. But an actual afterlife? I mean, who knows what that even looks like? Or if the soul even stays intact? Lots of Wiccans think the soul fragments and rejoins the universe, so I don't think there's any coming back from that."

She suddenly paled. "B-but, I mean, you can believe whatever you want. I would never disrespect someone else's belief. I mean, no one really knows, right?"

"Right," I said, exchanging significant looks with Lilith and Crowley. No one knew except, you know, us.

"So," started Sean, "I'm not sure how to do this. Do you guys need the ghosts-are-real talk, or are we good? Because I get the impression you know more than you're supposed to."

And wasn't that the question? What did humans know? We weren't passing as "normal" humans, but then again, apparently Sean and Charity weren't normal either. So far Halloween had seemed a cheap imitation of our holiday, but Charity had just called it Samhain, which I hadn't heard any other humans do. I started to worry that Lilith was right, but just because something seemed up with them, did that really make them untrustworthy?

"Let's move to step two," Crowley suggested.

"Anyway, like I was telling you, Charity," Sean continued. "What appeared next to them didn't look like our normal Limbo escapee, and unless you guys are carrying around a possessed object, it's not a wake-up call of someone who's been long dead."

"Recently deceased and not passed over yet?" asked Charity.

"Not unless it died at a costume party," Sean continued, popping a grape from a nearby bowl of fruit into his mouth. "Which, I acknowledge, is possible."

"Why do you say that?" Charity asked. "Was it dressed like a *T. rex*? One of those inflatable costumes with tiny little arms? They're so funny. I laugh every time!"

"It's Samuel Parris," I said. Charity's smile fell from her face so fast, it would have been comical if the room hadn't gone deadly silent.

"What?" asked Sean. "How do you know that?"

"Wait," said Charity. "That name is just a coincidence, right? Not—not the one who was a really horrible human being a really long time ago."

"It *was* dressed as a Puritan," Sean said to Charity, who paled even further.

"I don't understand," said Charity. "How do you know that?"

"The same way you guys know about ghosts," I said. "We know stuff too."

"Oh my goddess!" Charity said. "I hate that guy! As a Wiccan, I find that man so offensive. He didn't even try to go after any real witches. Just people who were different. It's so easy to convince people to go after others who aren't like them. Ugh!"

"The guy from the Salem witch trials?" Sean asked.

"Yeah, all that mass hysteria was seriously profitable for him. It was like he fed off the chaos he unleashed," Charity huffed. "Seriously, Sean, your mom hasn't talked about that guy?"

"Of course she has, but uh, ixnay on the ovencay."

Sean looked shifty, and I had no idea what that meant. Must have been human words, though I could have sworn we were speaking the same language.

A siren wailed. Red and blue lights flashed on the walls as it screamed past.

Lilith gasped. "Oh, my unholy darkness. *Eighth circle.*"

"Manipulation," I murmured. And there it was. That niggling idea in the back of my mind exploded into full vision. Guilt decided to flare right along with it. Brimstone. Parris was already affecting this world, and it was all our fault.

Crowley let out a soft, "Ah."

"You said it's not normally like this, right? So just how unusual do you think this chaos is?" demanded Lilith. "Twice as much?"

"Like, ten times as much. Easily. We come here every year, and I've never seen anything like this," Sean said.

"You can't think Parris is doing this," Crowley said to Lilith and me, though it sounded more like he was trying to convince himself. "It's just a soul. He may have been a manipulator once upon a time, but he can't influence anything now."

"I wouldn't be so sure. Everyone was freaking out at home. We had—*supervision*," I said, more to my friends than the humans, who were staring at us with confused frowns. "The parental units were worried for a reason, right? Maybe it's just residual energy from his circle, but it's something. This can't be a coincidence."

"Whoa, what now?" Sean asked, holding up a hand.

I looked at Lilith and Crowley. If they were going to disagree, now was the time, but they both nodded. I took a deep breath.

"We believe the soul of Samuel Parris is causing all the trouble in Salem," I said. "We need to find an object to trap it, something that would have a spiritual connection to him, and that should stop the madness."

"I don't see how a ghost can do that," Sean said. "The only way they can make people do stuff is through possession, and this is only one soul we're talking about."

"Let me tell you right now," Charity said. "The adults are talking about everything from curses to demons. Eve was even talking about Mercury being in retrograde, but everyone knows that's just crap. How that woman is a wit—" She turned to Sean with a scowl. "Stop kicking me!"

"I should call my dad," Sean said. "If I know something, I need to tell him."

"Do you, though?" Charity asked. Sean's face was a twisted mix of anger and irritation, like this was a conversation they had argued to death. "He can be a little—"

"Please don't tell any adults," I interrupted, before either of them could start talking again. "Not yet."

"Seriously," said Crowley. "Adults ruin everything."

"It is known," agreed Charity. "Especially bullheaded . . . Well, you know."

"I'm not sure." Sean sounded wary. "They should know what I know. If my dad knew I held something back . . ."

"Just wait," I pleaded. I gave him a look I referred to as puppy-dog eyes number four. Lilith gave me a betrayed look for only a second before turning back to the humans. I felt guilty and elated all at once.

That was weird. Was Lilith jealous? Did I want her to be jealous? Yes, I did. But no, she couldn't actually be jealous, because to be jealous she'd have to actually like-like me. Right? I'd have to analyze that later.

"Besides," put in Lilith, "we might be wrong. If your parents are already looking at something, it would be best for us to be going in different directions. To cover more ground."

"That's an excellent point," I said. "Maybe it's something else entirely. All we know is that we need to capture Parris, whether he's causing this or not."

"But you need something with personal significance, right?" asked Charity, like she already knew the answer. She nodded to herself and started pulling out books. "This is so cool. Instead of destroying a cursed object, we get to make one."

Lilith and Crowley looked my way with worried glances.

"Cursed?" I asked. "That doesn't sound good."

"Okay, maybe 'cursed' is the wrong word," Charity corrected herself. "It's just an object imbued with a soul. In this case, a prison."

"Sounds like a plan," I said. "How do we start?"

"First we get more snacks!" Charity said, skipping into the kitchen. "Then we talk about souls and research possession and then maybe—"

But whatever she said after that point was lost, thanks to her head being inside her refrigerator.

"Maybe I should call my mom," said Sean.

"No, no, no!" I said, placing my uninjured hand on his shoulder. "Trust me. We got this." Our eyes met for only a moment before we both seemed to look away simultaneously. I dropped my hand. It tingled slightly.

When I looked up, Crowley had an eyebrow raised and Lilith was scowling.

"Help!" Charity called. Her arms were filled with mounds of food. She tried to kick the refrigerator door closed with her foot, but I gladly took the opportunity to escape and jumped to help.

By the time we had the feast laid out on the table— Charity with a disclaimer of "This isn't our normal Samhain stuff. My moms are just busy!"—it was decided that Charity and Crowley would research the effects Parris seemed to be having on the town and how to find a way to combat them. Lilith would research any possible other way to capture a rogue soul, though Charity seemed to agree with Cassandra that the best way to do so would be to find an object with a spiritual memory of Parris.

Sean and I would focus on researching Parris himself to find something that would have been significant to Parris, to use as a soul trap. Even more important, that object still had to exist, hundreds of years after Parris had died.

We weren't thrilled with our chances.

We spread out in the house as well as we could and still be within easy reach of food because, priorities. We had piles of books scattered around that Charity had yanked from various hiding spots. Apparently only some of the good ones were out in the open. We were alternating between old handwritten journals and glowing screens, though I wasn't a fan of the not-mirrors. Completely counterintuitive. I was in the middle of reading about Tituba's migration to Salem when Crowley swore and stood up so fast, he knocked his chair back.

Everyone else jumped to their feet, immediately scanning for danger.

"I'm cursed," Crowley muttered.

"What are you talking about?" I asked.

"Look at my face!" he growled.

We all looked at his face.

"I'm not seeing the problem," I said.

"Look!" he yelled, pointing at his face, as if that would somehow help. He looked down and very nearly snarled. This was bad. I had no idea why he was so upset, and his eyes were going to glow at any moment. I wasn't sure that was going to go over well.

"It's just an app," Charity said, leaning over his shoulder. "You must have opened it accidentally."

"Oh my goddess," said Sean, throwing himself back down onto the couch where he'd been researching.

Charity twisted the not-mirror so Lilith and I could see our faces. I jumped when I saw mine, now featuring whiskers and cat ears. I felt my head, but there was nothing there. Thank Hades! I could do without swivel ears. Lilith, on the other hand, looked adorable, which really shouldn't have been surprising.

Charity laughed and looked at us with a puzzled expression. "It's just a filter. You don't really look like that."

"You haven't messed with my face?" asked Crowley warily. He looked at us for confirmation, and Lilith and I shook our heads.

"No. You seriously don't know what this is?" asked Charity. "Do you guys live in a commune?"

I looked over her shoulder to Lilith, who just shrugged.

"Yes?" I chanced.

"Huh," she said, frowning, before brightening. "I knew your clothes were weird! And you haven't said anything about my cool *Chilling Adventures of Sabrina* collectibles! Not what I picture when I think commune kids, but well . . . what do I know?"

I wasn't sure whether to be insulted that Charity thought our clothes were weird but decided not to worry about it. We shrugged and went back to poking at the not-mirror.

"I think I found something," Sean said. "Apparently, when Parris was made reverend, there were a bunch of disputes over his pay."

"Money's not very personal," Charity said.

"Yeah, I know, but listen," Sean said. "'This was significantly worsened when he bought gold candlesticks for the meetinghouse.' I've got to believe they wouldn't have thrown them away, right? It seems the candlesticks were important. At least a turning point, and someone deemed it significant enough to write it down."

"That sounds promising," I said.

"Maybe we can do a locator spell," suggested Sean. For a second he looked panicked, like he had said something he shouldn't have, but I wasn't sure why.

"Ehhhh," said Charity, cringing. She stood in front of a purple bookcase, scanning book titles. "When's the last time anyone saw them? I mean, without some focal point, a locator spell would point to every golden candlestick ever made. We don't even have a picture. To use a locator spell or summoning, we would need something to focus the call to the *right* candlesticks."

"We have to find them," said Lilith. "Assuming they still exist. We already looked for the meetinghouse, and they let it rot into the ground. Who's to say they didn't melt the candlesticks down?"

"We can't be sure, but it's not like all the artifacts from the trials were destroyed," Charity said.

She stepped onto the bottom shelf of the bookcase, then stretched on tiptoes for a book far above her head. I raced forward to steady her as her fingers brushed the spine of a book and pulled. She didn't have a firm grip and it fell, bringing a box down with it. I managed to keep us on our feet, but we slammed into the wall, and I earned an elbow to the ribs in the process. The book and the box fell to the ground, and both opened on impact.

I wasn't sure which one the glow came from, but before I figured it out, I found I had an even bigger concern.

Sean held a very pointy dagger pressed up under my chin.

"What are you?" he snarled.

TWENTY-FOUR

The point of Sean's dagger forced my chin up, which coincidentally gave me a perfect view of Charity's glowing hands. Huh, Charity was a magic user. Which made a lot of sense now that I thought about it. The things I should have found in the Witch House were in Sean's and Charity's houses instead.

A sharp pinch underneath my chin reminded me that I still hadn't answered Sean's question. Charity's magic was making the room smell like ozone.

Lilith had already shifted her weight like she was going to pounce. I knew if we still had our wings, hers would have been arched high over her head. In fact, I could almost see the shadow they would cast. Crowley was desperately trying to kick-start his magic, if the sparks around his palms were any indication.

My friends' eyes were just about to glow, and I didn't think that was going to help matters.

"Wait, wait!" I said. "When I said we weren't locals, I didn't just mean from Salem."

"Yeah, me neither," said Sean. "But that's not what I asked you. What are you?"

Lilith bit her lip in that way I always liked. *Not the time, brain, not the time.* Crowley laughed wickedly. But despite their reactions, they stayed at the ready, and my heart warmed. If things went bad, I knew I could count on them, wings and magic or not.

"We're from a different dimension," I said slowly.

"Okay . . . ," Sean said. The dagger didn't move, but he did turn his head to look at Charity. Her hands stopped glowing, and she shrugged.

"The amulet could react to something like that," Charity said, picking up a brightly glowing talisman that had fallen out of the box. "It's really keyed to 'other' more than anything else. That normally means vampire, werewolf, and all that jazz, but I suppose if someone was from another dimension, that would be 'other' enough to trigger it to glow too."

Sean didn't look completely convinced. His eyes narrowed as they swept my face. *Please, eyes, stay boring.*

"You're not monsters?" he asked.

"Define 'monsters,'" I said, bristling at the implication, but Sean pressed the dagger a little harder. "No, definitely not."

"Why are you here?" Sean continued. He lowered the dagger, but he didn't put it away.

"We're on vacation?" I said, which was technically true.

"You decided on a vacation to Earth?" asked Charity. "Do they make brochures? What do they say about us?"

"It was kind of an accident," said Lilith. "We didn't actually choose Earth."

"Then why don't you go home?" snapped Sean. "Why get involved in all this Parris nonsense, if this isn't even your dimension?"

My feelings probably shouldn't have been as hurt as they were.

"Parris is causing problems *here*," I said, before smirking and throwing back Sean's own words: "Helping is kinda what we do."

He didn't smile, but his face smoothed out a little, and he hadn't stabbed me yet, so yay for charm!

"Besides, the opening isn't there anymore," Crowley said.

I didn't face-palm, but it was a close thing.

"Which really has very little to do with anything," I said, with a glare at Crowley.

"No ulterior motives?" Sean asked. "You're just helping, out of the goodness of your hearts?"

"If you're from another dimension, how do you know who Samuel Parris is?" Charity asked.

"He came through the same opening we did," said Crowley.

"Really?" I snarled. I turned, fully expecting my eyes to start burning, but when I looked at Crowley, he looked shocked, like he couldn't believe he had said that either. He shook his head, and when his eyes met mine, they were apologetic. I frowned. What was going on?

"He did," I said, as I changed tactics. "But we can't tell you all the details. Rules, you know? Just trust that we have to capture him and bring him back to where he belongs."

"Okay," Sean scoffed. "Let me see if I'm getting this right. You came through here on 'vacation.' But when you came here, you brought along Samuel Parris, who for some reason was in your dimension. I'm betting that's something you would be in trouble for. All this 'helping people' stuff is really helping yourself. Did I get that right?"

"Don't think you know us!" I snapped, with such force that Sean lifted his dagger again.

"Malachi," Lilith cautioned.

"You have no idea who we are," I said.

"And isn't that just the problem," snapped Sean.

"Sean," cautioned Charity.

"Our entire lives are protecting those who can't protect themselves," I said. "You just happen to be those people right now."

"I can protect myself just fine," Sean growled. "In fact, you'd be bleeding out to nothing if it wasn't for me. You think we can't do this without you? You think I don't know what I'm doing?"

"I never said that!" I yelled. "He has to go back! But even if we didn't need him, we'd still be doing this, because it has to be done. Because it's the right thing, because it's what we're fated to do, and because everything else matters more than us."

"Okay," interrupted Lilith. "I think we're not really talking about what we started with. . . ."

"You need him?" asked Sean, quieter now.

"Yeah," I said. "But nothing has changed. Capturing Parris will make all this stop. Win-win." I took a big breath and felt all my fight leave with the exhale. "I swear, we're not the bad guys."

"Maybe," agreed Sean. "But we've been going through the idea of capturing the soul on your insistence, when maybe what we should be doing is looking to destroy it."

Sean gestured to Charity to follow him out of the room,

but then paused to look over his shoulder at us. "Don't go anywhere."

"Are you all right?" Crowley asked me.

"Yeah," I said. "I don't know what that was." I totally knew what that was.

I had stopped talking about Salem and Parris and started ranting about the unfairness of everything the Fates had put on me and my squad. Everything I had been squashing down was roaring to get out, but now was really not the time, and I shouldn't have let it get the best of me.

I could hear voices through the wall but couldn't make out what they were saying. I hoped it was along the lines of: *These people are totally trustworthy. We should help them,* and *The devastation in this town is clearly not their fault,* and *Wow, did you see how great Malachi's hair is,* and not along the lines of: *We should kill them while they sleep.*

"If they try to destroy Parris, we're not getting home," Lilith said. "Or we can ask for help, but we're going to the Cage."

"Maybe we should make a run for it," I said.

"We don't have the resources," Crowley said. "I can contact Aleister again, but any information about Parris from home is going to be heavily guarded and focused on his intentions and choices, not on physical objects."

"Let's see what they decide," I said. "If they agree to help capture Parris, great. If they want to destroy Parris, we'll just go behind their backs to work on our own plans."

"And if they decide we're the bad guys?" Lilith asked.

"We outnumber them," Crowley drawled, clenching and releasing his fist.

I nodded, agreeing, but I *really* hoped it didn't come to that.

The door opened to the room Charity and Sean had gone to for privacy or possible plotting. The phantom feeling of my wings puffing in anxiety distracted me just enough that I didn't panic. We didn't know the extent of Charity's magic. There was a real possibility that outnumbering them wouldn't make any difference at all.

"Okay, so let's get back on track," said Charity as if nothing had happened. "It sounds like the candlesticks are the best option, but we can't use a locator spell without a focal point. So now what?"

"Now what" turned out to be something that no one agreed on, but the arguments did get us past the awkward tension.

"Enough!" I said loud enough to be heard. Even I was surprised, but I just kept going. "We're going to split up. My team will come with me, and we will look for the candlesticks in the locations Charity suggested. Sean and Charity will stay here and research any spells that might be helpful or find any other objects that might work and still be around."

"Hold on," Sean said. "I know this town better than anyone else here, and no offense, but this is my world."

"And I'm not leaving the spell work to the humans," drawled Crowley. "No offense."

"Fine," I snapped. "Crowley, you will stay here and help Charity. Sean, you will come with us and tell us where to look. Any questions? No? Good. Let's get started."

Sean muttered quietly to Charity. I tried to listen in, but beyond hearing something about "lapels," I didn't catch what they were talking about. I put my hands into my pockets, one of them more gently than the other, and almost startled when I felt the velvet bag in my left pocket. I squeezed it, and the sharp edges dug into my palm.

My heart froze. The spark of creation could do almost anything. The powers of an archangel were nearly immeasurable, and I had one-time access to them in my pocket. I could create a morningstar. We didn't need to find these candlesticks that might or might not exist or might not even work to trap a soul or whatever it was that Parris was now.

But if I did that . . .

If I did that, *I* would be trapped. And not in the way we were trapped now, in a strange dimension that still had connections to home; that still had alternatives. Trapped as in forever. Molded and trained and tracked, separated from my friends in any meaningful way and, more important, separated from what made me, *me*. My awesome personal flair was not desired or required for a leader. Neither were close personal relationships with your squad.

If I used the spark for this, I would give up all control over what I would be, what I was. It would be over.

But . . . but I didn't have to decide right then. If things went bad . . . if we couldn't find the candlesticks and things were looking like they were heading for the worst . . . then I could still act. I could use the spark then. When there was no other choice.

That was okay. Right?

"There he is," said Lilith, shoulder-bumping me on the way out. "Knew there was a leader in there somewhere."

"Whatever," I said, shoving my nausea down. "Don't get used to it."

TWENTY-FIVE

The chill in the air was cold enough to turn the end of my nose red, but at least the familiar scent of dead leaves kept me calm while we waited for Sean to pick the lock of a tourist attraction called the Witch Dungeon Museum.

Sean jimmied it easily, and we pushed the narrow door open. A siren wailed in the distance, and I could hear a man on the corner ranting about the end of days.

The room was dark and crammed with merchandise: books, shirts, pens, and toys crowded the shelves. A counter with a cash register stood off to one side, looking forlorn with no one waiting to take money.

"Are you sure about this?" I asked.

"They do re-creations of the trials here," said Sean. "The candlesticks were bought for the meetinghouse, and that's where the original trials were. This town is super touristy, but they try for authenticity, so the candlesticks might be here to make the room as accurate as it can be. I'm not sure, but we can try one of the other museums after to see if they're being displayed as historical artifacts, or maybe Charity will figure something out. This way." Sean pushed open a door marked ENTRANCE.

He hadn't looked directly at me since the whole threatening-me-with-a-dagger situation. I tried not to let it bother me. It did anyway.

The door opened into a large room with rows and rows of benches and an elevated platform at one end. The platform had a large wooden chair in front of a tall podium where a wax figure of a man sat so that only his upper body was visible. There was a bench to the back, and more wax men filled out the seats. Red velvet curtains framed the sides of the platform, and lights hung from the ceiling with flickering bulbs of artificial flame. I didn't know if this was what the meetinghouse had looked like originally, but unlike the obviously fake haunted houses, this looked authentic. As we walked down the aisle separating the rows of benches, I could see it.

And then I could *see* it.

"Sarah Good, what evil spirit have you familiarity with?" demanded a man who had suddenly appeared on the platform at the front of the room. He was dressed much like Parris had been, and had a shimmery quality like Faust, there but not there.

"None," pleaded the woman, seated in the large chair. She had the same not-there quality. The memory of tears tracked down her face. Her hair was covered in a bonnet, and her long dress swept the floor.

"What the Hell . . . ," muttered Sean.

"No, not there," I muttered back, but I understood now. Sean had said they reenacted the trials here. We were looking at a court, and the large chair the woman sat in was the witness stand. The wax figures didn't look wax anymore, and their sneering faces flickered like glitching videos.

"Have you made no contract with the devil?" demanded the man.

"No," wept Sarah.

Lilith pressed closer to my side, and I leaned into her as if that would somehow protect us. I didn't know what was going on, but I didn't get the sense that it was part of the usual show.

"Why do you hurt these children?" The man was hostile,

intimidating, hungering for an admission of guilt. He gestured toward the front row, where I saw shadows appear, squirming and reaching toward Sarah with snatching fingers. But unlike the shades and gremlins we had seen roaming the town, these weren't really here, just shadows of the past.

"I do not hurt them. I scorn it," Sarah pleaded, looking very alone on the witness stand. She looked around, searching for a friendly face. My heart ached for her.

"Who do you employ, then, to do it?" the questioner continued.

"I employ nobody." Sarah shook her head.

"How is this happening?" murmured Sean. "Are you seeing this too? Is it just me?"

I shook my head, uneasy at repeating Sarah's gesture. "It's not just you."

"What creature do you employ, then?" The examiner stepped forward, trying to catch Sarah in a game of words.

"No creature, but I am falsely accused." Sarah leaned toward us, both hands on her knees, her body curling in on itself.

"Why did you go away muttering from Mr. Parris's house?"

"I did not mutter, but thanked him for what he gave my child," explained Sarah.

"She did, you know."

I spun to face the voice behind me, my heart nearly in my throat. And there he was. Samuel Parris walking down the aisle toward us. I could almost hear footsteps. I could barely see through him.

I had seen souls gasp, scream, and wail. I had heard them murmur words and half sentences that made no sense, in conversations with people who weren't there, but I'd never seen them interact as though they were alive. It wasn't possible.

We grouped together and stepped closer toward the front of the room and away from the former reverend. Wherever Parris passed, the seats filled with the shadows of witnesses, all in those same strange clothes, as if a bubble of the past followed him wherever he went.

"Thank you, children," Parris said, his eyes now turned to where we stood, watching. "When I found you by the veil, my only goal was escape, to flee my endless torment, but this . . . this is so much more than I expected. I can never thank you enough for helping me."

"We didn't do it on purpose," snapped Lilith.

"Still," said Parris, bowing his head slightly.

"You have to come back with us," I said. My voice didn't shake.

"No, I don't," said Parris, spreading his arms. "In fact,

I have a proposition for you. You gave me my freedom; I can give you yours. That's what you want, isn't it? Freedom? Freedom to be who you choose to be? *Give in.*"

My stomach turned to ice with the thrill that the suggestion sent through my heart. I heard a gasp from my left. I wasn't sure if it had come from Sean or Lilith, but I didn't think I was the only one affected by Parris's attempted manipulation. Thankfully, we knew what Parris was.

"You're a soul belonging to the eighth circle, and we will get you back there," I said.

"We'll see," said Parris. A smug smile spread slowly across his face.

"You are a liar!" Sarah's shout made us jump. I had forgotten she was there.

I turned to the side, trying to keep an eye on Parris as I looked to the front, my heart racing faster than I thought possible. The trial was over and Sarah's image, dirtier and worn, stood on a hillside, a noose hanging loosely around her neck. I could see the room through the hazy overlay of grass and sky. "I am no more a witch than you are a wizard, and if you take my life, God will give you blood to drink."

There was the sound of a lever being pulled, and Sarah's image fell. Her body hung from the noose, now pulled tight, her head cocked at an unnatural angle, her eyes lifeless.

I turned back in shock. Parris sneered, and with a snap of his fingers, he disappeared.

The room came back to its empty, dark self, and I tried to steady my breathing. The adrenaline I had tried to keep at bay was surging in all at once.

"We are way out of our league," Lilith said.

TWENTY-SIX

W hat dimension did you say you were from?" asked Sean, looking very suspicious.

I was not nearly recovered enough for that conversation. I tried to stop the shaking that was trying to take root in my limbs, but before I could come up with an answer, another voice spoke. "Oh dear."

Speak of the seraph.

"Things just keep getting worse," said Cassandra.

I turned. Cassandra was pristine and sparkly white, her halo straight and glowing dimly above her head. Lilith was silent but staring at Cassandra. Sean was still looking at me, which was weird, considering the glowing seraph in front of us. I waved my hand in front of his face. Nothing.

"What did you do to him?" I asked.

"Oh, he's just frozen. Appearing before humans is forbidden without the right paperwork."

Well, that was one way to avoid the conversation.

"Are you ready to come with me now?" asked Cassandra hopefully. "Please?" she begged. "Although why I should have to say 'please' to bring someone to Heaven is beyond me."

Were there any adults who trusted me to know what was best for me? Any, at all, in any dimension?

"Okay, that is an idea," I said diplomatically. "But maybe you could help us capture Parris first."

"Oh, I can't do that." Cassandra shook her head.

"We're not asking you to open the veil or anything," Lilith jumped in. "Just help us capture him, and we can make sure he gets right back where he belongs. Then everything will be all better."

"Well, things *are* going to be better. I told the home office that Parris was loose," said Cassandra, as if any further argument was impossible.

"And?" I asked.

"And the home office will take care of it," said Cassandra.

That could not be good.

"How?" Lilith asked.

"Probably something involving smiting. Floods, plagues, maybe a big dome over the whole city," said Cassandra with a wave of her hand.

"How does that help?" I asked incredulously.

"Well, we can't let this spread. Just look what Parris has done here in only hours. Of course, this is his home base. It's probably why you ended up here, but Heaven certainly can't let his influence spread. We really should get going. You don't want to be smited." Cassandra frowned. "Smoted? Smote? Smitten? No, that's not right." She shook her head. "Anyway, you don't want to be here when Parris is taken care of."

"But we need his soul to get home," I said. "We *want* to go home."

Cassandra looked at me. This time she really looked, her deep brown eyes searching my face for something. The seraph's expression became serious and a little sad.

"It's my job," she said apologetically. "I'm not always that good at it. The reapers take the new souls, you see. I just deal with the ones left behind or the odd cases like you. I was excited about you and your friends. I thought I'd be good with children."

"I'm sorry," I said. "I could . . . give you a recommendation or something?"

Cassandra smiled and placed her hand against my cheek.

"You're sweet," she said. She ruffled her wings and stood straighter. "You'll fit right in in Heaven."

"Um . . . okay," I said, carefully hiding my shudder. "How about before we finish talking about that, you find out the details of the home office's plan. It's only fair that we tell our friends, you know, before we continue talking about . . . that."

"All right, I suppose so. I'm so glad you're seeing reason." Cassandra brightened. Literally. I had to squint my eyes, which, having become accustomed to the dark, were finding the angel's radiance a bit hard to take. "Naomi owes me a favor anyway."

Cassandra disappeared, and I wondered how Heaven got all the easy transport. Just another of those unfair things.

"Well?" asked Sean, now unfrozen and apparently not having forgotten his question.

"You wouldn't know it," I said, getting back to his question of where I was from. "And it's one of those things we're not supposed to talk about. Hey, let's look around for those candlesticks."

"We can't let Heaven have Parris," I whispered to Lilith.

"Absolutely not," she agreed.

We searched the Witch Dungeon Museum thoroughly, and even though we found tons of cheesy knickknacks, dusty books, and employee supplies, we did not find anything that looked like golden candlesticks.

"Should we be worried that Parris knows about us?" Sean asked when we finally admitted defeat. "This is not what ghosts do, at least not here. I don't even know what that was. Have you seen this before?"

"No," I said.

Lilith frowned and bit her lip. Her hand tapped out a rhythm on her leg. One two three four, one, one two three, one two three four . . . The same rhythm she always tapped when she was nervous. We never spoke about it. The same way we never spoke about how she spun her locker dial five times before opening it, never four or six.

I rubbed her arm with my hand and smiled.

"It spoke," Lilith said. "The soul spoke."

"Yeah," I said.

We stepped out onto the street. The cold air helped.

"Look," Sean said. "I *have* to call my dad. This is way more serious than I thought."

"Maybe you should," Lilith said. "If you think he'd know more about this."

"What?" I protested. "Why? We know what we need to do. We just have to do it."

The last thing we needed was more adults who thought

they knew better, but apparently, I was the only one who thought that.

"Mal, look what he's done to this town," Lilith said. "Didn't you feel it? His influence? He's changing, and I think we need to get him trapped before he's finished changing."

"Changing into what?" I asked.

None of us had the answer for that. A shade slipped through the trees above me. I looked up, hoping it would make eye contact. It was hard to tell whether I was successful.

Sean put his "phone," which I had learned it was called, to his ear and walked away from us.

Cassandra flitted in to fill the silence with a rustle of feathers again.

I looked nervously to Sean, but he wasn't paying any attention. Whether that was because he was distracted or because Cassandra had done something to him again, I wasn't sure.

"The thrones will be here tonight," Cassandra said. "They're going to cleanse the town."

The thrones were a choir of angels that dealt with justice. Not quite as personal as sending an archangel, but just as dangerous. There was another rustle of feathers, which was weird because Cassandra's wings hadn't moved.

"Why do I think 'cleanse' means 'destroy'?" Lilith asked.

"We're going to be able to take Parris with us as part

of this cleansing, right?" I asked Cassandra. "Get him back where he belongs?"

"Oh, I doubt it," Cassandra said. "There's going to be lots of smiting, so nothing to take with you. Come along."

"Awesome," I said. Not awesome. "Wait, um, do you know, just for academic reasons, is Parris still a soul? He's not a demon or anything, right? If we had an object or—or a morningstar, would that still work?"

"Of course," Cassandra said. "He's very powerful, and only getting stronger the longer we wait, but yes, he's still just a soul."

"Why is he getting stronger?" Lilith asked. "He shouldn't be."

Cassandra smiled. "Well, I would tell you to ask your nice friend over there. He could tell you, but we should really get going."

"That was super helpful," I said. "But you can't take us to Heaven with Sean here, because he'll notice, and I'm pretty sure you still don't have the paperwork for a human appearance."

Cassandra pouted, and I had never been so glad for bureaucracy in my entire life.

"Guess you'll just have to wait till we're alone to kidnap us," Lilith said sweetly.

Cassandra scowled, but thankfully disappeared. A child's giggle sent chills up my spine. I looked around but didn't see anything. Freaking heavenly angels were making me literally insane.

Okay, no problem. We just had to constantly be with Sean. Or Charity. Or any human, really. Nah, probably best if it was Sean. It was just logical. Not for any other reasons.

"What was that supposed to mean?" hissed Lilith as soon as Cassandra was gone. "Sean knows why Parris is getting stronger. I knew we shouldn't be trusting some random stranger."

"He's done nothing but help," I protested. "*She* has done nothing but try to kidnap me all night. Who are you going to trust? Besides, Crowley is still with Charity. What are we going to do, bail on him? There's no going back without Crowley. Not even if we capture Parris."

"Of course not," Lilith said. "I would never leave Crowley behind."

Sean continued talking into his phone like our feathery intruder had never appeared, but now that she was gone, I realized that I could hear him speaking clearly.

"Dad," Sean said. "I know. But—No, sir, of course that's important. I'm not saying that."

I could vaguely hear a gruff voice coming through his phone, which was not exactly like a pocket mirror. I don't know why he had it facing his ear, but then again, the conversation didn't seem to be going well. I'd probably hide my face too.

"I'm not a kid," Sean said. "It's not about missing Halloween. . . . I know how to deal with a ghost, I'm telling you—Yes, sir. Yeah. I know. I will."

Sean sighed and put his phone into his pocket.

"Does he know anything?" I asked, almost afraid to interrupt the tension.

"He wouldn't even listen," Sean said. "Like I don't know how to deal with a regular ghost! Like I would call him for anything that wasn't an emergency. Why *would* I when he acts like I'm—whatever."

"Sorry," I said, because I wasn't sure what else to say. I wasn't necessarily upset with how it had worked out, but I knew what it was like when talking to your dad was more like talking to a wall. A wall who thought you needed a babysitter.

"Do you know why Parris is getting stronger?" asked Lilith.

Sean frowned. His face darkened with anger. "If I knew, I wouldn't be calling my father."

"We know that," I reassured him.

"Do we?" asked Lilith.

"Yes, we do," I said.

The air grew tense, and I almost couldn't believe this was where we were right now. Lilith was wrong, though. Sean wasn't the one keeping secrets.

A song broke the silence between us, and Sean pulled out

his phone again, his angry scowl smoothing out a little as he answered. "Tell me you have something, Charity."

"Sorta, kinda," Charity said, her voice barely audible. "Remember that thing you were asking about? The lapel thing? I figured it out. Where are you?"

"Just leaving the Witch's Dungeon," Sean said. "No luck. I called my dad—don't even ask. I was going to head to the Witch History Museum next."

"Don't," said Charity. "Meet us a block from Gallows Hill."

"Wait, why?" Sean asked. "Hello? Darn it, Charity."

He put his device back into his pocket and sighed. "If you want to trust me, come with me. I'm going to meet up with Charity and your friend, but I'll tell you right now, I don't know what's going on or how Parris's ghost is more than a ghost."

"We're coming," I said.

Lilith nodded but looked resigned. I nudged her. She raised an eyebrow, but eventually snickered and shook her head. She threw her hands up into the air.

"Where to?" she asked.

TWENTY-SEVEN

I think my feet are bleeding," I said, in an effort to lighten the mood.

"What? Why?" asked Sean distractedly. "Did you step on something?"

"Yeah, the ground," I said. "I've done more walking today than I ever have in my entire life."

"That's probably true," Lilith said. Her arm brushed against mine. Was it happening more than normal? Did her fingers always curl like that? I looked at Sean and felt my stomach twist for no apparent reason.

"Why do people live where it's so cold?" I said, reaching

for the next available topic to grab. My thoughts were in a dangerous place.

"Fan of global warming, are you?" Sean asked.

"If that means making this place warmer, yes," I said.

"It's going to get worse. It's not even winter," Sean said. He glanced at me quickly before looking away. "Is it—is it warmer where you guys are from?"

"Our world is literally on fire," I said. Sean mumbled something that sounded suspiciously like, *So is ours.*

Awkward silence fell between the three of us again.

I was going to have to tell Lilith about the spark.

We were wandering a human dimension as it moved ever closer to total apocalypse, or at least *citypocalypse*, leaving us with three options.

Option 1: We'd be destroyed with the rest of Salem.

Option 2: Cassandra would be successful, and we'd be ~~imprisoned in~~ adopted into Heaven.

Option 3: And perhaps worst of all, without Parris, we'd have to have Aleister contact our parents, who would then know that not only had we violated Hell's lockdown but we'd allowed an escaped soul to enter the mortal coil. And if that happened, what would happen to Aleister?

I had the solution in my pocket. We didn't need to wait.

It was selfish and awful, but I didn't want to give up my only escape from what was waiting for me at home. Whether I used the spark or not, knowing it was there was everything. And beyond that, I didn't want to admit to my friends that I was still keeping secrets.

"Why would you say that?" whined a girl across the street. It was a welcome distraction.

"I'm not sorry. Those shoes are terrible," said the one standing next to her. "But I like your hair."

"You do?" asked the girl, who looked immediately happier.

"Yes, you should cut it off and give it to me," said her friend.

"Okay."

I hesitated because *hair*, but Lilith nudged me forward.

"That has to be because of Parris, right?" Sean asked, pointing to the two girls.

"Do people often trade their hair here?" Lilith asked.

"No, that is not a thing," Sean said.

"Then it's probably Parris's chaotic influence," Lilith said, shrugging. "It may not be intentional, though. Just contamination, maybe?" She tapped her fingers against her leg. One two three four, one, one two three. She didn't know the answer.

We knew Parris was a manipulator, but he wasn't here, and even with my sometimes problematically large imagination,

232

I couldn't see how trading hair or dancing on tables could possibly benefit anyone. What would be the point? But somehow Parris was getting stronger. I just wished I knew how.

Cassandra says Sean knows, I thought. *Yeah, Cassandra says we'd be better off in Heaven too.*

I glanced back at the hair girls. Their auras glowed a steady blue, so they were apparently the harmless variety of weird.

My eyes jerked to the side when I heard a flutter of feathers. There was a flash of white in the bushes. Was Cassandra following us? Had she decided that stealth was a better option?

"What's the deal with Gallows Hill?" Lilith said, tugging me away from the girls and the flash of white feathers.

"You heard that?" Sean asked. "Um, I'm not sure why we're going there, but Gallows Hill is where they executed the people who didn't confess to being witches during the Salem witch trials."

Wait, what?

"The ones who *didn't* confess?" I asked.

"If they confessed, they weren't killed," explained Sean. He shrugged. "See, Puritans thought that if the witches confessed, they were repentant, and if they were repentant, then the people should leave any other judging to the afterlife."

"Why wouldn't everyone just plead guilty?" I asked.

"The people back then thought that lying sent your soul

to Hell," said Sean. "For the innocents it was a choice: Do you want to tell the truth, and go to Heaven? Or do you want to lie, and go to Hell when you died of old age?"

That was not how that worked.

"The ones the townspeople accused were different enough that people were willing to believe the worst," said Sean. "People always attack the ones who are different, whether it's skin color or religion or the fact that you're always the new kid or have the entire first three episodes of *Firefly* memorized. And I'm sorry, but that show was amazing—" Sean abruptly cut off his rant, which had become more and more animated as it went on, and blushed. "Anyway . . ."

"Are you saying the trials were rigged?" I asked.

"Yeah, pretty much," agreed Sean.

True anger flared in me for just a moment. Justice and protection of those who couldn't protect themselves was sacred. I didn't need sharp black wings or a halo to tell me that. I turned my head to hide the flames I knew had sprung to life in my eyes. The wind kicked up for a moment, sending fallen leaves swirling. One particularly bright orange-and-red leaf stuck to my shirt. I picked it off, spun it by the stem, and let it drop to the ground. It stayed there, lifeless.

I sighed.

We had to go home.

TWENTY-EIGHT

We arrived at our meeting spot before Crowley and Charity, which gave us more opportunity to stare awkwardly at each other. There was a bookshop across the way, and Lilith didn't as much wander over to it as she fled to it. The store was closed, but looking through the glass was undoubtedly preferable to the tension that had fallen over the three of us. I sat next to Sean on the bench anyway.

"Is it always like that with your dad?" I asked.

"Yup," Sean said.

"Mine too," I said.

"He's just—"

"Yeah." I hesitated. "My dad and I had a fight before I

came here. He thought being out of the house was reckless. I'm rather irritated that he seems to have been right."

"Well," Sean said, "my dad's not right about this."

"Didn't say he was," I said.

Something tickled my hair. I brushed it with my hand and felt something silky soft and barely there. I whipped my head around. I didn't see anything. I looked at my hand. Something shimmery? And there was a giggle again. High-pitched and young?

"What?" asked Sean. His hand went to his pocket, where there was probably a weapon hidden. He looked behind us.

"I thought I felt something," I said. "Maybe a bug."

"All sorts of things show up tonight," said Sean.

"But not like this?" I asked.

"Well, the things showing up are probably pretty normal for when the veil gets thin like this. Most aren't a problem. Honestly, we usually just celebrate with friends and family. Remember all that food at Charity's? We eat over there, but . . ."

"Parris screwed everything up," I said. Brimstone.

"If this is because of him," said Sean. "Yeah. I guess. Maybe Dad's right. Maybe Parris is just a strong ghost and whatever this is, it's because of something else. Dad said that when this is over, we're going to redouble my training."

Yeah, I could relate.

Sean stood up and kicked a trash receptacle. The clanging caused Lilith to spin on the spot. A nearby person cheered. A tiny voice whispered, "Uh-oh."

"Has he ever even asked if I wanted to follow in his footsteps?" Sean yelled. "God forbid I have a choice! Maybe I just want to be me? Not that he's ever tried to know who that is!"

Sean's breaths came in angry gasps. His fists clenched in rage, and his face turned an unhealthy shade of red. Lilith came up to the bench. I was too stunned to stand. Watching Sean lose his mind was like watching myself from the outside.

"Maybe it's time I make him listen," Sean said. He reached for his hidden weapon.

"Sean," I said, forcing myself to move. "Wait."

He was way too angry for the situation. Where was this coming from? His entire body trembled.

Before anyone could act, something flew in a blur of movement and jumped onto Sean's back. He staggered, and it took me an embarrassingly long few seconds to recognize the figure as Charity. She swiped her hand across his forehead, muttered something, and jumped down.

"That was a close one!" said Charity. "Feeling better?"

"Yeah," Sean said. He shook his head like he needed to clear it. I had seen that before. "I need to sit." Charity helped him sit back down on the bench, while Crowley ambled his way over to us.

"We figured something out," announced Crowley when no one had said anything further.

"Oh right, yeah," said Charity. "We totally did! So, remember the thing you asked me about?"

"Yeah," said Sean. "But it may not apply to this. You know the psychic thing's not exactly a science."

Sean must have been more frazzled than he looked, because he didn't blink at admitting something personal, and he didn't even try to kick Charity.

"Yeah, well, we think it does apply," said Charity. "Anyway, we looked into it: *l'appel du vide*. It's French, and it's actually an entire concept."

"I explained to Charity that Parris was stronger than he should be," Crowley said.

"Understatement," I said.

"Right!" said Charity. "And we already thought he was affecting way too much stuff, so my mind was racing. And I kept thinking about the thing you said, Sean. I mean, at first I thought it might have been some stupid fashion thing you saw on *Project Runway*, so I ignored it, and then I thought it was lyrics from that song on the radio that no one understands, but that didn't seem right either, and it was driving me crazy, and—"

"Speed it up, Char," said Crowley.

"Oh yeah, sorry. Anyway . . . Call of the void." Charity clasped her hands behind her back and rocked on her toes, looking pleased.

"Annndd, back it up a little bit," said Crowley.

"Okay, the literal translation is 'call of the void,' but it's not just random words your psychic little brain cooked up. It's the name for that feeling when you're high up, and you feel like jumping, or jerking your bike into traffic, or even pushing someone off the subway. But people don't really do it. It's just a feeling, and the feeling has a name: the call of the void."

"We think Parris is amplifying it," explained Crowley. "Normally people's consciences would stop them from acting on the call, but instead people are just listening."

"That would explain the crazy," Sean said. "But not everything people are doing has been that kind of . . . evil."

"We think that's part of the amplification," said Crowley. "Not just the giving in, but the kinds of things people give in to. Imagine having no impulse control at all."

"Yeah, so let me put this on you," said Charity. She smeared something across Lilith's forehead and muttered a few words. It glowed and left a sparkling streak to match the one on Sean's forehead.

"But does it explain how he's getting stronger?" I asked.

"Remember how Parris got rich from the witch trials, essentially feeding off the chaos?" asked Crowley. "We think he's doing that here, except literally now. Instead of gaining wealth, he's gaining power."

"If we can cut off the power source, we could weaken him," said Charity. "For now, we can at least protect ourselves, but we need to figure out how to spread this protection to the entire town—and really soon. You would not believe the stuff we saw on our way here! And we have an idea about finding the candlesticks."

"Gallows Hill," said Sean, like he was just realizing something important.

Lilith gasped. "You said that was the execution site, right?"

"Right, so it has a connection to the trials and Parris," Charity said. "I should be able to use that as a focal point to summon the candlesticks or something similar, assuming they still exist."

"It's worth a shot," Sean agreed. "Better than aimlessly looking."

Or revealing the spark of creation in my pocket.

"How come you're not glittery?" I asked Crowley, trying not to wipe off the gunk Charity smeared on me.

"Because I chose where mine went," he said, moving the collar of his shirt to the side.

"Jerk," I snapped.

But I couldn't really be mad. The fact that Charity and Crowley had figured this out was a *good* thing. Parris was way stronger than he should have been, and while it was obvious the town was being affected, seeing Sean lose himself to rage had scared me more than I wanted to admit.

The fear and anxiety were completely wiped out of my mind when we turned the corner and very quickly learned what it looked like when an entire town lost its impulse control.

"Wow," Crowley said.

"That looks like fun," I said, gesturing to a man riding a bike with one small wheel in the back and one enormous one in the front.

"Do people here usually keep those fluffy rodent things as pets?" asked Lilith, pointing to a man aggressively hugging a small fluffy gray animal.

"Squirrels?" asked Sean. "No, not usually."

"Oh," said Lilith, flinching as the squirrel clawed its way out of the hug. "Never mind. It doesn't seem to like that."

Charity and Sean seemed just as distracted as we were, so apparently none of this was normal human behavior, and while that was probably for the best, I admit I was a little disappointed. Some of this stuff looked awesome!

As we walked, we filled Crowley and Charity in on the

details of Parris's latest appearance in the Witch Dungeon Museum, and then reluctantly explained the deadline imposed by Heaven. Except of course I didn't mention Cassandra or the thrones by name specifically. "They're like this cosmic police thing."

Sean laughed bitterly when I finished, and then said, "More weight."

"Seriously," agreed Charity. "Good thing I work best under pressure."

"More weight?" Lilith asked.

"It's something we say when bad stuff keeps piling up," explained Charity. "One of the victims of the witch trials, Giles Corey, was pressed to death under rocks during his interrogation. He wouldn't confess. He just kept saying, 'More weight.' Kinda awesome, really. In a disgusting, painful way."

I was a big fan of *less weight*.

We didn't know if any of this would work. Was it even possible to capture a soul without a morningstar? Could we protect a town? Stand up to Heaven? Get back home? I swallowed back a moment of panic that threatened to overtake my cool exterior. When panic arises, you should squash it down, down, down so that later it can burst out in a humiliating bang of overdramatics. That was my philosophy, anyway.

Crowley and Charity talked simultaneously about expanding the protection spell (since smearing the town one by one was not going to work), and how to channel the mark of death left at Gallows Hill to focus on Parris and thus the candlestick. Magic wasn't my thing, but it all sounded very professional.

When I had pictured Gallows Hill, I'd imagined something isolated, cozy, and dark with old-growth trees. Something that made the night seem alive with the whispers of secrets and darkness incarnate. Something like the hill we used to play on as little kids. I had not imagined a neon sign with the word "Walgreens" on it. I frowned.

"Is Walgreens the name of an executioner?" I asked.

"No, it has stuff on its shelves," Lilith said. "Must be a supply shop."

"Organic nooses?" I guessed.

"Artisanal guillotines," Crowley stated.

"I don't think any of those things exist," Sean said.

"Hmm, untapped market," I said. Good to know.

"You guys are so weird," Charity said. "The store is not our destination. But now I have images of free-range attack lions in my head."

We snickered over that, and I wondered what they'd think of Damien. Aleister's hound was practically free-range, but maybe not so much of the attack variety.

"Heads up," shouted Crowley, and we all looked up to see a woman taking a step onto the street . . . from the third story.

I pushed Lilith out of the way. My hair flipped from the whoosh of air behind me. I waited for the sound of meat hitting pavement, but there was nothing.

I cautiously looked over. Charity was holding both hands out in front of her—her eyes huge, her face a sickening shade of not normal—while the woman hovered three inches from the ground. With trembling hands Charity lowered her to the ground.

"Well done," Lilith breathed.

The woman lay on the ground perfectly still for a long moment, and I was sure she was dead, until she lifted her head and twisted to look behind her. We followed her gaze straight into the face of Samuel Parris.

"Have you decided to join me?" asked Parris. "Is that it? Or are you trying to run away?"

He leaned down and ran his finger along the woman's neck. She blinked vaguely but didn't respond otherwise. A black line raced up his veins, and his eyes glowed for just a second before they dimmed. He looked even more alive now.

"Fascinating," murmured Parris. He turned his hand over and stared at it, before clenching and releasing his fist. He looked up, and there was no question that he was studying us. He tilted his head. "No. Neither of those is right. You're looking for something in this place. You shouldn't be here."

He stepped closer, and we all took a step back. I knew it was a mistake the second we did. *Way to show the bad guy you're afraid, Mal.*

Tension held me impossibly balanced between immobility and flight. My heartbeat roared in my ears. I couldn't think. The emptiness of Samuel Parris's dead black eyes had me completely frozen.

Until I wasn't.

TWENTY-NINE

I squinted, blinded by the sudden lack of darkness.

It was daytime, and the surf lapped gently at the edge of a white sand beach that had not been there before. Birds hopped along the sand, leaving faint footprints and filling the air with a happy piping sound. The light breeze made palm leaves rattle.

"What the He—" said Sean.

"Oh, no, no. Not there," interrupted Cassandra, before she turned to look at me. "I filled out the paperwork."

Cassandra's glow brightened to majestic proportions as she tried to introduce herself to the humans—now that she had the proper paperwork for a human appearance—with all the heavenly pomp and circumstance that was apparently required.

Sean stepped back as if he was going to run.

"Or not. We don't have to do that," said Cassandra abruptly, as the choir and the light immediately shut off. "Please don't run." She held her hand out like she thought Sean might do just that. Then she seemed to consider. "Of course, if you did, you wouldn't be able to run very far, since this is an island."

"Is this Heaven?" Lilith asked slowly, nervously.

"No," said Cassandra, dropping her hand. "It's close, though. We're on a small island off the coast of Australia. Beautiful, isn't it?" She sighed and sat on a nearby rock, while we remained standing, staring at her warily. "Cookies?" she offered, holding out an empty hand. A plate appeared half a second later, steam wafting from a pile of cookies—oatmeal this time.

"This is so cool! What are you?" squealed Charity. Well, most of us were wary.

"She's a seraph," I told Charity, since Cassandra seemed more interested in trying to protect her halo from Charity's curious fingers.

"Seraph? Like an angel? That is so cool!" Charity reached out to touch a feather, and Cassandra flinched. "I'm so sorry! I should have asked. Consent is everything. I really do know better, I swear!"

"How did we get here?" asked Sean. "You just zapped us here or . . . whatever? Why is it daytime?"

"Well, yes, I suppose you could say 'zapped,'" Cassandra said. "That's not really the word, though, but anyway, you were in real danger of being hurt. Parris has grown very powerful. . . ." Cassandra stared into the distance before shuddering. "Don't worry, you haven't lost any time. It's daytime because we're in a different time zone. It's exactly the same moment as it just was in Salem."

Cassandra held the plate of cookies toward us. They smelled awesome, warm and inviting. I could detect the faint scent of cinnamon, and I was instantly reminded of home.

Sean took a cookie. Charity grabbed two. Crowley, Lilith, and I watched them take their first bites. When the humans didn't immediately collapse or act like they had been drugged, we grabbed our own. The cookies were crisp on the outside and chewy on the inside. It was hard to stay mad at people who gave you cookies like that.

Besides, we all needed a moment to settle our nerves after our Parris encounter.

"I knew you would be angry if I 'zapped' you to Heaven, so I brought you all here. I thought we could talk. I thought maybe if you saw what Heaven could be—"

"And like we've told you," interrupted Lilith quickly,

"all we want is to get home, and we need Parris with us to do that."

"Oh, I can't help you with that," Cassandra said. "Even if I wanted to. It's not my jurisdiction."

"Can you just put us back in Salem?" Sean asked. "My family is back there."

"I can . . ." Cassandra twisted her hands. "Or maybe I could find you a new family?"

"What?" asked Sean in disbelief. "I don't want a new one. Who does that? You can't just replace *people*. I want to be with *my* family."

"Yeah, that seems to be the theme," Cassandra muttered, before pleading with us. "It was so terrible, and there really isn't a lot of time. Look at how beautiful this is. You can have this and better in Heaven. I can't bring you back to Salem. Parris is too strong. It would be dangerous and honestly wrong to leave kids there."

"We have to go back and fix things," Lilith said.

"How?" Sean asked Lilith, turning his back completely on Cassandra. "We're still trying to find something to trap him. Can he be killed? Ghosts can be destroyed. If we found his body . . ."

"Technically he's already dead, but he's not really a ghost, because he crossed over. . . ." Charity fell into contemplation.

"Though, now he's back on the mortal plane, so does that turn him back into a ghost? It's all so existential."

"We can forget about the deep questions for the moment," Crowley said.

"We can't just search the known universe for gold candlesticks that may not even exist anymore," Lilith said. "We need a focal point, and if Gallows Hill is it, we have to get past Parris."

"Can Parris actually do anything to us?" Charity asked. "Not that I want to find out, but his power is manipulation, right? And we're protected from that, so if we ignore him . . ."

"The rest of the town isn't immune," I pointed out, thinking of the skeleton men and the man who pushed that woman toward the speeding train.

"Once we have a focal point, it will take me time to find and summon the candlesticks," Charity said.

"We won't have time if we're fighting people off," Sean said.

"Is there anywhere else we can look? Anything else we can use?" Lilith asked. "Once the thrones are sent out, they don't suddenly reverse course. We can't let them 'cleanse' the town."

Hell may have a bad reputation, but smiting? Oh, no, that was all Heaven. The humans would be lucky if the thrones stopped at the city. If one person influenced by Parris made it out of the town limits, the thrones would make sure they were thorough, no matter how many people they had to eliminate in the process.

"But you don't need to do any of that," Cassandra said, looking absolutely baffled. "I can give you paradise."

I cast my gaze on the paradise Cassandra had brought us to. The sun was warm against my face, and it was soothing if I ignored the bright blue of the sky. The breeze smelled like flowers, and there were things by my feet that I had never seen before—I guessed they were seashells. (Little-known fact: not a lot of oceans in Hell.) It was beautiful and peaceful. I won't lie: staying was tempting.

Especially because it meant never having the conversation I knew I would have to have with my friends.

Whether we'd meant to or not, we had let Parris loose. It was our responsibility to get him back. We didn't have time to wander. Parris knew we were looking, and it didn't sound like we'd have access to Gallows Hill. He or the people he influenced would try to stop us. But I could use the spark to create a morningstar, and we could use that to trap Parris's soul quickly and easily.

"We have to go back," I answered for all of us. "Now, before we run out of time."

Unfortunately, even though we were all of the same mind,

Cassandra was not. She folded her arms across her chest and pouted.

"I can't be here!" snapped Sean. "I have parents I have to get back to, and there's no cell service wherever it is we are. And I do not want to explain this to my parents." He paused. "Though, this is kinda nice, so maybe some other time . . ."

"Please, Cassandra," Lilith said. "I know you only want what's best for us, but really we have to do the right thing, and the right thing is going back there and getting Parris back where he belongs. Somehow."

"Cassandra, you can't save us from this," I said, reaching out to her and hoping that I could find the part of her that understood.

Cassandra stiffened. Maybe not.

"Well, I *can*, actually," Cassandra said, looking up at us. "I can save you from this. That's my whole point."

THIRTY

W h-what are you going to do?" I asked.

I had been so busy worrying about Parris and my own existential drama that I had forgotten Cassandra wasn't my friend. She was just another adult who thought she knew what was best. The realization was instant and perfectly clear: I would never see it coming if she simply zapped us to Heaven, and there was nothing we could do to stop it. We were hostages.

Hostages who needed the help of their kidnapper, because without her we'd never make it back to Salem. We needed her, and we needed her to be on our side. But just because she was objectively good didn't mean we could trust her, and it certainly didn't mean she'd help us. At least not in the way we wanted to be helped.

"Isn't this lovely?" Cassandra asked, twitchy and high-strung. "We can spend a little time here, and then . . . we can get you to your new homes."

She studied our reactions, and we smiled reassuringly.

Lilith raised the virgin piña colada Cassandra was currently bribing us with. "My mom loves these. She adds ice cream when she makes them for me."

"That's a good idea," Cassandra said warily.

"And she makes really good cookies, too," Lilith said. "She makes these ginger ones when I'm sick."

"That's . . . nice of her," Cassandra said.

Lilith looked at me intently. I looked back at her stupidly. And then her plan penetrated my skull in a flash of insight. I was a little embarrassed that it took me so long to get it.

"Yeah, my mom always notices when I get sick before I even know it. It's like a sixth sense. And my dad makes me soup and sets me up on the couch with a blanket and movie," I said, and paused before continuing, "I'll miss that in Heaven."

Crowley grimaced, and I wondered if I had taken it too far. I stilled my breathing completely.

Cassandra jerked like I had hit her, and then she blinked furiously, a suspiciously wet gleam in her eyes.

"My parents are gone a lot," Sean started tentatively, like he hoped he'd gotten the plan right. "And my dad . . . we don't always see eye to eye, but he's always there for me. We had a fight last time we talked, and me disappearing without a word? That would kill him." Sean stopped and looked away. Was that acting or something else?

A sound suspiciously like a sob came from Cassandra before she recovered, ruffling her wings in agitation and clearing her throat like that was all she had needed to do.

"It's Samhain," Charity said. Her voice was quieter and less exuberant than I had heard so far. "I know it's just a day, but it's special and my family always spends it together. Me and my moms are all we have, and . . . and this is the first time that . . ."

"It's not over yet," Sean said when Charity fell silent. He wrapped an arm around her shoulders and squeezed.

Charity sniffed. "It's just, it's the first time that we haven't—I know, it's fine, whatever, it's just food and decorations and—it's just that it's the first time we haven't celebrated. It's the first time I'm alone for it."

"You're not alone," Sean said softly, barely audible.

"I know, it's stupid," Charity said, wiping her eyes. "I'm being ridiculous."

I thought about the lack of decorations at my house. The

fact that it smelled like old man instead of nutmeg and cloves, roasting meat, and baking apples. That I was fighting with Dad, and Mom was exclusively in work mode. The canceled celebrations and the ruined vacation, and my own missing holiday events and decorations that had made me feel very alone. Abandoned even, if I let myself be melodramatic.

"It's not stupid," I said.

Crowley leaned forward from the white hammock Cassandra had conjured into existence, and nudged Charity with his foot. She looked up and wiped her nose on her hand. He held up his palm, and after a moment or two of nothing, a fine mist rose until it twisted and turned into the shape of a unicorn. It sparkled and pranced on his hand, and Charity laugh-sobbed behind her hand. It was normally a simple piece of magic that Crowley had done since we were little to cheer us up whenever we were down. Today a bead of sweat dripped down his temple. The unicorn flickered and disappeared.

"Well," muttered Crowley. His cheeks pinked, and Charity threw her arms around his neck. "All right, human. Enough of that!"

Wow, mouthed Lilith. I smiled.

"Huh," said Sean. He was unnaturally still, and I worried we were going to be at an impasse yet again. "Can you all do that?"

"Just Crowley," I said. Sean seemed . . . impressed. I guessed we could work with that. I wanted to tell him that was nothing, they should see Crowley at his full power, but maybe saying that would raise questions we didn't want to answer.

And Crowley certainly didn't need the ego boost.

"It's a big holiday for us, too," Lilith said. "And our first one without all the trappings and family stuff. We can be alone together."

Our plan had slid by the wayside, but it didn't even matter, because while we'd moved from overdramatic pulls of the heartstrings to actual real conversation, Cassandra had burst into messy, wet sobs.

"You have to know," she sniffed, rubbing the back of her hand against her nose. "I just want to protect you. I'm not trying to make you miserable *or-or-orphans.*" She wailed.

Crowley fell through his hammock, which disappeared in a wisp of white vapor. "Son of a—"

"I'm terrible at this job," Cassandra sobbed. Her halo sank lower around her head, as if it could comfort her in her time of distress. "All I was supposed to do was pick you up and bring you to Heaven. I thought I would be making you *ha-ha-happy.*"

"It's not that we don't appreciate it," Lilith said, looking at me for help. I shrugged, and she shot me a look.

I quickly knelt in front of the weeping angel and cleared my throat.

"There, there," I said, patting her shoulder awkwardly. "I'm sure you're very good at your job."

"I'm not," she sobbed, the words muffled by the sleeves of her gown as she cried into her folded arms. "I screw everything up. All the time. No one ever listens to me in Heaven! Ever! Now you're sad. And I don't know why demons . . . why your *parent*s would be so nice to you, but . . . I made you saaaad."

"There, there," I said again as Cassandra's wail rose to epic levels. "But I've told you, like, a lot of times now, that our parents are not demons, so you don't need to worry about that. Maybe, I don't know . . . maybe there's just other ways to do your job."

"Yeah, besides kidnapping," muttered Crowley.

Cassandra's face snapped up. Her face was wet with tears, but she still managed to look majestically beautiful, not snotty like most people would be.

"Another way," she whispered.

And without any warning or movement at all, the world went dark and cold.

THIRTY-ONE

We stumbled into each other, and I discovered a side effect of frequent zappings as my stomach tried to revolt.

Sean gagged, and Lilith groaned, "Ugh, some warning would be nice."

It was dark, but I could make out the shadows of tables and chairs. A long bar top with stools and bottles that glowed faintly was at the far end of the room. There was a doorway exiting the space, the bottom stair visible through the opening. We were surrounded by a murmur of voices, like NPCs in a hologame, where words weren't audible but there was the distinct impression of conversation. The clinks of glasses and utensils, coughs, and laughs gave the feel of a fully functioning tavern, but the room was completely empty.

"Where are we?" I asked.

"Beadle's Tavern," Cassandra said.

"Beadle's Tavern doesn't exist anymore," Charity said.

"True," Cassandra said, laughing nervously. "Best not to look out the windows."

"Why are we in a bar that does not exist?" Crowley asked.

Cassandra bounced on the balls of her feet. Her hands twitched in the folds of her gown, and her halo was suspiciously missing. I had seen Cassandra smile before. It was soft, sometimes gentle, other times beatific. Right now it was nothing short of gleeful. I recognized that smile. I saw it in my mirror, often.

"What's up, Cassandra?" I asked cautiously.

"I'm going to help!" she announced, before slapping her hands over her mouth and squealing in excitement. "Is—is that okay?" she asked when none of us responded.

"Help us do what, exactly?" Lilith asked, casting nervous looks around the bar. That apparently Did. Not. Exist.

"Help you . . . do what you said," Cassandra said. She fidgeted. Her eyes darted between all of us so quickly that I was amazed she didn't fall over. "I still think it would be better to just take you to Heaven, but I don't want to make you sad.

So maybe if I help you capture Parris and save Salem, you'll change your mind."

"Yeah . . . ," I said. "Maybe." No, definitely not.

"Why would you take us to Heaven?" Sean said. "Because I can't go there, either—not islands off Australia, not Heaven, and also preferably not bars that don't exist."

"Well, not you," Cassandra said. "And not Charity."

"Ouch," Charity said.

"Oh, I just mean not yet." Cassandra made a wide gesture. "I mean, just look at you! You're clearly ours, although maybe I should . . . no, that would be breaking the rules. You see, because you're humans and they're—"

"Can we get back to the helping thing?" I interrupted, because yeah, I did not want to continue that train of thought. "And why that requires us being here?"

"Oh yes," Cassandra said. "Well, we can't make super-secret, potentially blasphemous plans out in the open where anyone could see!"

"And someone would see on a *deserted* island?" Sean asked.

"*Especially* on a deserted island," Cassandra said. "Besides, Salem is too dangerous right now, and this tavern used to be in Salem. Parris probably came here. They kept prisoners here during the trials."

Cassandra's face fell as she spoke. "Which is so sad . . .

but . . . that means you can use this, right? A link without any of the danger."

Sean turned to Charity and asked, "Can we use this place as a focal point?"

Charity walked the room slowly, trailing her hand along the surfaces. I held my breath. If this was an option, I would never even have to mention the spark in my pocket. I didn't have to give up my chance at freedom.

But as Charity remained silent, I knew I wasn't that lucky.

"This place isn't real," she said. "There's nothing to latch on to."

Everyone sagged noticeably with disappointment.

"Oh," said Cassandra. "I really thought I'd found the perfect solution. . . ."

"All right, seraph," Crowley said. "What else you got?"

"Um—well—I—" Cassandra spluttered. "I don't know! It's hard to come up with original ideas!"

"What about . . . ," I thought out loud. "You froze Sean when you wanted to talk to us privately . . ."

"You did what now?" asked Sean.

". . . so can you just freeze everyone around us? At Gallows Hill. We should be okay from Parris, so if you just freeze the humans—"

"Yes!" Lilith said. "That would be perfect!"

Cassandra was already shaking her head.

"Why not?" I asked. "You said you wanted to help."

"I do," Cassandra said earnestly. "One human is . . . easy. But I'm not an archangel. I don't have that kind of power."

But I did.

"Which leaves us with no plan at all," Lilith said.

"Hellfire," Crowley cursed.

"I have something—" I started, and that was when the ceiling above us creaked. Everyone looked up.

The sound was different from the murmured conversation around us.

"If this bar doesn't exist," I said, "there should be nobody here, right?"

"Right," said Cassandra, but she stared at the ceiling too. "I mean, the original one was haunted."

There was another creak, and then there was the patter of feet running across the ceiling. A chill ran up my spine.

"What is that?" I asked.

"Let's go see," Crowley said.

We left the room and ran up the stairs, Lilith right behind us, the humans and the seraph yelling caution. There was a window at the top of the stairs, and despite Cassandra's warning, I looked out. There was a void of nothing. Not blackness, but a *nothing* so deep that it threatened to suck me in. I shuddered and pulled my eyes away. Would that be Salem when the thrones were done? Was that what we were fighting against, not just here but at home, too?

The upstairs of the tavern consisted of a narrow hallway with rooms branching off. The running had to have been down the hallway. There was nowhere else with a span long enough.

"Here, ghosty, ghosty," called Crowley.

"It can't be a ghost," said Lilith. "This isn't a real place."

"The simulation of a ghost, then," Crowley said.

A giggle rang out, unlike the muted sounds below. It was high-pitched and young and very familiar. I had heard that giggle before . . . outside on the streets of Salem.

"I don't think so," I said. I walked down the hall, pushing open doors and peering in. Each one was empty, with windows looking out into that awful nothingness. Crowley did the same on the other side. My fingers were trailing the textured wallpaper as I was moving on to the next door, when I heard another giggle behind me.

I backtracked and reentered the room, trying to ignore the window. There was a bed and a small dresser with a basin on top. I stepped farther in, and the wood creaked under my foot. Another giggle and the bed skirt rustled.

I lay down on the floor and tried to look under the ruffle. There was an inch or two gap between the wood plank floor and the bed skirt. I thought I saw movement, but I wasn't entirely sure. What could possibly exist in a place that didn't?

I pushed with my toes and slid forward. Another giggle. That time it was quickly muffled. I put my finger at the bottom edge of the ruffle and lifted it up. My pulse raced, but my curiosity overrode any fear. Wide brown eyes caught the light and then closed quickly. I lifted the ruffle completely out of the way and was faced with soft brown ringlets.

"You want to come out from under there?" I asked quietly.

"What did you find?" Lilith asked from the doorway.

"I see you," I said. Another giggle, but no movement. Hmm. "Wanna come out and play?" The eyes popped open and two chubby arms reached for me. I slid my hands under them, my injured hand complaining, and pulled the bundle out.

I had never seen an angel as young as the one currently sitting on my hip. She tucked her head onto my shoulder, and her fat baby arms clung to my neck. She fluffed her tiny white wings and let them settle around my arm.

"Oh, unholy darkness," muttered Lilith.

"That should not be here," said Crowley.

"No, she shouldn't," I said. "But you've been following us for a while, haven't you? Or have you been following *her*?" I asked, pointing toward the doorway. The angel giggled and her wings rustled again. They left a shimmery streak on my arm.

"What—oh," Cassandra said from the doorway, Sean and Charity behind her. She paled into corpse territory, and somehow still managed to look ethereal. "What are you—will you put her down?"

"Aww," Charity said, peering around Cassandra's wing. "She's so cute. What is she?"

"Please put her down," Cassandra said. Tears formed in her eyes, and she edged forward.

"I've got her," I said. "It's fine." But that didn't seem to make Cassandra feel any better. In fact, she looked scared. Of me. "What do you think I'm going to do with her?"

Lilith and Crowley stepped closer, and suddenly we were divided, with us on one side and Cassandra and the humans on the other. Cassandra was the only one who seemed to have *ideas*, but I didn't like the symbolism.

"How did you lose this?" I asked, bouncing the angel toddler on my hip. "You should be at home. Did you let her out, Cassandra?"

The toddler giggled, cupped my face with tiny fat hands, and said, "Pwetty."

"Thank you," I said. Everyone laughed. Except Cassandra.

"I don't know. She must have—I can take her," Cassandra said. "Please give her to me."

"No!" said the toddler.

"I thought you were helping us, Cassandra. I thought you liked us," I said. "What are you so worried about? Are you worried about getting in trouble for letting a baby out where she's unprotected, or are you worried about something else?"

"Do you honestly think we're going to hurt a baby?" Crowley asked, anger making the question more of a statement.

"No," said Cassandra, but her wings tucked closer, giving away the lie.

"You do," I said. My eyes flared with anger, and I ducked my head to hide them from the humans. The little angel's eyes grew wide, and then her smile grew wider. I huffed a laugh. "You gonna come live with us when you're big?"

Cassandra gasped. An angel hadn't fallen for millennia, but it *had* happened even after the first.

Obviously. And this little one was showing all the right signs of straying. And funnily enough, despite Cassandra saying she wanted to help us and wanted us to be happy, she didn't seem too keen on one of her own joining us. Of course not. She didn't care about us, only what she could change us into.

"She needs to go home to Heaven. That's where she belongs.

At least for now," I added with a smirk that I didn't quite feel. "Just like we need to go where we belong."

"Yes," Cassandra said, her hands twitching like she still didn't trust me. "She does."

"Here's what's going to happen," I said. "I'll give her to you if you leave us alone."

Sean and Charity wanted to object. I could hear the intakes of breath and half-started words, but Lilith and Crowley were motionless beside me.

"I'll take her home," Cassandra said. "But I'm helping."

"Forget it," I said. It would have been more impressive if the tiny one hadn't taken that moment to squish my cheeks together. I pulled my face away and pretended to bite her little fingers. Cassandra, honest to Lucifer, gasped. I rolled my eyes. "We don't need your help. Put us back in Salem, and you can have the baby."

Even as I said it, I couldn't believe that Cassandra took me seriously. How could she not realize I'd hand her the baby anyway?

"Please don't hurt her," Cassandra said.

I know the pain flashed across my face before I could hide it. Crowley made a disgusted noise next to me.

"You honestly think I'd do that?" I asked in disbelief, and suddenly Cassandra's face changed. Shame dripped from her expression. I shook my head. I kissed the baby angel's forehead. Her soft curls smelled like vanilla. "See you soon, troublemaker."

I handed the baby to Cassandra. Chubby fingers clenched my shirt before finally letting go to wave. I turned my glare to the seraph. "Now put us back."

THIRTY-TWO

It was still nighttime when Cassandra dropped us back into Salem and disappeared. There was still the noise of conversation, but now there were actual people to go along with it. Maybe it was the benefit of dropping from somewhere that didn't exist rather than transporting between places, but my stomach and feet stayed steady as we appeared back in reality on a street filled with people.

"What just happened?" asked Sean. "Because quite honestly, some celestial help would be awesome, but the energies around everyone were . . . a bit wonky."

"Yeah, serious tension," agreed Charity. "Does she know you? Goddess, how weird is that? People are just friends with angels?"

Crowley laughed.

"She wasn't our friend," I said.

"Did she really think you were going to hurt a baby?" Sean asked.

I shrugged, pretending that the conclusion Cassandra had jumped to didn't hurt.

"Oh my goddess, we saw a baby angel," Charity said. "This is the weirdest Samhain ever."

"Not that I'm doubting you, Mal," Lilith said, crossing her arms. "But I hope you have a plan, because small-minded or not, we could have used the extra power."

"You heard her," I said. "She doesn't have the power we need. And now we don't have to worry about being kidnapped."

Charity and Sean both checked their phones. Sean returned his to his pocket almost immediately, but Charity held hers to her ear and listened, walking off a few paces for some illusion of privacy.

"Charity's moms might know something," Sean said. "They talk with her all the time, like she's an actual person, so yeah . . ."

There was a flash of movement in the tree above us, and I glanced up on instinct. Something invisible slithered and twisted on the branch. I could just see the shimmer of the unseen to track the movement. Lilith looked up and said, "Brownie."

Brownies weren't dangerous, but add them to the shades and gremlins and other critters that didn't belong here, and we just had a smorgasbord of interdimensional visitors. Some I had never actually seen before, since they weren't native to our dimension, and I was surprised by how many young ones there were. Was that important?

The brownie edged down until it was hanging from the branch above us. Right in Sean's face. He frowned but didn't seem to see it. The brownie leaned closer. Lilith and I froze. Sean shook his head and backed up.

"It won't hurt you," I said.

Sean froze. "What won't hurt me?"

"Can you see it?" I asked. Sean shook his head, slower this time. "But you know it's there, right?" Sean nodded. "It's a brownie, a type of hobgoblin that travels between Faerie and the mortal realm. They're sometimes helpful, sometimes not, but always harmless."

"Okay." Sean laughed nervously and rubbed his face.

"Do humans ever go through?" I asked.

"What do you mean?" asked Sean.

I gestured to the brownie. "All sorts of things come through the veil. They're coming through from somewhere, right? Do humans ever find the opening and go through?"

"Not that I've ever heard," Sean said. "Though I suppose

if it was a one-way trip, we probably wouldn't know."

Not that we could leave without Parris, but if everything went downhill, it would be nice to be able to take Sean and Charity and flee.

"What do you have, Charity?" Crowley asked.

"A message from one of my moms," she said. "I wish I could just call her, but magic and tech don't work so well together, so she and Mama will have their phones off. She just told me to stay inside, keep burning sage, and they'll see me tomorrow. They seemed to know something is up, but I'm not sure they know what exactly."

Lilith's fingers started tapping.

I slid my hand into my pocket and clenched it around the soft velvet bag. The sharp edges of the crystal were barely blunted by the material. I felt like I was going to vomit. My heart raced. I ran through the words in my mind; my voice wouldn't cooperate. I was vaguely aware of everyone brainstorming, but I knew they wouldn't come up with anything. We were out of time and options, and I couldn't be so selfish as to let my friends down, not to mention the rest of Salem.

Maybe if I hadn't met Sean and Charity, I wouldn't have worried about the humans. Earth was just a temporary stop anyway. What did it really matter in the long run? But they had families too, and something told me, though I couldn't say why, that if the humans in Salem were sorted into their respective afterlives right now, it wouldn't be fair. It wouldn't be justice.

"I—" The word was out before I was ready, and then everyone was looking at me. I didn't want to do this, because I knew with absolute certainty that this was going to go over very, very badly.

"I may have an idea," I said. I took a huge breath. I reached into my pocket and pulled out the bag. I tugged the string. My hand shook. I emptied the crystal into my hand. It glowed in the dim light of the night.

"What is it?" asked Charity.

"Why do you have that?" asked Lilith sharply.

There was a brief moment, no longer than a blink, when her wings flared and her eyes flashed red. At least, I thought they did. When I blinked again, it was Lilith, wingless like the rest of us, blue eyes glaring.

"You know," I said. I swallowed hard. "I find things."

"You have a spark of creation and you're just mentioning it now," Crowley said. His voice was flat and cold. I had never heard it so empty before. "How about when we realized we were trapped? What about when we first saw that Parris was more than he should be?"

"I know," I said, my voice tight and strained. Oh, Lucifer, was I going to cry?

"Why do you have that?" Lilith repeated. Her voice was clipped and her expression was carefully blank.

"I . . ." I swallowed again and blinked rapidly. "You know why."

Because I could see it on Lilith's and Crowley's faces that they knew. They knew that if I had a spark of creation and hadn't told them about it, they would hate the reason why I had it. I knew it too.

"But it was just a . . . a backup plan," I said, before turning my attention to the humans. "It's a spark of creation. It's almost infinite possibility. We should be able to use it to capture Parris."

"How do we use it?" Charity asked, but her voice was soft, like she wasn't confident she should be joining the conversation.

"It works by intention," I said. "I should be able to create a morningstar. That's what we use to trap souls in our world."

I flicked my eyes over to Crowley and Lilith. They stood side by side and were pointedly not looking at me. Crowley's jaw was clenched so tightly, his jaw muscle twitched. Lilith was standing stiff. Her hand wasn't tapping out its nervous rhythm; instead it was squeezed into a fist. I had promised her there were no more secrets, and now she knew that I had lied. The fight was still to come, but I could only hope they would wait until we got home.

Oh, Lucifer, I might have ruined everything.

"What do we need to do now?" Sean asked.

"We find Parris," I said.

In the end, finding Parris was easy. He found us.

THIRTY-THREE

The brownie reacted first. It froze completely for a heart-stopping moment before bursting into a frantic, scrambling dash away from us. Even Charity and Sean noticed the rustle of the leaves in its wake.

"That can't be good," I said.

Then the humming started, a low baritone over the breeze, and then there were barely audible words: "In every angel a devil hides . . ." A figure moved between two trees and emerged into view, looking as smug as any glutton in the fourth circle.

". . . and in every devil an angel strides," murmured Parris.

Nothing should have stopped me from reacting to the threat that was Samuel Parris. Especially not now that I had made the decision to use the spark, when I had the weapon in hand, holding it tight enough to nearly break my skin. But I didn't do anything. No one did.

We were all staring in shock.

Parris had changed. His hair was slicked back. His clothes were sleek and modern-looking. The white ruffle thing was gone, and in its place was a red tie he ran his fingers down.

He wasn't alone. Other figures emerged behind him. A woman wearing a leather jacket and a sharp smile, a man in jeans and a T-shirt, with a hungry look on his face. Another, completely androgynous, figure, in a full black bodysuit that covered their face, who would have been invisible if not for the red of their aura. In fact, all of them had red auras.

I flicked my eyes only enough to see Charity and Sean still glowing reassuringly blue.

"Where did you run off to?" Parris asked. "There's so much to see here, don't you think? So much has changed . . . but you didn't wander off, did you? How did you disappear?"

His three followers began muttering ominously. I didn't know what was showing on my face, but Parris's gaze changed from indifferent to focused. Right on me.

My hand twitched and Parris frowned. For a fraction of a second, he flickered back into his old style of clothes, before solidifying again into his new improved version 2.0.

Sean took three tries to breathe my name out, "Mal."

What was I doing? Now was the time! He was right here!

I pictured the morningstar in my head. How the thick edges had felt in my hand, how it had felt electric and alive, how there was no mistaking it for a simple piece of metal. I imagined the way it drew souls in, slowly and inexorably, no matter how they resisted. The way the medallion would twitch while the soul settled into captivity within it. I imagined every detail as clearly as possible, with no other intention in mind. Parris captured. It had to be my only thought, my only intention.

It wasn't.

What if this didn't work? What if I failed? Parris's compatriots edged forward. We could fight them off. We could protect Sean and Charity, right? But we couldn't fight off a whole town. We couldn't stop the thrones who would inevitably come. This had to work, and it was all on me. That kind of pressure was why I had the spark in the first place!

The woman chuckled. Low and slow. The phantom chill of my feathers rising made me shiver.

Pure intention, pure intention. Parris captured. A morningstar appearing and sucking him down.

I exhaled. "You're coming with us."

Pure intention.

I took aim, and I could already see every step happening the way I'd pictured as I threw the crystal at Parris's feet. It exploded with a light so blinding, I brought my arm to my eyes. Parris's friends screamed and threw themselves backward, as though the light caused physical pain. I squinted through the glare, determined to see Parris vanish. I needed to see it happen, to know that we were safe. That we could go home.

"Yes!" shouted Charity.

My eyes hurt, but it was all worth it to see Parris lose that superior gaze. He was scared. He flickered like Faust on a bad donut day. The white ruffle thing was there and then gone again. And then the light started to fade and retreat into the ground.

But not Parris.

Parris was still there. Tall and solid and somewhat bemused now that he realized the light was gone and Hadn't. Done. A. Thing.

The ground where the crystal had smashed was covered in a slick of rainbow metallic swirl and tiny shards of glass that turned into dragonflies as we watched. The rainbow puffed up and then vaporized into clouds of color that sparked with light.

We watched as it dissipated into nothing. Parris's followers stood warily. Oh, unholy darkness . . .

It was fake. My last best hope was fake.

THIRTY-FOUR

I couldn't move. My mind froze in disbelief. It was fake. The spark was fake.

Parris smirked. His followers flanked him.

"We have to run," Crowley said.

It was fake.

"Now, Malachi," Lilith said.

How could it be fake?

"Mal!" snapped Lilith. She gestured away from Parris. The light and screams had drawn the attention of the people around us, and we were completely outnumbered. "Get with the program!"

"What do we do?" asked Sean.

"I don't know if I can deal with this many people," said Charity, panic clear in her voice.

There was a startling number of red auras around us. I looked back at Parris. He smiled broadly, victory in his eyes. A knife blade caught the light in the leather-clad woman's hand.

"Run," I said.

Parris laughed, full-bodied and deep. The sound was picked up by those around us, like a pack of wild animals, and I realized I had never before felt real terror.

We ran. Parris's laugh followed for far too long, but it wasn't any better when it faded away, because there were yells and jeers and footsteps pounding behind us that didn't give us a moment's break. I looked over my shoulder to see that the man in jeans and a T-shirt who had been at Parris's side led the pack. He threw back his head and howled, which seemed to excite those still pursuing us, who added their own noises to the mix.

"Run faster," I panted.

"Where are we going?" gasped Lilith.

"I don't know," said Charity. "Why won't they give up?"

Movement above us caught my eye, and between watching my feet, which were never going to forgive me for this, and keeping track of the pack of wild humans behind us, I just barely recognized the movement for what it was.

"Hey!" I shouted to the movement above. "A little help, please?"

Sean and Crowley shot me confused glances but kept moving. It took so long for anything to happen that I started to doubt what I had seen, but then there was a rush of movement in the trees above us. The howls behind us turned to confused exclamations. I chanced a backward glance, to see the brownie bouncing frantically from one head to another of our pursuers, attacking with teeth and claws, and okay, yeah, I was going to have to reassess that "harmless" description.

"Hell yes!" I gasped. A stitch stabbed me in the side, but finally, finally we were leaving our pursuers behind.

"This way," Charity yelled. I followed blindly, stumbling up stone steps without any regard for where we were going. We shoved through heavy wooden doors and fell across the red carpet of the empty building, as the doors closed behind us with a loud thump.

I lay on the floor, concentrating on regaining my breath. Once I caught it, I wished I hadn't.

While I'd been running for my life and panting on the floor, I hadn't had to think about my friends' anger or the fact that our only hoping of escaping Earth and my one shot of everlasting freedom was gone. It had never been real in the first place. My stomach ached. I didn't think it was from the running.

When I couldn't wait any longer, I sat up. The rest of our group was already upright, leaning heavily against wooden benches or sitting cross-legged, looking toward one another.

"So . . . what happened?" Charity asked. "I'm guessing the plan didn't work."

"No," I said. I swallowed hard. "Apparently it was . . . fake."

"Yeah," snapped Crowley. He rose to his feet. "We noticed."

"I didn't know it was fake," I said. I stood up too. Crowley towering over me was surprisingly intimidating.

Crowley laughed. "Obviously! That doesn't make it better! Why did you have it in the first place?"

"Look," I said. "I'm sorry I didn't tell you sooner, but you know what this year is. And you know we didn't choose this."

"And your solution to that was what exactly?" Lilith asked. Her voice shook. Lilith had never been this angry with me.

"A spark can do anything," I said. "A real one could have—"

"Could have what?" Crowley demanded. "Could have ripped away your wings? And what would have happened to us? Did you even think about that? About us, your friends?"

"Oh, like you care about that?" I scoffed. "You barely tolerate us, and it's not like we ever had a choice. They threw us together and called us a squad. We didn't choose our friendships any more than we chose what our destinies would involve."

Crowley looked at me like I had slapped him. Lilith gasped. Wait . . . that wasn't—

"What?" asked Crowley. "So, we're not really friends, just assignments?"

"That's not what I meant," I protested. Crowley shook his head.

"Do you remember when I was friends with Abraxus? When we were little?" Crowley asked. I nodded. I vaguely remembered a time when Crowley had hung around other kids, before he'd decided he would rather be alone. Before he'd decided he would rather be the aloof guy no one knew how to read. "I went over to his house once after school. I heard his parents in the kitchen. They didn't want their son to be friends with 'one of them.' I was six. Never mind bigoted angels, we deal with that crap at home, too! And the only people who know what that's like is us! My squad, who is supposed to have my back, and what? You don't like being told what to do? We're not really friends?"

"I never said that," I said.

"But we were assigned?" he asked.

"You know we were," I said. "But that doesn't mean we're not friends. It doesn't mean that I don't love you guys. It just means we were never given a choice."

"Of course we have choices!" yelled Crowley. "We don't have

to play hologames or go to concerts or do anything more than our assigned work, but we do. And I thought that mattered."

"It does!" I shouted back at him.

"But you were going to leave us," Lilith said quietly.

"No," I said, just as quietly. "That's not what I wanted. The opposite, really."

"I need a minute," Crowley said, walking back to the doors. He turned with a hand on one of the doors. He tossed something at me that I caught on reflex. It was the scrying mirror. "I'm glad Aleister isn't here. You would have broken his heart."

"We're not sure it's clear out there," Sean warned before Crowley could open the door. Brimstone, I'd forgotten we weren't alone.

"I'll be fine," Crowley said.

"Where are you going?" I asked.

"I need a minute," Crowley repeated. "Alone." He pulled open the door and left.

THIRTY-FIVE

L ilith," I said tentatively, turning toward her.

"Mal," she started, "we'll talk more later. I just . . . I don't know how to feel about this."

"It was never about getting rid of you," I said. "Any of you."

She nodded, then wandered farther into the building, past row after row of wooden benches. Charity followed.

I sat down on a bench, giving Lilith her space too. I had really screwed up. I had never thought about what it would have meant if I had used the spark to take myself out of the equation. What would have happened? They would have been assigned a new leader.

If one was available.

More likely, they would have been split up to be added to new squads. Brimstone. But I hadn't even been sure that I was ever going to use the spark!

Sean sat down next to me and nudged his knee into mine. I looked up to see a gentle smile.

"I didn't understand all that," he said. "But it sounds like maybe things got blown out of proportion."

I nodded. "Do you ever feel like you have no control over anything, and you just need one thing, one thing?"

Sean laughed. "Uh, yeah. Like, all the time."

"I kept a secret I shouldn't have," I said, looking back down at my lap. "And explained things really badly."

"Well," he said, "maybe you can explain better next time."

"Yeah," I said. "Maybe."

"Or, you know, we could die in this church," Sean said. "And you'll never have to talk about it again."

A startled laugh escaped my mouth, and I looked up to meet Sean's eyes again. "Not sure which one I should root for there."

Sean smiled, and I began to feel that abnormal swoop of spell work. I didn't think it was intentional, now that I knew about the psychic thing, but I didn't need to let it happen either. I was giving away plenty of insider information all by myself. I dropped my eyes to his lips, and my stomach swooped for a whole other reason.

"So, what is this place?" I asked, looking around the room.

"What?" asked Sean. "Oh, um, yeah. This is a church; specifically, First Church in Salem."

"First?" I asked. "Does that mean it was around when Parris was alive?"

"Yes," said Charity as she and Lilith joined us. Lilith looked at me and smiled sadly before hopping onto the back of one of the benches. "Sort of, but also no. The church was around, as in the people and the congregation, but this building was built long after scary dude died."

"No focal point?" Lilith asked her.

"No," Charity said. "That invisible thing that helped us before when we were running—anything else like that roaming around we can call in for the assist?"

"No," I said. "That was pure luck. I've seen some other . . . vacationers here, but they're not always able or . . . willing to help."

"Can I see that?" Lilith asked, gesturing to the scrying mirror in my hand. I had been absentmindedly playing with it, and even though I hadn't been planning on contacting Aleister, handing it over still felt like losing another friend. "Thanks."

She hopped back off the bench and walked away. Apparently, I was not forgiven yet. I had really screwed up.

"We can try to find my moms," said Charity, flicking her eyes between me and Sean to see how we'd react. "I can't get through by phone, but I can probably track them. I doubt they're behind a secrecy veil. Although I can't be sure."

"Or," Sean said, clearing his throat, "we could go to your house and wait it out. Mine too, but yours is probably better warded, since it's a permanent home. Let the adults handle everything."

"Wait it out till when?" I asked. "Things are getting worse, and Heaven is probably still going to send in the thrones. We don't have a few hours, much less all night."

"We could leave town," Charity said. "Maybe we can find our moms on the way, and your mom can tell your dad and we can all—"

"He will never believe that *Heaven* is going to wipe out the town. Certainly not if the information was coming from me," Sean said bitterly. "And even if he did believe that, he would refuse to leave the town until the job was done anyway. Since we're doing the whole caring-and-sharing thing? Charity and I, our moms, we're all witches, but my dad is in a 'secret' order. He says it's allied with Heaven, which I always kind of thought was a philosophical thing, but now I'm not so sure."

"Is he going to be a problem?" I asked.

"Doubtful," Sean said. "He'd have to believe anything I said for that to happen."

Lilith rejoined us as we held the world's worst pity party. I gave her a questioning look.

"Aleister's fine," she said. "But he did say that something seemed to be going on. He didn't have a lot of info, but he thought the Powers That Be might be onto something."

I nodded and almost felt relief, because if the upper echelon at home had any inkling as to what had happened, that would mean my mom would know as well. Of course, just because Aleister thought there were mutterings didn't actually mean that there were or that they were right about what was happening. The front door opened and closed quietly. Crowley slunk carefully back into the room. I looked up eagerly, hoping we were okay. His eyes met mine, but his face stayed blank.

A rustle of feathers followed, and I couldn't even find it in myself to muster up enough energy to yell. "I thought we had a deal."

"I know," Cassandra said quietly. She wrung her hands as she approached us, like one would approach wild animals. I shook my head. Why was she back if she thought so little of us? "I am so sorry. I don't know why I reacted like that. I mean, I met you and you were nice. You never gave any sign that you were anything but innocent. It's just that they say

291

things . . . and I know they're probably stereotypes . . . and I never thought I would fall into that, but I just . . ."

"You heard things about them specifically?" Sean asked, frowning.

"No," Cassandra said. "About . . . you know, people like them . . . and I shouldn't have listened. I didn't think I had." She shook her head. Her halo was dull and crowding her hair. "No, that's not true. I did. I believed them . . . but once I met you, I should have realized."

"That you shouldn't make conclusions about someone because of a stereotype?" snapped Charity. "Yeah, you should have realized."

It was the angriest I had heard her, and I wondered if she was speaking from experience.

We already knew there had been witch hunts here. Maybe there still were? Or maybe the witch hunts now were less literal. I had noticed only one kind of people here, just humans, but I didn't get the impression that that united them. Whatever it was that humans used to separate and prejudge each other, I got the impression that Charity had experienced it personally.

"If you're here to apologize," I said, "it's accepted."

"I did. Want to apologize, that is," Cassandra said. "But I also want to help."

"How . . . exactly?" Lilith asked.

Cassandra smiled tentatively. Her halo popped back up, glowing happily, before she reached up and grabbed it. She spun it once and then put it into the pocket of her robe. Whereas my parents' halos were powerful weapons, Cassandra's halo was apparently a good mood indicator.

"You need a vessel for Parris, and you can't find one, which makes sense, because he died forever ago, and you weren't even alive then, much less here." Her gown jerked to the right, and she clamped her hands down over what looked like her halo trying to escape.

"We are aware," Crowley said.

"So we need a link to find the perfect thing," she said, taming her wayward halo. "Someone with a connection."

"That's why we were at Gallows Hill, before you zapped us away," I pointed out.

"Anyone with a connection is dead," Sean scoffed.

"I know! Isn't it perfect?" Cassandra squealed.

We stared. And then I got it.

"You want to do a summoning?" I asked. "Are you allowed to do that?"

Summoning a soul from its final judgment was a major no-no. In fact, it was such a major no-no that it was one of the few rules both Heaven and Hell agreed on. For those souls in

Heaven, summoning them away was cruel. For those in Hell, it was downright dangerous.

"Well, technically no," Cassandra said, and her halo made another bid for freedom. "But I've never *personally* been told not to. But . . . we could also go to Heaven. I know, I know, just temporarily. Then we wouldn't *really* be breaking rules. I promise, I will bring you back. Right away."

Even I could see that the reassurances were weak, but . . . it couldn't make things worse. That's the problem with facing total annihilation: there really is no way to escalate the threat. The question was, could we trust Cassandra to bring us back?

"I promise," she said, standing perfectly straight and lifting her hand. "I'll bring you right back to Salem. I won't keep you there."

This was a terrible idea.

"Wait," Sean said. "What are we doing?"

I looked at Lilith and Crowley. Lilith bit her lip but shrugged. Crowley raised an eyebrow. Charity looked slightly confused but also really excited.

"Let's do it," I said. My feet hurt, I was wingless and under threat of smiting, and . . . all the friendship angst was stressing me out. Bring on the summoning.

Cassandra had to prep the humans somehow, so I had a couple of minutes with my squad mates.

"I'm sorry," I said. "I should have thought things out, but really, I don't think I would have ever used the spark anyway. Even if it was real. I just needed to feel like I had a choice in my own future." And once I started talking, I felt the need to be completely honest. "It's a lot about you guys too, not just me. My parents don't hang out with their squads. My mom makes hers cry, like, *all the time*. I don't want that for us, and school changes after this week, which is almost over! We won't be together. We'll be separated into our tracks in different schools. And then what happens to us? To me? Will we be the same? And what about everything we want to do that we can't? I don't want to lose you guys. I don't want things to be different."

"You're an idiot," Crowley said. "Yes, we'll be in different schools, but we're not at school all the time. We'll still have after school, weekends, and vacations. And then when we're all adulty, doing adult things, we'll be together all the time, but we still won't be *working* all the time. I fully intend on writing that comic book. It's going to happen."

"And as for your parents," Lilith said, "they're not friends with their squads, but they do have friends. Your mom and my mom talk all the time. They do spa days! And your dad has that not-so-secret society that he always hangs out with. They're ridiculously dorky with their *friends*. My mom said that your mom was never friends with her squad at all. In fact, she and Ruby hated each other in school."

"Exactly," Crowley said. "We're not them. And I for one am not letting Fate get in the way of anything I want."

"I'm sorry," I said. Maybe I should have talked to my friends about this before. "Are we okay?"

"Yeah," said Lilith, nudging me with her hip. "We're good."

"For all that is unholy," Crowley groaned. "We love you, you enormous idiot."

I pulled them both into a giant hug. Crowley protested, but it was half-hearted at best. "I promise," I told them. "No more secrets. I'm serious this time."

"We're going to rule the place," Crowley said, with a mischievous glint in his eye.

"Don't say that in front of the Lightbringer," Lilith said, using Lucifer's old moniker.

"Why do you think I'm saying it here?" Crowley said. We laughed, and even with all that was still to come, I felt freer than I had in . . . weeks.

"Okay," said Cassandra. "I spoke to Charity, and we're going to try an in-between process. We'll part the way to Heaven but stay physically here."

Sean looked absolutely shell-shocked.

"Yeah, we need to be on this side for the object, assuming

one still exists," said Charity. "This 'Heaven' thing will be, um, yeah."

"You don't have anything you use to trap souls on your end?" Lilith asked Cassandra. "Something you could just snag for us?"

"Well, no, dear," Cassandra said. "Souls *want* to come with us."

We sat on the red floor of the altar and placed a white candle in the center of our circle. Cassandra pulled a feather from her wing with an undignified squeak and handed it to Charity, who looked absolutely in awe at her spell ingredient. Charity muttered something in Latin, and the candle lit with a flame far too big for the tiny wick. A gust of unnatural wind roared through the room, sending the flame even higher.

"Think about home," Charity instructed, reaching her hand out to the seraph, and Cassandra nodded.

The world around us faded at the edges. The scent of vanilla came strongly into being, and I knew we were closer to Heaven than ever before.

I was in the middle of thinking how impressive this whole thing was when Lilith's hair whipped me in the face, and Sean spluttered as he got a mouthful of feathers from Cassandra's wings. Crowley rolled his eyes like he couldn't believe he was sitting with a bunch of amateurs.

Charity's eyes practically glowed with enthusiasm—actually, now that I looked closer, they may have been literally glowing.

"Sarah Good," whispered Cassandra.

Her eyes closed, and she frowned in concentration. Nothing happened for a long time, and we shifted uncomfortably at the whole lot of nothing that was happening. The rest of us looked at each other, and then back at the flame, which still rose far higher than physics demanded. Cassandra muttered softly in Latin, her eyes still closed, and again I heard the summon for Sarah Good.

Gallows Hill was supposed to be our focal point to find a soul trap, but Parris wasn't going to let that happen. Now, Sarah Good, someone who had personal and profound experience with Samuel Parris, would be our focal point instead.

If this worked.

The fog around us crept farther in. There were the vague outlines and movements of something in the distance, and then, suddenly, the woman we had seen pleading for her life at the Witch Dungeon Museum was right there, sitting in the middle of our circle.

"Oh my gods," breathed Charity. Sarah wasn't wispy or transparent; she was as solid and real as any of us.

"Sarah!" Cassandra said, before excitedly clapping her hands. "I knew this would work! I'm helping!"

Sarah smiled at Cassandra indulgently. She turned her head to meet eyes with all of us, her smile never falling.

"Of what assistance can I be to thee, kind seraph?" asked Sarah, before moving her gaze to Charity. "Young one."

Charity beamed.

"I didn't think we'd get this far," said Cassandra.

"Sarah," I started. "Can I call you that?"

"Of course, angel," said Sarah, with that same peaceful smile.

I smiled back. It was hard not to.

If Cassandra had been trying to convince us that Heaven was a great place, Sarah Good should have been exhibit A.

"You knew Samuel Parris," I said gently.

Sarah's smile faded slowly, and then she nodded. I looked at my friends, and they gestured for me to keep going.

"We need to obtain a possession that would be important to him, something to use to capture his soul and get him back where he belongs. You want that too, right?"

"He should burn," said Sarah without ever losing her serenity.

"Um, yeah . . . sort of," I said, because Hell is excellent at punishment, and it's not all fire. Although, now that I thought about it, I was pretty sure Parris spent a lot of time as a pillar of flame. "We were thinking about these golden candlesticks we read about. It seemed they were important to him."

"The *only* things he cared for were wealth and power," replied Sarah. "I know these candlesticks."

"But see, the problem is that we have no connection to them. We don't even know what they look like, and if we just try to summon golden candlesticks, we'll get every candlestick that's ever been made," I said.

Sarah cocked her head to the side. "How can I help?"

"We just need you to focus on Parris," said Charity, calmly and gently. "Focus on the meetinghouse, and the candlesticks in particular, if you can. If you can picture them in your mind, I can find them. I can maybe even bring them here if everything works. You'll be our focal point."

"I can do that," she said, and smiled serenely again. "If it will bring him to justice, nothing would please me more."

Charity made complicated hand gestures and muttered something I couldn't understand before placing a hand on Sarah's shoulder. At first nothing happened, but Sarah kept sitting, calm and still, as if everything was as it was supposed to be. Then her brow furrowed in concentration, and Cassandra silently clapped her hands in glee. Charity's eyes widened, and she extended her free hand in front of her.

We waited. The air started to feel heavy, and then there

was a *pull*. We all swayed, just a tiny bit, toward the center of the circle. Something was happening.

The floor inside our circle started to glow. A pale yellow, like the very edge of hellfire, drifted up in twisting wisps lighting the space from within. We held our breath. There was something in the glow. Sarah's serene look was gone. Her frown of concentration turned to effort and something that looked very much like unhappiness.

The "something" in front of her crossed legs started to darken and become defined, the silhouette of the candlesticks coming into view as that pulling sensation got stronger, and I had to work to keep myself in my spot.

"It's working!" Cassandra squealed.

I kept my eyes on the forming candlesticks, being pulled to our location from wherever they had ended up over the last several hundred years. Our weapons to capture Parris and return him to the Pit were so close! We could do this. This was going to work.

And then the room started to shake.

I looked at Charity, hoping to see her reassuring glee, but she looked confused, and that was never a good thing when violating divine law. She didn't look scared, but the expression on Sarah's face was more than terrified enough, and it was catching.

The floor vibrated beneath us. The windows rattled in their frames.

Sarah lunged backward, away from Charity's hand, and scrambled to the very edge of our circle, where Sean and Crowley sat. Crowley put his hands out as if he was going to stop her from going too far, but Sarah didn't cross the edge. I didn't know if she stopped on her own or if an invisible wall held her back. I was guessing the latter, because she looked like she wanted to be anywhere but here.

The glow that had lit our circle went out, and with it our only way of capturing Parris. The candlesticks were gone.

"He's here," Sarah hissed.

"Sarah . . ." The voice murmuring over the wind was way creepier than anything that had happened so far.

"No," Sarah spat. "No."

Charity started muttering and pulled a vial out of the bag on her hip. She sprinkled some powder into her hand and blew across her palm. Instead of scattering forward, the powder moved up and around us. Everything beyond our circle lost all focus.

"You must work faster, young one," Sarah said to Charity. Charity nodded sharply.

Sarah shifted to her knees and closed her eyes, bowing her head in concentration. Charity rushed to touch her once again. The circle glowed, and the *pull* was back, stronger than ever, as though the call of the void had somehow been altered by the universe to become something more literal, something more physical. Lilith slid forward, and I grabbed her arm, which slowed her slide but didn't stop it completely. Cassandra's wings flapped inward hard, once, before she pulled them in tight to her back, while Sean grabbed my waist to keep me outside the circle.

And oh, that was his arm around my waist and his chest against my back and, oh wow, now was *not* the time to be distracted.

"Sarah . . . ," came the call again, but it sounded distant and distorted, like listening to someone speaking underwater. Parris couldn't know what we were doing. He was still taunting her. He wouldn't be doing that if he knew we had a way to stop him, right?

Charity screamed in one last expenditure of energy, and Sarah shoved the candlesticks, now solid, forward to the very edge of the circle. Lilith grabbed them. Sarah looked up at the ceiling, as if she could see Parris somewhere outside, and she was shaking in fear. I wasn't sure what to do, but before I could try anything, Cassandra snapped into action.

"Rest now," she said, placing one hand on Sarah's forehead and snuffing out the candle with the other. "Thank you."

Sarah smiled in relief and disappeared.

But that didn't stop the church from rumbling. The air felt so thick, it hurt to breathe. Parris was getting louder, and there were more noises following. There were sounds from outside of people approaching, and loud engines, hoots and hollers, and it was all warped and muffled, except for the doors when they burst open. No, that sound was loud and clear, like our ears had popped.

The heavy doors slammed against the wall, and Charity screamed as the church around us vanished.

THIRTY-SIX

With an audible snap, the scene around us solidified in 100 percent high-def. We were in a room with large glass windows that looked out toward rolling fields of green grass covered in an impossible number of bright-colored flowers. The sky was lavender and held puffy white clouds with edges of sparkling silver. It smelled like vanilla and something fresh and frozen. Snow?

"You zapped us to Heaven?!" snarled Crowley.

"I panicked," said Cassandra apologetically. "I couldn't hold it."

"Are we dead?" Sean asked faintly.

"This is legitimately Heaven?" Charity asked. "It's not just a metaphor? I always thought it was a metaphor."

Okay, I could deal with this.

Out the window there were seraphs flying, shining like comets and leaving trails of light behind them. There was a group of cherubim off by a sparkling pond. Each had four faces and wings covered in eyes, which not only was completely freaky but also made it difficult to figure out what they were looking at. In the distance a squad of thrones flying in formation zipped from one building to another. I didn't see any kids or houses.

Okay. Business sector. I knew where we were. That . . . that solved absolutely nothing!

My shoulders twitched where my wings wanted to flare in panic, and for the first time since falling through the veil, I felt them respond. I gasped, which made them flare further. They weren't my normal black, but they weren't Cassandra's white, either. They were translucent and sort of multicolored.

Sean and Charity both let out startled sounds, but I ignored them because that was when the alarms starting sounding.

Blue lights flashed, and a gonging like large bells rang out. They didn't sound the same as Hell's Bells. They were more melodious and less clanging, but I was smart enough to know an alarm when I heard one.

"I broke the rules," whimpered Cassandra. At her feet lay

her halo, dull and lifeless. She bent and picked it up. It didn't glow or float or respond in any way.

"What is happening, Cassandra?" I asked.

"Oh dear, oh dear. I panicked." Cassandra twisted her hands together. Her halo was still dull and lifeless, hanging around her wrist. "Sean and Charity are still alive. They're not supposed to be here. Even when I try to follow the rules, I still mess up! This is terrible. Okay, if I return them and turn you all in, maybe then my halo—"

"Stop!" I snapped. "The only thing you've done wrong is bringing us here!"

"No, no, no." Cassandra shook her head. "I was *supposed* to bring you here, and if I had done that right away, none of this would have happened. Look at my halo! Look at it!"

"The right thing is capturing Parris and protecting the town," I argued. "The right thing is helping us get home, and you were doing that. You promised!"

"I didn't bring you here right away. I summoned a soul away from her eternal resting place! And now I brought two living souls into Heaven. I knew demons were dangerous, but I didn't think they'd be adorable children."

"We are not demons!" Crowley yelled in an ironically demonic voice. Then, more softly, he added, "Or . . . you know, adorable."

"Cassandra, listen to me before someone does something about all those alarms going off," I pleaded. "The rules can't possibly apply in every different situation. Okay? They're more like guidelines. It's more important to do the right thing. To listen to that voice that tells you what's right. Didn't you feel that when you were helping us?"

The alarms were still ringing, and there was bustling beyond the door.

"I—I don't know," Cassandra stammered.

"Yes, you did," Lilith added. "I know you did. Remember how bad you felt when you thought about making us orphans? Remember how excited you were to help us find a way to trap Parris? Remember how you realized the stereotypes aren't right? You *know* we're not evil."

"I . . . um . . ." Cassandra wouldn't look at anything but the windows opposite, which was really a shame, considering what was happening with the halo around her wrist. The celestial metal was beginning to glow and brighten. It trembled with so much energy that I was amazed Cassandra didn't feel it.

"Aren't there some things that are so universally good, you don't need a rule to tell you to do them?" asked Charity. She gestured to Cassandra's wrist, but the seraph was staring blindly out the window, her fingers twitching nervously.

"If we stay here, everyone in Salem dies," added Crowley,

much more gently than I had ever heard him speak.

My eyes stayed locked on Cassandra's wrist, while my mind repeated one word, a quiet, frantic *please*. And then Sean put the chant to voice.

"Please."

We didn't even need an answer. Cassandra jerked as her halo came roaring back to full glory, glowing bright and shining, and flew straight up to float above her head where it belonged. Of course, since it was still around her wrist when it decided to spark to life, it dragged her arm up in its bid for freedom, but that was all okay, because Cassandra knew who she was again. She was on the right path, and her halo was just letting her know.

"See? All good." Crowley patted her arm. "Just a little shock." Which was when the door blew open, revealing three seraphim, one of whom was holding a massive golden book.

"Cassandra, what is the meaning of this? These two humans are not due to pass over for another . . ." The seraph waved his hands, and the pages of the golden book raced open before falling flat. "Right, I see . . . oh, it's been updated. Only forty minutes?"

Charity's and Sean's mouths dropped open. Learning you had less than an hour to live had that effect on a person, I guess.

"Well," he continued, "I suppose no real harm has been done, but that will be a negative on your performance review."

"Forty minutes early, sir?" Cassandra asked weakly. "Oh, well . . . that just won't do."

She waved her fingers, and a door appeared in the room. It swung open to reveal a black starlit sky on the other side.

"Save them," Cassandra said to us, smiling gently, her halo glowing peacefully over her head. "Go home, children, and I'm sorry . . . for everything." It was the first time she had ever acknowledged Hell as our home. My relief was overwhelming.

Cassandra waved a hand, and we were shoved through the open door and into the star-filled sky.

And then we were falling.

THIRTY-SEVEN

As soon as we were out the door, our wrong-colored wings disappeared. Free-falling with wings is the best feeling in the world. Free-falling without wings? Not so much.

"AAAHHHHH!" was quickly followed by "OOF!" as we all landed hard against the Salem sidewalk. We raised ourselves to sitting. Crowley gently shifted Charity off his lap. I was tangled up awkwardly with Sean again. "We've got to stop meeting like this," I said.

I flicked my eyes over my shoulder, and even though I knew those wrong wings were gone, the soul-crushing disappointment nearly overwhelmed me.

Squashed candy and popcorn littered the street, and the

remnants of broken glass crunched under our shoes as we stood up. We saw huge machines sending streaks of light into the air with every abrupt sweep of motion. Other machines spun, filled with people, their lights spiraling together with the speed of movement. Every now and then a scream broke through the aggressive music.

"We found your torture Pit," I said vaguely. "Finally."

"Pathetic," Crowley said, just in time for someone to stagger to a trash can and throw up into it.

"Start talking," said Sean. His voice shook. "Because I was apparently in the afterlife, and I'm getting a bad feeling about stereotypes and demons and wings."

The breeze kicked up, but that wasn't what made me cold. "You knew we were from another dimension," I said warily.

"Yeah, and what dimension is that exactly?" Sean stepped toward me. I stepped back. I did not want to fight him. "You're demons?"

"No," I said. "Why do people keep saying that?"

"All this talk about circles and souls and Heaven," Sean said. "And the amulet glowed around you! You're demons from Hell."

"Seriously?" snapped Crowley. "We have movie theaters and tacos. You people have some serious misinformation."

"So you admit it," growled Sean. "You're from Hell. That makes you a demon."

"No, it doesn't!" I yelled, because Sean wasn't listening, and he really needed to.

"Then what?" demanded Sean, in a voice equally as loud.

"We're angels!" I shouted. "Hell's angels!"

"Like the motorcycle gang?" Sean sputtered.

"Motor . . . huh?" I said. "We're angels who live in Hell. Guardian angels, to be exact."

"Guardian angels?" Sean asked doubtfully. "So, I'm supposed to believe you follow people around and keep them safe?"

"That's stupid," I said. "There are, like, eight billion of you, and maybe a hundred thousand of us. How would that even be possible?"

"Humans," scoffed Crowley.

I said, "We keep evil—and the demons you keep mentioning—locked away, so they can't influence the mortal realm or swing the balance. Or at least we will. We're not human, but we're not demons, either. We're powers."

Sean didn't look convinced.

"That *is* a type of angel," Charity said quietly.

"Have we done anything to harm you?" I asked.

"Apparently you failed at your job and unleased evil on my planet," Sean said.

Ouch. "Wasn't our job yet," I mumbled.

"I'm sorry," Sean said, shaking his head. "That was uncalled-for."

"Good. Because, guys," Charity inserted, "that angel basically said we're going to Heaven in forty minutes. Heaven, which is apparently a real place you go to after you die! In FORTY MINUTES!"

"She's right," I said. "We don't have time for this. I promise you that we are not the bad guys. You have to believe me."

"We have the same mission, Sean," Charity said, smacking him on the arm. "Don't screw it up by channeling your dad. Let's get this evil jerk before we all die!"

For a minute I thought Sean would fight. I thought he'd be like everyone else who judged us on myths, rumors, and stereotypes, and ignore the admittedly short friendship we'd developed.

"I'm sorry," Sean said. "It's not because I actually think you're evil. This has just been . . . a lot to take in for one night. I mean, afterlives are a thing." Sean pushed his hand through his short hair. "Which we know about now, on a factual level. And I need to rethink my dad's whole . . . thing. All his absolutes always rubbed me the wrong way before, but now . . . I think we really need to talk. At the very least, I can't be part of just blindly aligning myself with some authority."

"It's okay. Let's—" I stopped. The torture machines were admittedly distracting, but it was the people we needed to watch, and once I did . . . "Have you noticed all the red?"

"The lights?" asked Sean.

Crowley and Lilith scanned the crowd and inhaled sharply.

"What's wrong with the lights?" asked Charity.

"The auras," Crowley said vaguely, turning in a slow circle as he looked at the humans around us.

"I was seeing mostly blue and gray when I got here," I said. "But that group that chased us was completely red."

"Parris is tipping the balance," Lilith said, confirming a theory I very much did not want confirmed. Her voice sounded strangled, and I didn't need to look to know that her fingers were tapping out a nervous rhythm against her leg.

"Ghosts shouldn't be able to do this," Sean said. "This isn't how any of this works."

"He's changed," Charity said. "This whole time, he's been changing."

"We noticed," Crowley said.

"None of this should be happening," Lilith said. "He shouldn't even look like his former self on the mortal plane, but at least that makes sense. But to change? He certainly should not be able to do that. And he's apparently giving direct instructions, instead of just manipulating people now. We knew he was gaining strength, but this?"

"That sounds bad," said Charity. "Like, on a cosmic level."

"It is," I said.

Everything came together. Parris *was* the vague sparkles when we got here. The sparkles always at the center of a disturbance. But he'd been getting more real, more solid as the night went on. His solid form, his ability to speak, his changing clothes, his manipulation and ultimate control of the humans in this world—all of it was getting stronger. Parris was gaining power not just by influencing small actions but by swinging the entire balance of good and evil.

People were doing things they never would have done on their own. Charity had been right. Most people *didn't* answer the call of the void. Some of the things people were doing under Parris's influence were harmless, but other people were doing horrible things.

If the thrones did their job tonight, we were going to be seeing souls in the Pit that never would have been there otherwise. He was changing everything. This was indeed cosmically bad.

"Hey, Lil, we've been saying 'chaos' with a small *c*," I

said, feeling like I had to be absolutely wrong about this, but needing to say it anyway. "But are we sure we're not talking about Chaos with a big *C*?"

Before the balance, before light and dark, and good and evil, there was only Chaos. It had been the tightly held balance between good and evil, preserved by the efforts of so many, that had kept Chaos, the being, locked away. Celestial and infernal forces, and others beyond that, all maintained the balance that had prevented all of existence from falling to its influence and returning to nothing, like the deep blackness that had been outside the windows of Beadle's Tavern.

"This is only one town," Lilith said, but I could tell I had rattled her. "In one world. It would take more than that to let Chaos rise."

"Let's not make things worse than they already are," said Crowley. "They're plenty bad on their own."

"I don't know anything about a capital *C* Chaos, and I can't see auras," said Sean slowly. "But my magic manifests more with the psychic thing, and Salem has felt . . . wrong. And more wrong as time goes by."

He side-eyed me.

"It's not us," I said, exasperated. "It's definitely Parris."

"I know," he said, surprising me. "When I'm not freaking out, I don't get that feeling from you."

"Well," I said, blushing a little despite myself. "That's, uh, good. Yeah. I mean, of course not."

"No, yeah," Sean said. "I mean . . . you know."

"Great," Lilith said, stepping between us. "Very articulate. Crowley, can we use this to track Parris?" She held a candlestick between Sean and me, breaking our sight line.

"You managed to hold on to it?" I exclaimed. "Do you have the other one too?"

"Uh, yeah," Lilith said. "What kind of amateur do you think I am? Charity and I got this."

"You're amazing," Sean said.

"Seriously, well done! I'm sure we could use it to track him," Crowley said. "If we were home, definitely. Here? I don't know. I'm not . . . me, here."

Sean frowned. "What do you think, Charity? Charity?"

But Charity was gone.

"Charity!" yelled Sean. Panic turned my stomach so fast, I thought I'd be sick. The machines were still flinging people around, and the excited cries on top of the loud music almost completely drowned out the sound of a muffled scream.

"There!" I pointed. In the distance—how had she gotten so far away?—Charity fought, but she was outnumbered. A figure dressed as a clown held his white-gloved hand over her mouth. He turned to grin over his shoulder at us. There were others in bright colors dragging and pulling at her before they lifted her into the air completely.

We were already running when a group of people blocked our way. We tried to push through, but they were bigger, and Charity was disappearing quickly. The man in front of me laughed.

"Haven't you heard?" asked the man, leaning in close. His breath smelled like burning. "Thou shalt not suffer a witch to live."

"Get off me," I snarled. Anger and fear made my missing wings flare and my eyes blaze.

The man backed away, holding his hands up, a smirk firmly on his face. The others followed suit, and we pushed our way through, but they had done their job in distracting us. Charity was nowhere to be seen.

THIRTY-EIGHT

We have to find her!" Sean yelled. He was frantic. He rubbed his fists into his eyes and then scanned the streets around us.

We'd been right there. My whole squad had been right there, and still Charity had been grabbed.

It was my job to issue the orders. It was my job to keep control and keep my squad safe. And over and over again tonight I had frozen, I had done nothing. I had never *wanted* to be responsible for any of that, but sometimes, in the heat of the moment, Dad had made comments like I wasn't *capable* of doing it. I was too rash, not focused enough, too emotional. Maybe he was right. Despite my formerly black-feathered wings, I was not cut out for my predestined role.

Maybe there was a bigger reason why my wings were gone. Maybe I didn't deserve to have them back. Maybe Fate had changed its mind. Funny how only a day ago I would have loved that outcome.

"We have to stay calm and think," I said.

"Mal," Lilith said urgently. "She has the other candlestick."

"She could be anywhere," Sean said. "This entire town has gone crazy. She could be at any house, any building, anywhere!"

"I don't think so," I said. "That man said something weird. Does 'Thou shalt not suffer a witch to live' mean anything to you?"

"What?" Sean said. "Yeah, it's a quote, a complete mistranslation, that was used a lot in the persecution of women. He said that?"

"Yes," I said.

"Then it's Parris," said Lilith. "It's not a coincidence. It has to be Parris's influence."

Sean cursed.

"This doesn't change anything," I said, grabbing his shoulders and forcing him to stop frantically turning. "We're *looking* for *him*. We have a way to stop him, and we have to do it quickly, before the thrones take out everyone. Parris can't already know about the thrones coming. Or that we're ready for a confrontation."

"Exactly," Lilith said. "He probably thinks taking Charity will control us, that he'll have leverage. He knows we're trying to stop him, but he doesn't realize that time is running out."

"So where would he take Charity?" asked Crowley.

Sean shook his head, but then the movement slowed.

"First Church?" he guessed. "I think. It was his congregation, and that quote was religious."

"We have a way to stop him," Crowley said. "So let's stop him."

It seemed to take both forever and no time at all to return to the church. I hadn't studied it the last time we'd fled here, but now when we approached, the bell tower loomed over us, dark and intimidating. Unlike last time, the church was lit up now, and shadows twisted behind the windows.

"We should look for a side door," I murmured. A scream, recognizable even through the walls as Charity's, rang out. "Or the front, the front is good."

We raced to the massive front doors and slipped in as subtly as possible. Crowley guided the door, and it closed with a gentle thump. The church was full.

Parris was at the red-carpeted altar, standing between

two small staircases, almost exactly where we had summoned Sarah Good.

My eyes were immediately drawn to Charity. Her hands glowed in front of her, but the glow was contained close to the skin, like it was being held back. There was a rope around her neck that coiled and uncoiled in the air like a snake, and her eyes followed the movement with a look of terror.

Charity's bag was on the pulpit, and I could only hope the candlestick Lilith said she'd given to her was still inside, and not in the hands of one of his people. Because Parris stood solid and in control in front of his new congregation of manipulated Salem residents, like three and a half centuries had meant nothing, and Lilith was on the other side of the church.

"Brothers and sisters," Parris called out. "Dreadful witchcraft broke out here a few centuries past. Members of this church, hypocrites and liars, damning this town! As I've said before, let none then build their hopes of salvation merely upon this: that they are church members. This you and I may be, and yet devils for all that. I had meant this as a warning to not assume salvation, but it was a statement of fact. There are devils. There are devils among us whither one or ten, or twenty . . . My arm wielded the lash that ripped free many a name of those in league with darkness, and was I rewarded for my service? No, I suffered for my righteousness. Why resist our nature? Do as you will, and we'll tear it all down."

Parris stopped talking and looked directly into my eyes. He knew exactly where I was, and his expression? It was so clear. He didn't see us as a threat.

"Still, not all the old ways should be discarded." Parris smirked. "'Thou shalt not suffer a witch to live.'"

"Charity!" screamed Sean as the rope tightened abruptly around Charity's neck, and with a flick of Parris's hand, the rope was pulled into the air by an invisible force, dragging her into the air.

I ran down the aisle without a second thought, and if anyone tried to stop me, I didn't notice. Charity's face was turning a not-at-all-human shade of blue. I lifted her, and the rope bit into my fingers, pulling the stitches on my injured hand as I tried to create slack, but the rope stayed taut as it continued to rise. Charity gagged. No one stopped me as I struggled. My eyes caught Parris's. He sneered triumphantly.

There were the sounds of a struggle nearby, but Charity was dying, and contrary to logic, I pulled her down and straddled her waist to prevent her from rising. The rope was going to stay tight no matter what I did, and I needed room to work.

"Crowley," I called. "Do something!"

"I can't make it disappear," Crowley said. "Hold on, I might be able to . . ."

For a fraction of a second the rope froze and loosened just a smidge, and Charity gasped in much-needed oxygen. I grabbed the rope with both hands before it tried to pull tight again, and it bit into my fingers as I created as much space between her skin and the rope as possible. Sean appeared at my side and thrust a knife between my fingers and Charity's neck.

"Faster," I snapped.

The knife pulled through the last threads of the rope, and the moment the blade pulled free, the rope disappeared in a wisp of smoke. Charity lay gasping on the altar. Her throat had rope marks that were going to bruise horribly, and her eyes were red where blood vessels had burst, but she was breathing, and that was a win.

"Bravo." Parris clapped sarcastically. "Did you know this is my church?" he asked. "Oh, they updated the building and moved it, but it's still *mine*. Rebecca Nurse and Giles Corey belonged to this church. Witches hiding in my own flock. Can you believe that? But I found them."

"They weren't witches," Sean said.

Parris's face changed for a split second, and I wasn't sure what that reaction was. Had he not known that? Did he really believe he was the good guy back then? Did he think he was the good guy now?

My eyes flicked to Charity's hopefully untouched bag. Parris and the weapon to contain him were so close together. I could end this.

A smile spread slowly across his face.

"But she's a witch," he said quietly, and I shivered despite myself. "Did you enjoy my parlor trick? So convenient, even if you managed to get past it. Sometimes the old ways are best anyway."

He looked out onto his makeshift congregation, and they rose, looking at Charity with a hunger that was not healthy, but that was okay, because Lilith was almost to us, gold glinting in her hand. We had him surrounded, with weapons on both sides. Hopefully.

People took to the aisles, so focused on Charity that they paid no attention to Lilith creeping closer.

"We're not letting you hurt Charity," I said, trying to stall for time.

"They're not going to hurt her," said Parris. "They're going to kill her."

The congregation started yelling horrible things.

Parris was still smirking, still confident, right up until Lilith touched him with the candlestick. She didn't even get the words out before Parris's face showed true terror for the very first time.

"What?" Parris lurched backward, but not all of him went. Part of him stuck to the candlestick, and his modern look began reverting to the old as his body stretched away from the vessel like it was physically connected.

"Anima—" started Lilith, but before she could finish, one of Parris's followers clamped a wrinkled hand over her mouth. Crowley and Sean grabbed the man and wrestled him away from Lilith, but Parris had gotten free. I lunged for Charity's bag on the podium, hoping to help, but I stumbled as the church rumbled, and lost sight of the bag as the podium fell. I smelled ozone in the air—someone was doing magic. All I could hope was that whatever they were doing wouldn't make things worse. The congregation continued to surge forward. A few had stumbled when the building had shaken, and others trampled over the fallen. Some were climbing over the pews, heedless of the obstacles in their way, single-mindedly pursuing the witch they intended to destroy. I lost sight of Parris in the chaos.

Sean was trying to weave and duck his way through the mass of bodies, while protecting Charity, and it wasn't going well. He didn't notice the knife coming from behind. I jumped into action and intercepted the attack just as the tip of the knife snagged on Sean's jacket. With a quick flick I snapped the man's wrist, sending the knife flying. Sean looked back, startled.

"School?" he asked.

"Obviously," I said. "Seriously, dude, I worry about your education. Now get her out of here!"

He looked torn.

"She can't fight," I said. "We got this."

He nodded, and Charity smiled apologetically.

I had to be the leader my squad needed. We had to stop Parris. We had to end this now.

THIRTY-NINE

Mal! Crowley!" yelled Lilith. "This way!"

I ran and twisted my way through bodies as quickly as I could. Crowley pummeled his own path, and we arrived nearly simultaneously at a brown door to the side of the altar.

"He went through here," Lilith said.

"I didn't get Charity's bag," I announced, glancing back to see the area I had lost it swarming with people. A hand rose through the crowd, and I caught a glint of gold before someone else lunged for it.

"Leave it," snapped Crowley. "We'll lose Parris if we try to fight through that mess. Lilith, you still have the other one, right?"

Lilith held up the candlestick briefly before shoving the door open to reveal an alcove containing clothing and supplies and several closed doors.

I heard a yelp and shoved aside robes that were hanging in the nook across from me, only to find Furfur. The daemon was cowering on the floor.

"What are you doing?" I asked.

"Apparently hiding in the wrong spot!" he snapped.

"You could help, you know!" I snapped right back.

"No way," he said. "I'm just waiting it out until dawn and going home."

"This town will be gone before dawn," said Crowley.

"He went that way!" Furfur pointed to a door on the other side of the alcove. "What do you mean the town will be gone? Guys? Guys!"

I ripped the door open to reveal the bottom of a staircase. "Of course there are stairs," I groaned, thinking about all that my poor feet had had to endure since I'd landed on Earth.

The metal staircase was narrow and ran against the interior walls of the large square bell tower. I looked up. A heavy bell hung from the top. I caught a flash of movement and took to the steps before I even made the conscious decision. The staircase rattled under our racing feet, and the constant zigzagging of the stairs made me disoriented and nauseated.

"Ugh," grunted Crowley, pulling himself up by the railing. "I'm gonna die."

"Only if you don't move that butt," snapped Lilith.

We climbed until there was nothing further to climb. The massive bell, which had looked heavy from the ground, was enormous from eye level, easily taking several flights of stairs to encompass its height. There were decorative windows at the top of the tower that let in a bit of light but were too opaque to see through.

"There," Crowley said, pointing to a wall-mounted ladder off to the side that I had missed in the gloom.

He climbed quickly, and I held my breath as he popped his head through a door in the ceiling. He was still for a second before scurrying the rest of the way up. I grabbed the rungs and awkwardly climbed. Ladders weren't something I had a lot of practice with—when I wanted to go up in Hell, I flew.

We pulled ourselves through the narrow opening one by one, not knowing what to expect.

The top of the tower was open to the sky, and the sight that greeted me was so familiar that it took me a second to realize how wrong it was. There was light rising from the earth into the sky, but it wasn't the warm coziness of the flames at home. A net of holy light was being woven by the thrones, and it was rising rapidly.

It was enormous. Heaven was going to cleanse Salem right off the map.

"Wicked angels," snarled Parris. I snapped my head to follow his voice and cursed myself for having gotten distracted.

Parris gazed out at the thrones' work, fists clenched at his side. Whatever he had been expecting when he'd escaped up this tower, it wasn't this. The ground trembled again, and I held on to the low stone wall at the top of the tower. The scent of ozone accompanied a flash of light in the distance, separate from the work of Heaven's soldiers. The smell of magic. Big magic. More than Charity. At least, more than *just* Charity. I hoped that was good.

There was a muffled noise, and I realized we weren't alone. Three of Parris's makeshift congregation had accompanied him, but one of them wasn't looking so cooperative. The teenager shook his head like he was trying to wake himself up.

I nodded my head at my friends, giving them the signal to flank Parris. Yet again he didn't care that we were here. We were just kids, and he thought that meant we were weak, that we could be controlled. But we were going to prove just how dangerous it was to underestimate us.

The net of light was level with the top of the building now, and the energy radiating off it felt like the cold burn of ice.

"Almost there," Parris said. We hesitated. My friends looked at me nervously. Were we moving into a trap?

"Wait," said the teenager. "What's happening?"

The boy moved like a puppet, stiff and wooden as his limbs sent him jerkily up onto the stones of the short wall at the top of the bell tower. The other two stepped up gracefully, blank expressions on their faces.

"Help me," said the teenager. He looked frantically at me and my friends.

"You children should flee," Parris said, not even bothering to look at us. "Neither the witches nor those *wicked angels* have finished what they've started. I nearly have the power to stop it all. Heaven. Hell. I'll make them irrelevant. I just need a little more power."

"Wait!" shouted Lilith. "Don't let them do this."

"Why?" Parris demanded, and then he did look at us. "I've spent enough time around your kind to know your opinions on the subject. These people will just end up where they belong. They'll just be sorted to their endless reward or torment. What's the difference if that happens now or later?"

Parris didn't make any discernible movement, but all three of the people shifted their weight forward. The teenager whimpered.

"You can earn time," I said desperately; some souls did.

They repented as they paid for their crimes and moved on to a more peaceful existence in Purgatory.

Parris laughed. It was loud and a little mad. "I've been cooped up in that torturous circle for centuries. They're never moving me up. There will be no redemption. No earned reprieve. Do you think I don't know that? You think I don't know that I'll still be in that Pit when you take Mommy's and Daddy's place? When your children take yours? No. If you learn one thing from me, learn this: you must seize the future you want for yourself."

Parris looked right at me. *He knows,* I thought wildly. *He knows I'm a fraud.*

"And I plan to do just that," he continued. "This world will be my Kingdom Come, and Heaven, Hell, they will be nothing more than the outdated relics of a sanctimonious deity."

He raised his arms, his open suit jacket casting a terrifying shape against the brightly glowing net, which now reached well above the top of the bell tower.

The people on the ledge wobbled forward.

"No!" I yelled, and my cry was echoed by my friends.

"Of course, there is an alternative. . . . Give yourselves to me." Parris smiled, hungry, cold, and evil. "You're stronger than these mortals. One big gesture, that's all it will take. What will it be, children? You for them?"

I looked at the teenager begging for our help and mouthed, *Fight him.* I felt worse than I ever had in my life. It wasn't a choice. If Parris won, everyone died. He was fundamentally changing the balance, and that was more important than anything else. Any*one* else. If the balance fell . . . it was all over, for everyone.

My hesitation spoke volumes. Parris snarled before turning away and gesturing with his hand.

It didn't matter that we raced forward. It didn't matter how fast we moved; we were going to be too late. Parris, and gravity, were forces much too strong to overcome, and I just *knew* we were going to fail.

I was never so glad to be wrong.

An eruption of flame and a hot cyclone of air pulled Parris's three victims off the short wall, back to safety. I stumbled, and debris from the rooftop scraped my eyes in the hot wind.

Maybe he just needed the right motivation, or maybe it just took time to figure out this world's rules, but there in the center of the rapidly dying flames stood Crowley. Our magician was back! I swore I even saw the shadows of his wings.

Parris's face became feral with anger. The teenager ran for the hatch to the ladder, ignoring us completely as the two others still in Parris's thrall threw themselves at us. They were crazed, but clumsy and untrained. We outnumbered them, and even with Parris's influence overriding their sanity and sense of self-preservation, they didn't stand a chance.

Parris had nowhere to go and not enough protection. We were going to win. We were going to finish this!

Finally we would be able to go home.

But . . . why was Parris smiling?

FORTY

I flicked my gaze to Lilith, reassured to see the gold candlestick clenched in her fist. Crowley looked deep in concentration, apparently still struggling to get infernal magic to respond in the mortal realm but controlling it enough to pin the two humans flat to the roof beneath us. We clearly had the advantage, magic or no.

But Parris . . . Parris was smiling like everything was finally going according to plan. One of us was very wrong.

The scent of ozone grew stronger, and light flared in the distance beyond the net. The witches were at it again. Whatever they were trying to do was building.

I pushed down my panic at our expiring time and focused

on being careful. If Parris really did know something I didn't, then it was even more important to rely on tactics.

Maybe Lilith didn't notice Parris smiling. Maybe she missed his triumphant expression or didn't notice Crowley coaxing his magic back to life, ready to help us finish this.

Or maybe she just panicked.

She moved before we were ready. Parris twisted like smoke, and with a quick hand gesture wrenched the candlestick from Lilith's grip. He spun in a graceful movement that sent Lilith stumbling to the edge. She grabbed the rough stone wall, but even as Crowley released the two humans on the ground and lurched forward, Lilith's momentum pushed her over the side.

It took me a horrifying millisecond to realize that this was dangerous without wings.

"Lil!" I screamed, and ran faster than I ever had before. I grabbed her arms and felt them slip, before I tightened my grip as hard as I could, ignoring the pain in my hand, and stopped her fall.

"NO!" shouted Crowley. I jerked my head to see Parris's grasp cause the candlestick to become molten. Gold slithered over his fingers, down to his wrist, and wrapped around his forearm before it faded and was absorbed into his soul. His eyes flashed gold, and then it was gone.

Our weapon was gone.

I pulled and Lilith pushed her feet against the wall. On the next pull she was back over the wall to safety.

An iridescent glow surrounded Parris. Then he threw his head back and laughed with his entire body, and when he finally stopped, he winked. "This is going to be so much fun."

The light around Parris flared blindingly, and when I could see again, he was gone.

"We don't have time for this," I snarled.

"I'm sorry," Lilith said.

"This is why I make the calls," I yelled. "And where were you, Crowley?"

My friends' jaws dropped open. I snapped my mouth shut. I couldn't believe those words had come from me.

"I didn't mean . . . ," I said.

"Yes, you did," Crowley said. "And it's fine. We all have our roles, and don't even start arguing. This is our first test as a squad—well, sort of; Aleister will just have to catch up—but it's about time we act like it. I'm doing the best I can with my magic."

"I know, and you're doing amazing," I said before turning to Lilith. "Are you all right?"

"Yeah," she said. "I had a pretty good grip before you came and pulled me up."

She let out a shaky breath, but then she smiled, and I still felt terrible.

Lilith had almost been seriously hurt, and I had yelled at her. Why hadn't I fought harder to get to Charity's bag? I'd let our only other option be lost to a mob. There was nothing I could do about that now, but I felt sick with regret.

"We need to go there," I said. I pointed to the distance, where the flashes of light had been coming from. "I smelled ozone when the light flared, just like the ozone that comes when the magic users cast their spells."

"Sean's and Charity's mothers?" Crowley asked. "The witches' coven?"

"Gotta be," I said. "We have to make sure we're there with them. They have no idea what they're dealing with."

I shuddered. Parris's *This is going to be so much fun* echoed in my mind.

"But we don't have—" Lilith said, her voice strangled with what I was sure was guilt.

"We'll figure something out," I said. "We have to hurry."

And hurrying would have been great, but we were on the top of a tower and there were people between us and the trapdoor. More than just the two Crowley had pinned down. Leather jacket lady from before and the man who had howled when he'd chased us had already risen to their feet after climbing through. And more were still coming. We were trapped.

Unless . . . maybe we weren't.

I looked over the edge. It was a long way down.

"Off the side of the building," I said.

"Uh, Mal," said Crowley. "No wings. That's a really long way down."

"I have a theory," I said. I bit my lip nervously. I was almost positive I was right. It was that *almost* part that bothered me, but the more I thought about it, the smaller that part got.

I hadn't just imagined that I could see Lilith's wings arched over her head in Charity's house, and I knew I'd seen Crowley's wings when he'd used his magic just now. We'd had wings in Heaven. And when I'd first arrived, it had taken a look at my reflection for me to know that my wings were gone. If I'd been missing my fantastically majestic wings, shouldn't I have felt the weight missing from my back? I hadn't felt any different then, and I didn't feel any different now.

"We still have our wings," I said firmly. "We're letting this world change our perception of ourselves. Nothing about us has changed. We're the same as we always were. Crowley has his magic, and we have our wings. We have to jump."

If I was wrong, I was leading most of my squad to a painful end. Aleister would be so lonely.

No one said anything for a long moment.

"We know ourselves better than this world does," I said.

"Okay," said Lilith.

Crowley nodded sharply.

With my confidence shaken from my freak-out with my team, dread at what Parris had planned, and a large amount of panic at the distance to the ground, I took to the ledge. I had never been afraid of heights before, but that's not uncommon when you've been able to fly for most of your life.

I took a breath. I knew who I was.

Didn't I?

Yes, I did.

I jumped.

FORTY-ONE

For a fraction of a second, I panicked, doubt clouding my surety. The wind whipped my hair, the ground drew closer, the air made my eyes water, and then . . . I was flying.

I looked behind me. My wings, black, glorious, and razor-sharp, were back. I had never been so happy to see them. I promised never to take them for granted again.

"Yes!" Crowley shouted. "We're back."

I laughed and twisted in the air. Crowley's wings flashed iridescent green in the light from the thrones' net. Then Lilith's flight feathers brushed mine, and I sobered instantly. We had work to do.

Somehow.

"That has to be the coven over there." I pointed to the distance, where beyond the net of light a faint glow rose between the trees. Not that I needed to direct anyone. Crowley may have been our only magician, but we could all feel it.

The thrones' containment lit up Salem nearly as well as the daylight had when I had arrived. Trash cans fell over and a car alarm sounded as the ground shook. We flew faster.

There was the flash of human movement below us. Sean and Charity were moving quickly, and I was glad to see that Charity was okay. I whistled sharply and dove for the ground, knowing my friends would follow. We touched down lightly.

"Heading to your mothers?" I called, startling Charity and Sean.

Charity screamed. "Oh my goddess, you scared me! Ooh, black wings."

"Parris?" Sean said. His eyes flicked to my wings, and an unreadable expression crossed his face, but I didn't think it was negative.

"Escaped," I said. "We had him at the top of the bell tower, and then he was surrounded by a glow and gone. But . . . uh, we had a mishap with the candlestick."

"It didn't work?" asked Charity.

"It melted," I said, swallowing hard against the disappointment. "We didn't have time for the incantation."

"Good thing we have a spare," Charity said. She pulled the candlestick's twin from under her jacket.

"I love you," Crowley said.

We all shot him a look.

"Stop it," he said. "You know what I mean."

"Wait," Charity said. "What street are we on? Of course! I can't believe I didn't think of that. Our moms must be at Old Burying Point Cemetery. John Hathorne was buried there. He was a judge during the witch trials."

"Another focal point," Crowley said. "Something here to link to Parris for a binding."

"Exactly," Charity said, twisting her hands together. "I'm so sorry. If I had remembered . . ."

"I didn't remember either," Sean said. "It's not your fault."

"We've all made mistakes," I said.

I looked at Lilith and Crowley apologetically and hoped they'd forgive me. I wouldn't if I were them. I was never going to act like that again.

"It will be faster if we fly," I said.

"Some of us don't have wings," said Sean.

For the first time all night, my trademark smirk came out to play. I nodded to my friends. Evil grins broke out on their faces. Crowley and I each grabbed an arm, and Sean screamed as we dragged him into the sky. Lilith grasped both of Charity's arms and brought her into the sky after us.

Charity squealed, "This is awesome!"

I laughed.

"Do not drop me," snapped Sean. "Did you hear me?"

"Sorry, Sean," Crowley said. "Can't hear you. Wind and all that. Hang on."

We raced forward. The witches were not going to want to give up Parris once they had him, and I couldn't blame them for that. Not really. But we had to get Parris back to Hell, and it wasn't even just so we could get home anymore. These people didn't deserve what Parris was doing to them, and we certainly weren't going to let Heaven kill them for it.

Old Burying Point Cemetery was filled with gravestones smoothed with age and leafless trees with gnarled, reaching branches. A house with ivy clinging to its walls took up much of the property on one side. The cemetery wasn't large enough to hide the coven of witches chanting, and it certainly wasn't large enough to hide Parris.

"All right," Sean said. "I'm not so sure about this. My mom can be kinda—"

"We're all going to die when that closes," interrupted Lilith, pointing to the sky, where the thrones were closing their containment net around the city.

"Right, let's steal that ghost away from my mom," Sean said.

We peered through the gravestones. Five witches formed the points of a star surrounding Parris, who was cocooned in a thin membrane that resembled a soap bubble. Colors swirled along its shimmering surface. Several other witches stood farther back between the points of the star, watching and saying something I couldn't hear, but probably lending power to those keeping the containment. There was a tingle along my skin, and the feathers on the edges of my wings were floating. I ruffled them, uncomfortable.

Parris had grown rich persecuting fake witches, and now the real ones would make him pay. That kind of justice made my mischievous little heart positively gleeful.

Parris arched and stretched, and the bubble clung and moved with him. Occasionally part of him would poke through its surface, and the witches would stumble.

They were barely hanging on.

And then they weren't.

Parris inhaled and screamed against the membrane, which stretched across his mouth like plastic wrap. His arms strained, and his fingers burst through. The witches staggered, but Parris pushed, and then the bubble burst in a way that bubbles do not, with a bang like thunder. A ripple of energy slammed into us like a wall. The witches fell, and I spread my wings, barely keeping my feet.

"Curse you all," snarled Parris, grinning victoriously. "It's time you burned."

He glowed with energy, and I realized the danger before it hit. We might have been able to deny Parris the boost that our angelic energy would have given him, but he had found another source of otherworldly power. It was why he had been so gleeful when the witches had seized him away.

One of the witches stood, a jealous, wicked expression on her face.

Until now Parris had been influencing people to act out their suppressed, hidden urges. People with ordinary urges, and normal abilities.

The witch's hand began to glow. A second witch stood. His face went slack, then turned angry and hostile.

Parris's influence wasn't limited anymore to what *normal* humans could do, to the chaos and mayhem that *normal* humans could commit.

A third witch recovered from the rebound of the broken containment spell, while the other two staggered and shook their heads, as if fighting to clear their minds. The first witch now had a fully formed fireball in her hand. With a snarl she threw it at one of the other witches who hadn't yet recovered.

"Mom!" yelled Sean, running toward the witch still on the ground.

Parris had been feeding off that normal human power all night, and he could do the impossible. What were his limits when he used people with power? Real power, and real magic. What kind of fuel was that? What would he be able to do now?

Then everything happened at once.

The witches under Parris's influence flung fire and spells at the ones who weren't. Sean punched one of the enthralled witches, while another one not under Parris' influence tried to use magic to stop the others' attacks. One woman pleaded with another, and my stomach knotted as I saw Charity run in their direction. I could feel my fear, rage, and desperation swirling in a storm, and I clung to my lessons from school.

Tactics, not emotion.

Do what makes sense.

Parris began to glow, rising from the ground despite his solid state and lack of wings. We had to capture him now. The cemetery was a riot of noise, flames, and magic.

The ground began to tremble. I stumbled, but used my wings to help steady my balance.

And then the dead began to rise.

FORTY-TWO

Long-dead skeletal hands pushed through the dirt, snatching at the ground, stones, ankles ... whatever would help them dig their way back up. I had wanted to know what Parris could do with real power; I was getting my answer.

Somewhere there were spirits left behind. Spirits that wanted to come back, and Parris was letting them do just that.

Several of the witches were still fighting each other, but one had his hands raised. The net the thrones were weaving was still growing, and the light was cast over everything, but inside that started containment began a wavering in the air like a heat mirage. I recognized the sight. It was how we'd gotten to Salem. The witch was ripping the veil.

Behind the distortion was a familiar fiery horizon. Flames rose, tall and proud, from the metal sigil standing outside the gates of the Pit. I took to the sky and almost fell when I realized there was a second rip. I noticed a familiar lavender sky and the scent of vanilla. Heaven. Everything was open.

Shifting the balance in Salem was bad enough, but Parris hadn't just been gloating in the church. Throwing the balance off had cosmic consequences. He really could bring everything down. If he succeeded . . .

No. I couldn't let it happen.

My heart stuttered in my chest, but I couldn't freeze this time. Parris had noticed Lilith, and she spun in the air, fighting for control as her wings whipped in the unnatural currents he generated. She struggled to maintain contact with the candlestick she had taken from Charity, and then, in a fumble that seemed to move in slow motion, she dropped it.

I dove and grabbed it.

Parris watched us both.

I knew my eyes were glowing, and Parris just smirked. Who did he think he was? He was a threat to the balance, and I was a power.

He should show me some respect.

Crowley joined us in the air, and we were suddenly in the most important game of King of the Cage of our lives. This was *our* game, and we fell into practiced patterns and formations so that Parris couldn't possibly keep the candlestick in sight.

Crowley had it then, and I held my breath. Parris was still distracted by Lilith, and Crowley was right behind him, his eyes glowing with hellfire. He pressed the candlestick into Parris's back. His mouth opened to say the incantation that would bind Parris, and then Parris spun.

For a second time the candlestick was free-falling out of our control.

I dove straight to the ground, trying to fly faster than gravity. Parris kicked up the wind again, and we struggled to maintain control while the candlestick jerked and switched direction. We couldn't lose this one. It was our last chance.

I dove and spun, grabbing the candlestick out of a squall of wind and noise. I turned and flew straight toward Parris, who was currently occupied with Lilith and Crowley. Crowley was sparking magic in the air, and when our eyes met, he smiled victoriously. Parris started to turn, but Crowley yelled, "Over here, jerk!"

I flew faster than I ever had before and, using Crowley's distraction, pressed the candlestick to Parris's back and said the incantation, *"Anima coniuncta!"*

Flesh and gold merged where the candlestick touched. Parris tried to pull away. He failed. The candlestick knew

Parris, and it was not letting him go. His modern black suit changed back into the original old style, the white ruffles coming back into view, before everything started trying to force itself into the candlestick.

But it wasn't enough. For every gain the spell made in containing Parris, he took an inch back. Parris was still hanging on to this world. He had fed all night. He had juiced up on powerful witches, and he was still too strong.

We were going to fail.

Cassandra was gone. The squadron of thrones had us trapped. We had one object and no alternatives, and it wasn't enough.

My eyes frantically searched the sky to take one last look at my squad. Lilith, beautiful and resigned. Crowley . . . Crowley was missing.

More weight. I almost laughed, hysterical as the thought of Sean's expression came out of nowhere. My eyes fell to the ground to search the human out as I continued to push the candlestick against Parris's back. There he was, green eyes blazing straight at me. Charity was at his side. And so was Crowley. Why was Crowley on the ground?

Almost in answer to my unspoken question, Charity and Crowley pressed their hands together. Purple light pulsed from Charity's hands while the red from Crowley's twisted and slithered. Then the light expanded and spread across the entire town, crashing against the net like a tsunami. I felt the same heat as when Charity had smeared that glittery stuff on us.

They had figured it out! They had figured out how to multiply their protection spell to the entire town. Everyone in Salem was safe from Parris's influence. He couldn't sway them anymore!

The people on the ground stumbled and collapsed.

Parris screamed a wordless cry of outrage, and the candlestick glowed and shuddered. The heat was becoming unbearable. I struggled to hang on, but no amount of pain was going to make me let go.

Charity and Crowley had silenced the void. Parris was cut off, and finally, *finally* the candlestick with all its object memory was able to gain ground.

Parris's stolen power started releasing back into the world. I could feel it over every inch of my skin. I focused on holding my position in the air, keeping my contact with the candlestick and Parris, my feathers painful and charged.

I screamed as Parris resisted the pull, but kept my grip firm.

The candlestick burned my hand. For a moment I was terrified I would be fused with the candlestick too, but I still did not let go. If that was the price for stopping Parris and all his hate and madness, I'd pay it. I'd pay it a thousand times over to protect the balance, to protect good.

Parris was transparent again. His mouth formed a voiceless scream.

Then, in a final burst of wind, he was gone.

FORTY-THREE

I dropped lightly to the ground, stumbling slightly as my feet touched earth. I let the candlestick fall from my hand. Angry blisters lined my grip, next to the now-filthy bandage over my cut. I really hoped I didn't actually end up with gangrene.

The cemetery was littered with broken stones and broken skeletons. Several of the witches lay recovering on the churned-up soil, with another casting healing spells. Charity was helping with her own healing spells.

"Hell, yes," Lilith breathed.

Crowley strolled back to us, looking justifiably smug. I rolled my eyes but grinned anyway. We had captured an escaped soul *without* a morningstar. We were badass!

"Powers, huh?" Sean said. He smirked, but my stomach tightened, and my mood wavered. "Who calls themselves that? So pretentious."

"I didn't make up the name," I said.

"You can get Parris back?" he asked.

"Yeah," I said quickly. "He's trapped now. That wasn't the case when he somehow ended up in our neighborhood."

"The guards didn't notice right away," muttered Crowley. "If they had, he would never have made it to our woods."

He'd been in the woods.

"I thought Crowley pushed us through the veil," I said.

"Hey, we talked about this," protested Crowley.

"Or that Aleister had knocked us over," I said, continuing my thought.

"It wasn't Aleister," Lilith said, a hint of wonder in her voice. "It was us."

"Say that again?" asked Crowley.

"It was us," repeated Lilith. "Think about it. Parris was still a proper soul when we were home, so he couldn't have pushed us. But we've seen his power. After being cooped up for so long, we *wanted* to go through. He gave us the mental push."

"So we went through," finished Crowley.

"And Parris came with us," I said.

"Wow," Sean said. "So you suck at this whole guardian angel thing, huh?"

But then he smiled, and I knew we were good.

And then the net snapped shut.

FORTY-FOUR

O h, brimstone," Lilith said. "How did we forget about *them?*"

"Are you kidding me? They still closed it?" I asked. "Didn't they see all that?"

My ears popped as the pressure of the containment field shifted, and a high-pitched whine filled my ears. We might have stopped Parris's influence and trapped him within the candlestick, but apparently that wasn't enough for Heaven's soldiers. Parris was still not where he belonged.

"We've got to get home," Lilith said.

"Go," said Sean, looking worriedly at the sky. We gripped left hands awkwardly as I tried not to cause any more pain to my poor tormented right hand. Although, it might have been worth it.

"Thanks," I said, squeezing his hand and not immediately letting go. He nodded and, curiously, blushed. Lilith cleared her throat. I stepped back.

"Wait," I said.

"No, fly," said Crowley. "We have to get Parris back where he belongs."

"We won't get Parris to his circle in time. They'll still destroy Salem even if we make it to the gate," I said. "We have to try to talk to them. We have to convince them the situation is fixed."

I glanced at the sky and vaguely wished Cassandra was still around, at least to act as a go-between. There were figures beyond the net, and I was sure they would talk to Cassandra. Would they talk to me?

"No way," Crowley said, shaking his head.

"Yes way," Lilith said, smiling at me.

"I would like to not die," Sean said, raising his hand.

"Make. The. Call," Crowley said, slowly and emphatically.

Crowley and Lilith turned to look at me, expectation clear on their faces, but not disdain or petulance, and I knew for sure in that moment that we'd be okay. I could take my role, or not, and either way, my squad would be there. It didn't have to be the cold professional way my parents led their squads. It could be different.

"We'll talk to the thrones," I said. "Let's go."

We flew to the top of the dome. It was remarkably high and noticeably colder. We hovered back-to-back in a circle.

"Hey!" I shouted. "You can open this thing up. Everything's okay now. Can you hear me?"

"There's someone out there," Lilith said.

A throne flew closer, so that only the white glow of the net separated us. She had blinding white wings, and a golden halo hovering proudly over her head. Her silver armor gleamed more like a costume than functional armor.

"Just wait," I said, making hand gestures just in case sound couldn't penetrate the net. I held up the golden candlestick. "We've got him. Okay? Wait."

She didn't respond.

"Please," I said, panic clawing at my throat. "This isn't necessary. His influence is gone. The balance is safe."

She cocked her head, raised an eyebrow, then nodded and turned away. She made broad hand gestures to her warriors.

"We need to go," said Crowley.

"Yes, now," I said.

At the speed we flew, it took hardly any time to fly back to the statue. Lilith pulled the hand down, and the statue slid just as before. The flames glowed warm and bright, and I waited for the familiar sight of Terrence. We didn't have any candy this time, but we were probably beyond the bribery point by now anyway.

But Terrence was not hunched over his counter, greedily gobbling chocolate or staring vacantly at his clipboard. Instead he was looking rather pathetic, and maybe a little pouty, sitting on a tiny chair while a large, very buff imp sat in the proper-sized chair in Terrence's place. Even though imps rarely had anything more than wisps of hair, this one had a crew cut.

"Name, rank, and serial number," demanded the larger imp.

"What? We don't have serial numbers," I said.

"Or ranks," said Crowley.

"And our names aren't exactly on that list," Lilith said.

"No list, no entry," said the imp. He moved as if to lower the booth.

"Wait!" I said. "We have the escaped soul. We have to get him back to the eighth circle."

"I'll put in the proper paperwork," said the imp. "If it's approved, someone will be here to check your claim. In six to eight years . . . probably."

"Our claim?" I said. "We're not making this up. And did you notice that? That glowing dome? Heaven is getting twitchy. This whole place might be destroyed if we don't get him back in time."

"Terrence knows us," Lilith said. "He was just waiting for us to come back."

"Terrence." The imp snarled the name and gave a derisive look at the much smaller and dirtier imp behind him. "He's unfit for the job. Guilty of taking bribes. Trying to bribe a gatekeeper is a Cage-worthy offense. You wouldn't try to do that, would you?"

"No, no, no," we all said with as much sincerity as possible.

Before the imp could say more, a glowing sword dropped in front of me, separating us from the booth.

"Dad, no!" yelled Sean, breathing hard as he burst into our group.

The man holding the sword, which glowed just like the amulet had in Charity's house, was dressed in something like my parents' field uniform, but more ornate, like a knight brought to a new age.

"Step away from that portal," Sean's dad said. "I won't let you bring the forces of Hell into our world."

"We're trying to bring the forces of Hell back to Hell," I said.

"Negative," said the imp. "You don't have the proper clearance. We'll need to fill out forms 1205B, 13F, and 802HE at least."

"Override per Article Seventeen," said Lilith, "regarding emergency circumstances including apocalypse and near-apocalyptic events, and while we're at it, I will remind you that any interference in the recapture of an escaped soul and its return is a Cage-worthy offense."

Lilith crossed her arms, and I grinned. Leave it to Lilith to know obscure procedural overrides.

"Come on in, children," said the imp quickly. Terrence smiled on his tiny chair of punishment.

"Not so fast," said a new voice.

"Seriously?" Crowley asked.

It was the throne we had seen beyond the barrier.

I looked up. The top of the net was open again, and I noticed that the pressure had changed. I didn't feel like my head was going to explode, and the high-pitched whine I had been hearing was gone. But I wasn't quite relieved yet.

The light flared bright for a moment, and my eyes flicked to the gate. We had another newcomer, and this one I knew, oh so well.

My dad stepped through and cast furious eyes to the throne, who was not looking quite as confident anymore, and to Sean's dad, who was still holding his glowing sword—very near us, in fact.

"We have a situation," said the throne warrior. "This town is under an evil influence."

"No, it isn't," said Crowley.

"I have a morningstar," Dad sneered. "I'll have the prisoner recaptured in moments, if you can wait that long before your eradication event."

"With all due respect," said Sean's dad, "these demons must be destroyed."

"Touch my son and die!" growled Dad.

"We're the good guys," Lilith said to Sean's dad.

Why did we keep having to say that? It was like coming from Hell was some sort of mark against us.

"ENOUGH!" I yelled.

I swallowed. Was it getting hot out here? It felt like it was getting hot out here.

"We already took care of everything," I said. "Literally, it's all done. Crowley and Charity stopped Parris's influence and cut him off from his power. And as for Parris? I'm holding him. Right here. In this." I held up the candlestick.

"Ezra, he's telling the truth," said a woman with familiar green eyes. She had one hand on Sean's shoulder, and I recognized her as the one he had run toward in the cemetery.

Charity was standing next to her, looking tired.

"Don't be ridiculous," said Sean's dad. "This isn't something children can fix. Certainly not *demons.*"

"Get these children out of the way so we can remedy Hell's mistake," snarled the throne.

"I will take care of this, I assure you," argued my dad, his eyes glowing.

"Oh, my unholy darkness!" I growled. My wings arched high over my back, and I could feel the flames of Hell illuminating my eyes. "All of you have only made everything worse. Seriously? Mass extinction? That's your go-to move? I get that you are all Very Important Grown-Ups, but listen to me when I say: WE GOT THIS!"

I cleared my throat from where it had dropped to a deep growl, and blinked my eyes rapidly to force the flaming glow away.

"Well, what do you expect?" spat the throne. "Fallen angels."

"Fallen?" I demanded.

Maybe it was because I had been called a demon all night, but I. Was. Done.

"The first powers flew with great purpose to do a job that had to be done. They were the ones, and we are still the ones, who make the sacrifice to protect creation. And do you even appreciate it? No, you're all about the public relations. The myth that somehow you're good, and we're bad, because we dirty ourselves while you get to keep your hands nice and clean. What you were going to do tonight was not *good*. Just because it's easy doesn't mean it's right. If you think being a power means that I'm fallen, then you'd better believe I'm proud to have fallen. If you think protecting people and seeking justice is falling, then I will choose to fall every time."

Unholy night! I was proud to be a power. And I *wanted* to be a guardian, maybe even the Commander I was destined to be. I was good at this leader gig!

The throne looked as stunned as Sean's dad looked confused, but Sean's mom looked like she found all this very amusing. Charity was laughing behind her hand. And my dad? He was looking prouder than I had ever seen him.

"So mote it be," muttered Sean with a smirk. Charity held out her fist, and Sean bumped it with his knuckles.

"Well," said Dad. "I guess we're all set here. I'd drop that containment net if I were you."

"Very well," grumbled the throne.

Dad looked at me, and I swallowed again nervously. "Captured him without a morningstar, huh?"

He clapped his hands on my and Lilith's shoulders and with a gentle but firm push moved us toward the veil, where

Crowley was already waiting. Breathing a sigh of relief, I waved goodbye and grinned over my shoulder.

"Hey, Dad?" I asked. "That was a great speech, right?"

"Yes, it was," replied Dad. "But you're still grounded."

FORTY-FIVE

Parris was returned to his place in the eighth circle. My mother oversaw his new security measures, and if I never saw that look of absolute murderous intent on my mother's face again, it would be too soon. I was very glad not to have it directed at me. My mother was a scary woman, and it was suddenly very clear to me why she ranked so high.

For a week Parris screamed and raged; then he fell silent. My parents weren't sure if that was good or not, but since Parris had messed with the balance, he had earned Mom's specific attention, as did anyone else who personally threatened existence. Dad was incredibly proud of us both, which was kind of nice. The fence receded to its proper level; the flames returned to their homey glow.

Parris wasn't saying how he had done it, but as far as they could tell, he had manipulated several bored powers and hitched rides on residents of Hell before going through the veil with us. None of us were punished by the Powers That Be, since they deemed our actions unintentional and not based on corrupt hearts. Dad's testimony probably helped.

But . . . the reality was, Parris had been released to the mortal coil only because we had broken the rules. We may have been influenced at the veil, but it had been our choice to go there in the first place. I liked to comfort myself that if it wasn't us, it would have been someone else, and to a certain extent, people agreed. Thankfully, tales of our recapture of Parris had spread, and so our only punishment was parental and not infernal, and if anything, escaping official reprimand only added to my already awesome reputation.

I was still being punished a month later, allowed to go only to school and training, and I hadn't worked up the courage to ask how much longer that was going to go on. My parents were back to working normal hours, which should have meant I'd have roughly two and a half hours to goof off before they got home, but since I was grounded . . .

"Is that you? Is someone here?" asked Methuselah as I made my way toward the kitchen.

I took a deep breath. The house smelled like old man . . . again.

"Yes, sir," I said.

"Ah, good, good," said Methuselah. "You can do your homework and watch my stories with me."

"That's okay, I can just do it in my room," I said. Methuselah had a penchant for soap operas. Boring, boring soap operas.

"Ah, don't worry, boy. I won't tell your parents I let you have a little entertainment," said Methuselah. "Sit, sit. This is a good one."

I sat. I tried desperately to tune out the soap, which was probably why I didn't hear the sound at first. There was a tapping at the window. I looked over. There was a paper dove bashing itself repeatedly into the glass.

I hesitated, and then cautiously walked to the window. I took one glance at Methuselah and then slid the window open silently. The paper dove flew in and landed in my hand. It smelled like vanilla and snow.

"I, uh, gotta get a . . . something, in my room," I told Methuselah.

"What was that? Yeah, yeah, okay," he said without ever turning his head from his soap opera.

I flew to my bedroom and unfolded the now-motionless dove. It was a letter.

Dear Malachi,

Everything is fine. I am confined to Heaven for the time being for some retraining, but it's okay. I told Archangel Michael all about you, and he made sure I wasn't in any major trouble. It turns out he agreed that what we did was the right thing!

Anyway, I hope you are well ~~in Hell~~ at home. It was so wonderful meeting you, and I hope to see you again! I'm trying to convince the cherubim to start the interdimensional mixers again! Michael says there's been a lot of misinformation that needs to be cleared up, and it would do us good to mingle. I'm going to make the cookies.

Love,

Cassandra

P.S. I totally broke the rules to send you this!

I laughed. I had to admit I had been a tiny bit worried about the seraph, even if my feelings about her were still conflicted. In the end, though, she had helped and tried to do the right thing. I tapped my pen against my desk.

Cassandra had found a way to do her job and do it well, even if it wasn't the way it had always been done. I still wasn't willing to completely admit that my destiny was sealed, but if I took my place as Commander of my squad and remained a guardian angel for all eternity . . . well, I thought I was okay with that.

It didn't mean I had to do it the way my parents did. It didn't mean we had to follow their example. My squad and I could do things *our* way. I could be different. *We* could be different. No matter what happened, we would be in it together.

I pulled out some paper and held it up to my nose. After taking a deep breath of cinnamon to clear the old-man smell away, I laid the paper down and began to write. If a seraph could break the rules of interdimensional communication, then so could I.

Dear Sean . . .

Besides, that was the good thing about being grounded forever: there really was no way to make it worse.

And I was going to take complete advantage of that.

ACKNOWLEDGMENTS

This book is the work of a lifetime love of all things mythological and supernatural, and I am thrilled to be debuting with *Grounded for All Eternity*. I hope you love Mal and his friends as much as I do. I can't wait to continue their story! I owe a huge thank-you to my agent, Victoria Wells Arms, who helped me revise and flesh out this universe so well. Thank you for the critiques and the continuous cheerleading; I need them both! Thank you to my editor, Kristin Gilson, who understood exactly what I was trying to do from the very beginning and made this book even stronger, and to everyone at Aladdin who helped make this book a reality through the weirdness of a pandemic.

To K Callard, who beta-read multiple versions of this book: your commentary is always thoughtful, and I hope we'll get to be writing conference buddies again soon! Thank you to Clay, who was the first kid to read this book. It means the world to me that you liked it.

Covers are sensitive things, and I am in awe of the art of Nicholas Kole. Thank you for capturing Mal, Lilith, and Crowley so perfectly!

And, of course, thank you to my family, who encouraged my writing, often with random suggestions, and to the readers who came along for the ride.

ABOUT THE AUTHOR

When Darcy Marks was small, she went to the Salem Witch Dungeon Museum with her family and had to be carried out crying by her father when a woman screamed. When she was slightly older, she read every book her local library had on the Salem witch trials, and in 1992 the theme of her Halloween decorations was in honor of the three-hundred-year anniversary of the hysteria. It's only fitting that the villain of her debut would be the infamous Samuel Parris.

These days Darcy writes snarky fantasy books for kids from her beautiful Green Mountain State, where she lives with her husband, three genre-defying kids, and a very needy cat. When she's not reading or writing, she explains math and science to lawyers as a forensic toxicologist and smashes the patriarchy with the Safety Team.

You can find Darcy fangirling on Twitter @wheresthetime and perhaps wandering the streets of Salem on a clear fall day. She has never known it to be particularly smitey, but there's always a first time.